# SLEEPER CELL

By Doug Karlson

Dan —
Hope you enjoy it —
It you do be sure to
Till your friends!
Best wishes —
Doug

Thank you to the many people who read advance copies of SLEEPER CELL and contributed their thoughts and corrections: Nancy Silk, Katy Corneel Stromland, C.J. Conrad, Bill Seed, Lee McLendon, Carol Dumas, Jim Horvath, Scott Chandler, Amy Dykens, Matt Belson, Elise Johnson-Dreyer, Chris Karlson, and Liz Groves.

This book was set in Book Antiqua.

*For my mother and Ben,*
*and my father and Shannon*

# PROLOGUE

The remotely piloted aircraft rode the thermals. It circled slowly, gaining altitude. All the while it watched. But there was very little to see, just a dusty village that looked like it was decaying back into the reddish earth from which its walls had been formed.

Thousands of miles away, at Clovis Air Force Base in Clovis, New Mexico, the RPA's pilot, Air Force Lieutenant Garth Cunningham, sat in an air-conditioned control room. He stretched his legs and yawned.

Every few minutes, out of boredom more than anything else, the lieutenant toggled the camera controls to zoom in for a closer look at the village. Did anyone actually live there? Intelligence reports said yes, but for more than an hour he had seen no signs of life.

Two hours passed. Cunningham drank his third cup of coffee and tried to blink away the dryness in his eyes when a light flashed in the village. He toggled the optical controls for a closer look. A bright, silvery light flickered on and off. The lieutenant put down his cup of coffee, leaned forward and squinted at the screen. The light came from the back of a pickup truck, which was surrounded by half a dozen men. He zoomed in closer.

The light grew brighter, now a steady beam. Then his screen turned to static. Cunningham sat up in his chair and looked at the drone's flight instrumentation. He noted quickly that it was off-course and losing altitude, and then the flight data went blank. He looked at the radar screen. The aircraft was off course, out of control, as if it had snapped free of its tether, pulled inexorably toward a new master.

# CHAPTER 1

*Two months later, Afghanistan*

Through a moonlit sky, the MC-130 Combat Talon approached its drop zone deep in the Nangarhar Valley. Sergeant Lance Dennehy sat in his canvas seat. His equipment was so heavy – more than a hundred pounds - that he could barely move. He crossed his arms for warmth and felt the aircraft's powerful turbo-prop engines vibrate through his body. He studied the faces of the men on his special 18-man team, bathed in the dim green light of the aircraft's cabin.

Most of those men were barely out of high school, teenagers practically. Just like the teenagers back home. Except for one thing, thought Dennehy, his teenagers knew twenty different ways to kill a man.

Mike Peterson and Emilio Sanchez sat next to each other in silence. They'd been on three deployments together, two in Afghanistan, one in Iraq; combat veterans with nothing to prove. They finished each other's sentences and knew what the other would do before he did it. It was as good a combat pairing as Dennehy had ever seen, which is why he had Sanchez carry the squad automatic weapon, and Peterson the ammo.

Private Tony Luna chewed gum and listened to music on his iPod. Frank Lorenzo, the communications specialist, was actually asleep, his helmeted head jerked back and forth with the motion of the plane. Next to him, Lt. Aaron Hildebrandt, the unit commander, was absorbed in a map of the target area. Lt. Hildebrandt folded his map, then checked his watch and elbowed Lorenzo awake.

At the same time, the jumpmaster stood up, held his hands and arms forward and extended his fingers.

"Ten minutes!" he shouted, and pulled his hands back to his shoulders in closed fists. A well-rehearsed string of commands followed as the jumpmaster gestured for the men to stand.

They heaved themselves to their feet as the rear cargo door

dropped open. Dennehy felt a blast of cold air, and saw the faint early morning light breaking over the Hindu Kush Mountains.

The jumpmaster made a hook with his fingers. "Hook up!" he shouted. The men clipped on to the static line.

"Check equipment!" was the next command, as the jumpmaster tapped his chest with his fingers.

Sergeant Dennehy's eyes rested on Jason Hill, the newest member of the squad, from Mobile, Alabama. It was his first combat jump. Dennehy watched as Winston Washington (the men called him W) checked Hill's chute and equipment, then slapped him hard on the shoulder to indicate he was good to go. Washington turned and Hill did the same for him.

"Stand by," the jumpmaster shouted, and then gave Dennehy a sharp tap on his back. "Go!"

Hundreds of coalition forces were participating in Operation Tightnoose. Nearly three-dozen separate offensive thrusts penetrating deep into the heart of the insurgency. The tip of the spear was the Third Battalion of the 75th[th] Ranger Regiment, and Sergeant Lance Dennehy, 23, of Woodboro, New York, population 1,278, was the first man out of the plane.

# CHAPTER 2

*Ab Darak, Afghanistan*

Pazhman Khan woke with a start.

He threw off his blanket and rushed into the courtyard outside his room. The Afghan looked up at the sky but clouds blocked what little moon there was.

The fortified compound, or qalat, belonged to Farzad, chief of Ab Darak, Pazhman's host. It was surrounded by an ancient red mud brick wall. There was a mud brick tower in one corner of the wall. Within the wall, in the traditional layout, were living quarters for three generations of Farzad's family and stalls for his goats. The garden inside the walls consisted of three apple trees rooted in hard packed soil and a well where the women drew water by hand. For generations, little had changed in Ab Darak. Until Pazhman arrived.

Pazhman stood in the empty dark courtyard and listened. His face, with its hawkish eyes, hooked nose and graying goatee, looked up at the dark sky. He had survived for years by trusting his instincts, and now, once again, he sensed something was wrong. But all was quiet except for night sounds, crickets, and a barking dog in the adjoining village. Then the wind shifted and he heard it: the distant, receding hum of an airplane.

"What is it?"

Pazhman turned to see Farzad standing beside him. He was still in his nightgown. His long hair was disheveled, but his eyes were alert.

They were quickly joined by Jawid, Farzad's idiot cousin, who carried an old British Enfield rifle.

"American soldiers. They have come for me."

"Then you must go," said Farzad.

"We will drive them away," said Jawid, raising his rifle.

You are a fool, thought Pazhman, but a useful fool. You will buy me much needed time.

Sergeant Dennehy landed hard in a barley field and rolled to a kneeling position in the freshly plowed earth. As soon as he released his parachute harness he clipped on his night vision goggles. He saw the green image of a fellow Ranger ten yards to his left, then spotted a row of fig trees lining the irrigation ditch, and the mud-walled compound at the edge of the field in the distance. He was exactly where he was supposed to be. Within less than half a minute, the rest of his team landed safely. The men assembled around him and Dennehy did a quiet roll call. All present.

Dennehy led the way down a dirt path beside the irrigation ditch toward the compound. The Ranger team paused while Sanchez and Peterson broke away and began moving along the ditch to the south to set up their weapon. Their job was to protect the right flank while the rest of the squad assaulted the compound's main gate. From their position, they could stop anyone who tried to enter the compound from the nearby village.

The team moved quickly. Private Luna set the charge he carried and, within moments, there was a loud explosion and flash of light. The front gate collapsed open.

From the other side of the compound, Pazhman saw two soldiers dressed in the uniform of US Army Special Forces dash through the breached wall. He rushed back into Farzad's house.

Anyone who survived would be harshly questioned, and if the Americans suspected they were Taliban, which they would, they would be taken away. I would gladly die fighting the invaders, he thought to himself. But it was not time. Not yet.

He moved quickly to the room where he slept and picked up his small canvas satchel, kept ready for just such an emergency. Inside were a small parcel wrapped in bubble wrap and covered in plastic, a roll of money, and his 9mm pistol in a leather holster. He unhooked a plastic water bottle from a hook on the wall and placed it in the satchel.

Pazhman felt a momentary panic and clasped his hand to his belt. Where was it? Then his eyes rested on the bed. There, in its black leather holster, was his silver handled knife. He breathed a sigh of relief and placed it under his belt. He could hear gunfire in

5

the courtyard now. Short bursts of semi-automatic weapons, and the occasional single shots of what must have been Jawid's ancient rifle. There were about eight Taliban in the village. Pazhman knew they would fight. But suspected the fight would not last long.

There was a wooden cabinet in the room, recessed into the wall. Inside the cabinet was a trap door. Pazhman lifted the door to reveal steps cut into the earth. He started down, then turned to close the doors behind him.

The steps descended ten feet to a tunnel. In the darkness, Pazhman felt for and found the flashlight that was kept near the bottom step. He shined it forward. The tunnel was wide enough for one man, and just under five feet high. He bent his head down and hunched his shoulders forward, his arms hanging in front of him. In this way he could pass through the tunnel without rubbing against the walls.

The secret escape route ran straight for almost 100 yards, and then curved to the left, where it became so narrow that Pazhman had to angle his shoulders sideways. Finally the tunnel widened again where it joined with another tunnel, and smelled of freshly dug earth. Pazhman himself had ordered the tunnel improved when he first arrived in Ab Darak. He felt the ground beneath him begin to slope upward, and continued another 50 yards until he came to a vertical shaft with a crude wooden ladder. He turned off his flashlight and climbed the ladder. When he reached the top he felt a wooden door above him. Pazhman waited and listened. He heard nothing, and pushed the door open.

He was in a stable in the village outside the compound. The goats in the stable crowded into a corner away from Pazhman. One of the goats made a baying sound.

"Shhhh," said Pazhman. In the distance, the sound of gunfire had died down except for the sporadic firing of a single rifle. The idiot, Jawid. Pazhman smiled.

A figure appeared in the doorway. It was still dark, but Pazhman recognized Samira, the goat herder's wife. She staggered into the stable, and stopped short when she saw Pazhman.

The two had never spoken, but like all the people in the village, Samira knew who Pazhman was. His family had lorded over neighboring villages for centuries. After the Russians came, Pazhman had been sent to study abroad. It was said he knew the ways of the infidel, had lived among them. It was common knowledge that he was a man to be respected, and feared.

"Samira, do not be afraid, it is Pazhman Khan."

"What are you doing here?" she asked.

"Are the Americans in the village?"

"Yes," she said, then collapsed. Her body rested against the wall.

"You are injured?" asked Pazhman.

She nodded.

"There is shooting at the house of Farzad, and among the rocks. The men have gone to the gate."

Pazhman shined the flashlight on the woman. She was young, perhaps 16, which was not so young for an Afghan woman. Pazhman knew she was married to Azar, a goat herder.

He placed a hand on her back. It was wet, and he realized she was bleeding. She must have been hit by shrapnel, or perhaps by a stray bullet. He would not have been surprised if she had been shot by one of the men in the village, because they could be very careless, especially with automatic weapons.

"What are you doing here?" he asked.

"I came to collect the goats, and to take them and the children."

"Who told you to do this?"

"It is what Farzad has taught us, since we were children."

Pazhman understood, and knew it was not necessary. The American tactics were different from the Russians, but Farzad was an old and simple man and still thought in terms of the Russians. Her plan to escape would have made sense if the Russians were attacking from the air, but not now.

"Where are the children?" he asked.

"Outside."

"And where will you bring them?" He was thinking fast now, revising his plan.

"The olive grove, on the other side of the stream," replied Samira.

"I will send the children now, leave the goats. I will tend to your wound," said Pazhman.

Samira gasped. It was bad enough that he had addressed her, and that he had dared to touch her. Now he would treat her wound? She heard a burst of automatic rifle fire from the compound. Why was Pazhman not with the other men, defending the village, she wondered? But she was feeling weak from loss of blood.

Pazhman went into the courtyard where the children, bleary eyed and afraid, waited.

"Go to the grove where you pick the olives, and wait there. We will not be long," he said to the oldest, a boy named Babur.

Babur nodded and then spoke to the other children, who followed him into the darkness. Pazhman returned to the goat shed.

Samira felt a chill as Pazhman knelt beside her. Her strength was draining, and each breath brought a sharp pain.

"Do not be afraid, your pain will soon end," Pazhman said. He placed both hands around her neck, and squeezed.

# CHAPTER 3

"You think it's going okay?" asked Peterson.

"How the fuck would I know? You're the one with the radio," said Sanchez. It was the third time Peterson had asked the same question.

"So I should call in?"

"Are you crazy?"

"I just don't like sitting out here in the dark. We might be all alone. Maybe everyone else left," explained Peterson.

"Where the fuck would they go? We're in Afghanistan. Didn't they give you an intelligence test when you joined the army?"

Peterson smiled. "Yeah, I passed too."

"They must have lowered the fuckin' standards. I heard they were going to do that."

Sanchez said it with a straight face. It was reassuring to Peterson, and he felt less concerned about being alone.

Sanchez continued. "Your parents weren't related, I mean, before they got married?"

"At least they were married."

"At least I didn't grow up in Wisconsin."

"Yeah, you wouldn't have been able to buy all that crack you like to smoke in New York City."

"If I knew I was headed back to Wisconsin, Jesus Christ, I can understand why you volunteered for this shit."

"You've never even been to Wisconsin," said Peterson.

"Shut up a second."

Sanchez adjusted his night vision goggles, tilting them down from his helmet. "I got hajis coming out of the village."

Peterson seated the buttstock of the M-249 machine gun in his shoulder as he looked through the scope. He kept his trigger finger extended, outside the trigger guard, as he had been trained.

Sanchez saw figures moving down the rocky slope, away from the village, toward the trees below. The ground was rough, and they moved slowly, picking their way over the rocks in the dark.

They were about two hundred meters from their position.

"Don't make me wait all day," said Peterson.

"Hang on," replied Sanchez, adjusting the focus on the night vision goggles. "Definitely locals, hightailing it away from the village, but it looks like a bunch of kids and a lady in a fucking burka."

They watched as the small party climbed to the bottom of the ravine. When they reached the stream they turned and walked along the bank, headed toward the two soldiers.

"Shit," muttered Sanchez.

"Do we stop them?" asked Peterson.

"Better let them pass. We got a job to do."

The children were now close enough that he could see them clearly. There were eight of them, the oldest no more than about 10 years old. Then again, you couldn't be sure in Afghanistan. Children were mistreated, and malnourished, and tended to be smaller than the children in the States.

They observed a single adult, a woman wearing a burka that covered her head, and a long robe that covered her entire body. She was guiding the children to the woods on the other side of the stream.

"Should we check them?" asked Peterson, taking his eye away from the scope.

"They're a bunch of kids."

"What about the broad?"

"You don't mess with them."

"So what do we do?"

"Just relax, and sit tight."

The two soldiers watched, relieved, as the children picked their way across the stream and disappeared into the thick underbrush on the other side. The radio crackled, and Peterson put the handset to his ear. He listened, then acknowledged.

He looked at Sanchez. "All secure, the Lieutenant said it's time to go."

The compound was secured by the time Sanchez and Peterson arrived. The scene was chaotic. A half dozen Afghans sat on the ground, their hands bounds behind them with plastic ties. A woman shouted at the soldiers in Pashtun as Lieutenant Hildebrandt and Sergeant Lorenzo, the Special Forces translator assigned to the unit, tried to question two Afghan old men.

"What's he saying?" asked Hildebrandt.

"Says his name is Farzad, he's the head honcho. He says they're not Taliban," said Lorenzo.

"Of course they aren't," replied Hildebrandt. He'd been in Afghanistan for almost a year and knew the routine. These interviews always went in circles and ended up nowhere.

"Ask them if they have more weapons."

"He says no."

"So why are they so nervous?"

"He says they're goat herders. He says they don't make war on America, the usual bullshit."

"Tell him we know the Taliban have been using this place, ask him about all the meetings. Tell him we see what goes on. Tell him if we don't get answers to our questions we're going to have to bring everyone away from here. And I don't think he wants that."

Lorenzo spoke to the Afghan. The Afghan listened then replied, talking fast. He sounded scared. They went back and forth in Pashtun, then Lorenzo turned to the lieutenant.

"He says the guy we're looking for isn't here," said Lorenzo.

"Oh yeah?"

"That's what he said."

"You tell him we were looking for someone?"

"Nope."

The lieutenant was about to say something when Luna stepped out of one of the small huts that faced the courtyard. "Sir, we got a tunnel."

Luna had investigated several Afghan tunnels. They were called zalegs, and the country was laced with them. They were originally built as irrigation systems, vital in an arid country like Afghanistan, and it was said they dated back to the time of Alexander the Great. During the Mongol Invasion, Luna had read, the Afghans used them as a way of hiding from invaders. He had studied the history

11

of Afghanistan, which was a source of amusement to the other men in his squad.

Luna aimed his flashlight down the tunnel.

"Anybody home?" he shouted.

Private Hill shrugged and reached for a hand grenade.

"Nuh uh," said Luna.

"Dude, the lieutenant wants us to clear this tunnel," replied Hill.

"Dude, I'm not throwing a grenade where there might be women and children hiding."

"I'm not going down that fucking tunnel unless I blast it first," said Hill.

Luna frowned. "Just give me the rope."

Luna was an experienced rock climber, as were most of the Rangers. He tied one end to a beam that supported the roof of the hut and tested it with his weight. Satisfied, he attached a belaying clip to his web belt and through it he threaded the rope. Hill planted his feet firmly on the floor and slowly lowered Luna.

He rappelled slowly, using small steps, to the bottom of the shaft. There, the tunnel branched off horizontally. He aimed his flashlight and saw the tunnel went a great distance in what he thought was the direction of the village.

"Looks all clear, I don't see shit!" he shouted up.

Two minutes later Hill and Washington joined him.

Luna was probably too tall to be a tunnel rat. He crouched, pistol aimed forward, and started down the tunnel. The tunnel was narrow. Luna didn't like it. If they were attacked, they would have to fight their way out single file. Not a good situation.

They pressed on in the dark. Luna could smell the earth, and felt as if the world were closing in on him. He felt fear. Fear of suffocation. Fear of collapse. Fear of never seeing sunlight again. He pushed those thoughts out of his mind and hoped he would come to the tunnel opening soon.

At last the tunnel became wider, and they came to a chamber excavated into the red earth. In the center of the ceiling was a nearly vertical shaft. More steps were carved into the wall, and further up, a wooden ladder. Luna clambered up the ladder, eager to get out of the tunnel. His helmet hit a wooden door, which he slowly pushed open. He crawled onto the ground, breathing in relief. He smelled fresh livestock as he took a defensive position against the far wall, and listened as Hill emerged behind him. A moment later, Washington followed.

"Where the fuck are we?" asked Washington.

"In the village," replied Luna.

"Any locals?"

"Negative."

That's when Luna saw it. In the straw, beside the small herd of goats, lay a body. He turned on his flashlight.

It was a woman, half undressed, and she was dead.

He had been almost eight months in the Afghan countryside, and she was one of the few women he had seen up close. Whenever they entered a village, the women always hid indoors. Or, if it was during the day, there were only men in the village, smoking hashish and drinking tea while the women worked in the fields, harvesting the hashish. But there was something different about this woman.

She wasn't wearing a burka.

# CHAPTER 4

Pazhman and the children moved silently through the olive grove. This, he knew, would be the most dangerous part of his escape. How fortuitous it was for Samira to be there when he needed her, and how clever of him to think of what to do. It must be for a reason, he thought, part of a grand design, for he had in his possession something of incalculable value, something that must not fall back into the hands of the infidel.

They passed through a field of poppies after which the brush became thick and then there was a clearing. Here Pazhman stopped and removed his robe and burka, flinging it away in disgust. I banish it from my memory, and will never speak of it, he thought.

The youngest of the children, Babur, who was six, rubbed his eyes and sat down at the base of a tree. It was cold, and he clenched his arms together.

"Where is Samira?" asked Babur.

"She has been killed by the Americans, I am sorry," replied Pazhman. "You will have time to mourn her later." He paused. "After that, there will be time for revenge."

He smiled to himself as he spoke these words. Sometimes good fortune led to more good fortune. "You must be strong," he told the boy. "And if they ask you where I have gone, you must not tell them."

The boy stood up straight and nodded. He admired Pazhman, though he was confused as to why he wore a woman's clothes. He thought it must be to deceive the enemy, but in any case, it was not for him to question a man like Pazhman. He had listened to Pazhman speak of the far away places he had visited: Pakistan, France, which was in Europe, Iraq and Yemen, and even the United States. It was almost impossible to believe, and yet he knew it was true. Pazhman had told the children that when you commit to Jihad, life opens up new adventures, and great joy.

Pazhman said goodbye to the children in the clearing.

"Wait here until dawn," he instructed them. "Then you may

return to the village. If there are any Americans there stay away, and do not return until they have left. They will not stay for very long."

With that Pazhman disappeared into the thorny underbrush. He had arrived three months earlier, shrouded in mystery, thought Babur, and now he was gone.

Like a ghost.

* * *

After the sun rose, while those Afghans who had not fled or been killed were assembled in the courtyard, Dennehy searched their living quarters. He entered a small room that faced the courtyard. The walls were the usual mud brick, and there wasn't any furniture other than a chest and an ornately decorated armoire, both of which looked very old. On the floor were dusty Afghan carpets. He felt the floor give under the weight of his combat gear. He stepped back and pulled up one of the carpets. Another trap door.

Dennehy hesitated. He didn't like opening doors without knowing what was behind them. He'd met a few men, like Luna, who actually liked to explore tunnels, but tunnels gave Dennehy the heebie jeebies. He wished there was an engineer unit nearby that could help check for booby traps. But there wasn't. He was it.

He examined the door. It was made of rough-hewn planks, and could have been very old. Then again, this was Afghanistan, and everything looked old. Everything in the countryside looked old because there was no electricity and everything was still made by hand, and everything smelled and everything was always dirty and dusty.

He looked outside to the courtyard and saw that Lorenzo was fingerprinting the men from the village and Hill was taking their pictures with a digital camera. Everyone looked busy. Screw it, thought Dennehy. He reached for the trap door and pulled the brass handle, revealing wooden steps leading down.

Dennehy descended slowly. With every creaking step he stopped, looked, and listened for anyone who could be hiding. When he got to the bottom he shined his flashlight all around. He was in an underground chamber. It was about 12 by 16 feet and housed what looked like stacks of flour, and rectangular plastic packages piled three feet high. He removed his KA-BAR knife and slit one of the packages open to reveal brown gummy paste - unrefined opium. That's when he noticed a door in the wall behind the flour sacks. He pulled the door open with the barrel of his M-16 and entered.

It was a workshop of sorts. Dennehy's flashlight passed over electronic components, wires, and a tool bench, then his light rested on something, a broken piece of grey metal, and on that metal was a small American flag.

* * *

Pazhman had fled his homeland once before. The first time he had been filled with fear. Now, as he walked south, he felt anger. He had suffered an indignity he would not forget, and for that, and other things, his enemies would pay.

As he walked he was reminded of his childhood, when his father had taken him hunting with the falcon. That was before the Russians came, before his father was killed and before his uncle usurped his rightful place as the leader of the province. Sometimes, when he walked the fields around Ab Darak, he had longed for those boyhood days. It was hard to believe he had once lived in such simple, happy times. But always he put such thoughts out of his mind. He was seven when the Russians came, and life before then was ancient history, a world that no longer existed. And anyway, he told himself, there was greater joy to come, and the world was becoming a better place.

Pazhman wanted to put as much distance between himself and Ab Darak as possible, so he walked without stopping. The Americans would put out patrols. They probably had helicopters and infrared scanners and drones. They would go to great lengths to capture me, thought Pazhman.

He reached his hand into the satchel and felt for the pistol to make sure it was still there. He remembered the special training he had received, and the unique skills he possessed and knew he could

16

defeat anyone who confronted him.

Around mid-morning he came to a dirt path that led to the village of Ramazi. That meant he had walked at least ten miles. The men in Ramazi had only insults for the people of Ab Dakar. There had been a feud, too complicated to understand, though Farzad had tried, recounting one insult and one retaliation after another. Apparently one of the men of Ab Dakar had agreed to send two sons to Ramazi to work in a farmer's field, but one of the boys had been too lazy to work, so had been returned to Ab Dakar. The boy's father had taken insult and beaten the boy, and demanded a goat as compensation for the insult. But the farmer refused to provide a goat and then somehow one of his daughters entered the bargain and more insults had followed and on and on it went until it didn't matter how it had begun. Such were the backward ways of Afghanistan, more backward in some places than others.

Pazhman had once dreamed he would return to be a great lord in this country. But that dream seemed impossible now. Unless he was willing to live in a cave, or in a slum in Jalalabad (he was not), he would remain a fugitive, a man without a country. For now.

Thanks to the Americans.

# CHAPTER 5

*TOC (Tactical Operations Center)*
*Divisional Headquarters*
*Bagram Air Force Base, Afghanistan*

Sgt. Emil Vasquez, the communications specialist whose job was to keep the computers running, had his fingers crossed that the system didn't crash again. The officers in the TOC were on edge, kept busy by the steady stream of intelligence reports to be received and analyzed and logistics arranged. The TOC had been coordinating the operation at Ab Darak and a dozen other drop zones for the past four hours.

Lt. Colonel James Carver leaned back in his chair and stretched his arms. He glanced up at the bulletin board mounted on one wall where photographs of several dozen men, high profile targets, were pinned up. At the top of the board, above the photos, was a handwritten sign that read "Operation Tightnoose." If they were successful, someone would make a red "X" over the photo to indicate he had been either killed or captured.

Carver took a deep breath and looked at the rows of computers and the wires running everywhere. How incongruous, he thought, to see men managing a battle from a computer. But the TOC was where the action was. Where the general was. Where officers who had achieved senior staff positions worked.

What he wouldn't give to be back with his men in the field instead of breathing air-conditioned air, drinking bad coffee and sitting for so long your ass went numb. When he got home would he tell his son that he'd fought the war sitting in a folding metal chair staring at a laptop, typing on a keyboard?

Maybe that wasn't fair. He made sure he got out into the field as often as he could. Sometimes he pushed it beyond what was reasonably expected of him, which was how an officer in an elite unit in the United States Army was supposed to behave. The intel that came to him on his laptop was one thing, but it was another altogether to see the look of fear in the face of a village elder, the rags the villagers wore, whether the children looked like they had eaten that day, and gauge the hundred other things that couldn't be evaluated in a field report. Carver called it the vibe on the ground. And you had to feel it first hand.  But for now it was his job to monitor the feed from an MQ-1C Grey Eagle long range UAV circling above Ab Darak, and wait for pictures of the men who had been bagged in the operation. He knew the spooks in Washington were waiting too.

"Imagery coming in now, sir," Vasquez said.

The sergeant got up from his desk and walked to the printer, which had started humming. He didn't understand it, but Carver always wanted printouts, instead of looking at pictures on the screen. It was so analog, so 20th century, thought Vasquez. But whatever, Carver was the boss.

On the board was a photo of the man they wanted. Vasquez had studied it a hundred times. It was a grainy photograph, taken with a telephoto lens, Vasquez didn't know where.  Beneath it was written "The Ghost." It was what some of the Afghans called him in interrogations, and so that had become his code name.  A bit overly dramatic, thought Vasquez. Beside the photo was an artist's rendition of what "the ghost" looked like. It wasn't much to go on, but it was all they had.

Carver looked at the batch of photos he'd been given and shook his head.

"That's the whole bunch?" he asked.

"Yes sir."

"Call them and make sure."

He waited while Vasquez got on the satellite phone and established a link with the commander on the ground. It would be Lieutenant Hildebrandt, a very capable young man, West Pointer like himself, thought Carver.

Vasquez turned to the major and shook his head. "That's the whole gang, sir, looks like we missed him. But he said they found some kind of underground facility, they're sending encrypted JPEGS. Looks like your hunch about Ab Dakar was a good one."

"JPEGS?"

19

"Yes sir."

"Why can't you just say pictures, they're sending pictures?" Acronyms drove him crazy.

"Sorry, sir, they're sending more… pictures."

"Print them for me, will ya?"

Vasquez smiled. "Yes sir."

A minute later Vasquez handed the colonel a photo, and patched a video feed to a high-resolution screen on the wall.

The video was of the underground chamber discovered by Dennehy. It showed a large room with a long table against one wall.

"Hey Vasquez, can you tell them to zoom in on the left there?"

"Yessir."

Carver leaned forward in his chair to get a closer look as the image stabilized. There was no mistaking the markings, though the fuselage was badly damaged and the wings had been removed. He studied it for a minute before turning to Major Stan Simmons who sat beside him.

"Is that what I think it is?"

The major nodded. "Looks like the fuckers shot down one of our birds."

# CHAPTER 6

The squad cut its own path through a field of poppies. Safer that way. They'd been walking for two hours, going from Ab Darak to the neighboring village of Hurmu. Operation Tightnoose had been a success, for the most part, Hildebrandt told his men. The second battalion had captured a terrorist leader who was high on the list, and elements of the 10th Mountain Division had converged on three villages to the south, netting most of the high profile targets assigned there. The Ranger regiment had succeeded as well, but his team had failed in its primary objective, not that anyone could fault them. As a result, they decided to put out patrols.

Sergeant Dennehy was tired of Afghanistan. He wanted to go home. Home to Woodboro, New York. He wanted to be with his girlfriend again. He thought about her as he carried his heavy pack and weapon through the field. Her name was Jill. They'd been dating since senior year in high school. He wanted to marry her. He also wanted to stay in the Army, but wasn't sure if that was what Jill wanted. It would mean base housing, probably at Fort Benning. It would mean frequent deployments and long absences, maybe not much of a life for a married man, or woman.

If he left the Army, it would mean Woodboro, and then what? Maybe a job at Yorke Aerospace, the area's largest employer? Not likely. He wasn't trained as an engineer, and hadn't completed college. Maybe work as a policeman or maybe a fireman. His uncle could help guide the way, and his Army record would give him an edge in the application process. But did he want to be a policeman? Patrolling the back roads of his hometown would be a let down after the Army. But it was either that or the only other idea he could think of: web designer. He was good on the computer, and liked to surf the Internet. He often thought of going back to school and learning to design websites for clients, not that there were many clients in Woodboro.

Anyway, Woodboro was a long way away. For now he was in Afghanistan, and he had a squad to lead. Shortly after ten o'clock they stopped to rest by an irrigation ditch.

Sanchez drank from his CamelBak and looked at the poppies all around him.

"How much heroin is all this?" he asked.

"Thinking of becoming a drug dealer?" asked Peterson.

"Beat the shit out of humping my ass through this shit hole. I could make a fortune selling smack back home, all those rich fuckers from the suburbs eat this shit up."

"You've got a lot of hostility, Sanchez. You know that?" said Peterson.

"No shit, that's why I joined the Army."

"I think you're a very confused person."

"You got that right."

Sanchez took off his helmet and leaned the back of his head against the earthen embankment. The sun was bright overhead, and a hawk circled above them, riding a thermal higher and higher. Sanchez yawned. "I think I'm gonna fall asleep, like that chick in the movie."

"What movie?" asked Peterson.

"The one with the tornado, and the wicked witch and all those flying monkeys and shit."

Dennehy looked confused. "The Wizard of Oz?"

"Yeah."

"What would make you think of that movie?" he asked.

"All these poppies, I guess."

"Sanchez, you scare me sometimes," said Peterson.

"Sometimes I scare myself."

They rested quietly for ten minutes until Hildebrandt said it was time to move on. The squad stood up and hoisted their packs back on. Sanchez adjusted his helmet.

"So we find this dude, we get to go home?" he asked.

"I doubt that."

"This patrol's one big shit show if you ask me."

Peterson adjusted his pack. "This war's one big shit show."

"This country's a shit show," said Dennehy.

The patrol passed a small settlement in the distance. The people living there watched but did not wave. Shortly after noon the soldiers came to Hurmu, a stone and mud village, where they met elements of the 10th Mountain Division who had come up from the South.

The houses were ancient, built with stones from the hills into which the village, with its many steps and terraces, was tucked. A scrawny dog nosed around in the main square where five men sat smoking a pipe. One of them, an old man without teeth and with wrinkled, dark leathery skin, greeted the squad with a smile and a wave. He was stoned, thought Dennehy.

An officer from the 10th Mountain Division and his interpreter approached the men smoking the hashish.

"Assalaamu alaikum," he said, giving the customary gesture with his hand to his forehead. He received the same greeting in return. Then the interpreter stepped forward and the usual translation began.

"Tell them we've come to see how they're doing today," said the lieutenant.

The interpreter translated. The men nodded.

The old man smiled, and gestured for the lieutenant to sit with them. The lieutenant sat cross-legged. The old man offered him his pipe. The officer smiled and shook his head.

"You should smoke it sir," said the interpreter, "they might take offense."

"I'm not smoking. Tell them I don't smoke."

The interpreter spoke, and the men laughed. One of them said something.

"He says all the men smoke in Afghanistan," said the interpreter.

Dennehy had seen countless similar conversations and thought they were ridiculous.

The lieutenant asked about the Taliban, and the villagers hemmed and hawed and questioned how the Americans could protect them from the Taliban. Then the lieutenant told them the Americans were there to help, and it went back and forth like that for a while. Then he asked if they had seen any strangers from Ab Dakar. The men shook their heads. Finally the lieutenant smiled and they shook hands all around.

23

Same old shit, thought Dennehy, total waste of time.

The Rangers said goodbye to the other 10th Mountain Division soldiers and took a different path on the way back. Dennehy was dog tired, hungry, thirsty, and his feet hurt. They walked single file through the poppy field until they came back to a stream. He wanted to take his boots off and put his feet in the water but that was out of the question. Instead he chose a place to cross, deliberately avoiding the small wooden footbridge, three rickety planks spanning the water. He stood to the side of the stream and watched as the rest of the patrol passed. Hill brought up the rear. Dennehy turned to resume his march, then looked back at Hill, who was about to cross the footbridge.

He started to warn him: "Jason, don't ---"

The blast catapulted Dennehy back through searing heat and dirt. He landed on his back among the poppies. He could hear nothing. He felt a stinging pain in his leg. He opened his eyes, and saw dark smoke wafting across the endless blue Afghan sky.

# CHAPTER 7

*Near the River Gul, Afghanistan*

Pazhman sought cover wherever he could, moving through gullies and orchards, wooded areas and brush. He avoided roads and open fields. He had considered traveling by night instead of during the day, but quickly realized that was impossible. The terrain was too rough.

The fields he crossed had once been cultivated with barley, but now lay fallow and neglected. He recognized the ground on which he traveled, for he had visited here several months earlier to show his followers how to plant a roadside bomb, to be ready if the Americans came. They were simple bombs, designed for simple men. He had showed them how to find a suitable location to bury the explosives, and how to detonate them. The idea was that these men would, in turn, teach others.

Pazhman was a disciple of Professor Al Fariz, known to some as the Lion of Peshawar, the spiritual leader of an organization called Pachaas Talwaray. Translated into English, it meant Fifty Swords.

He had been among fifty men recruited many years earlier, and trained in the mountains not far from here. Those first recruits had endured the most punishing training, after which they had dispersed. It was said there were cells in Europe and the US, but no one spoke of these. Only the leader, Professor Al Fariz, knew everything. It was safer that way.

Pazhman walked through the morning and afternoon and into the early evening. He had not eaten in more than 24 hours and was hungry, and thirsty too. Perhaps he was being tested, he thought. Perhaps this is a message, that it is time for me to bring my struggle to another place, into the heart of the enemy. As the sun went down Pazhman, one of the original members of Pachaas Talwaray, found a place beneath a juniper tree and lay down. Within a few moments he was asleep.

In the morning Pazhman moved into territory he was not

familiar with. He had traveled nearly thirty miles, and was no longer in the lands once ruled by his family, but in territory that belonged to the Bandar tribe. From here, until he crossed the river Gul, he would be in danger. The Bandar was a tribe of cheaters and scoundrels, who stole young boys and who had been lackeys of the British long ago. That is what was said of them.

If he ran across any Bandar tribesmen Pazhman decided he would tell them that the Americans had raided his village to the east and so he was making his way to Pakistan. But he was sure if he came upon any Bandar they would almost certainly slit his throat and take his money. At least they would try. He reached under his robe and took his weapon from its leather holster, checking to make sure it was loaded.

And, of course, he had his knife.

He spent the rest of the day moving through dense woods as the terrain grew more mountainous, thick with conifer forests. Whenever he came to a clearing, he watched carefully before proceeding. He saw no one except once, some women and children working in a field at a distance. He passed them undetected.

At the end of the day Pazhman lay down in a rocky gully. He was, by now, so weak from hunger and thirst that he was delirious. He fell asleep almost immediately. When he woke the sun was going down, and it was getting colder. He knelt to say his prayer. When he had finished his prayers he looked up there was a man standing over him. The man wore the robes and headdress of a Bandar villager and he carried an old hunting rifle over his shoulder.

"Who are you, and what are you doing here?" he demanded. He kicked Pazhman in the leg. "You are crossing on Bandar territory. Where do you come from?"

Pazhman started to speak. Then something hit him hard on the head. When he regained consciousness his hands were bound behind his back. He was sitting in the dusty courtyard of a house, and his head hurt. He had trouble opening his left eye, and realized it was because it was sealed shut with dried blood.

Two young boys approached and spat on him, then cursed him. One of the boys, who was about eight and wore a hat and filthy shirt and vest, saw a small stone on the ground and picked it up. He threw the stone, hitting Pazhman's chin. The boys looked for more pebbles and threw them at Pazhman. They made a game of it until a toothless old man, with a revolver and Pazhman's silver-handled knife tucked into his belt, appeared in the courtyard. The boys fled.

"Who are you?" the old man demanded.

"I am Pazhman Khan."

"And where are you coming from?"

"Ab Darak." If he was going to die, he would do so proudly, but Pazhman was not ready to concede that.

Pazhman saw that the old man had his satchel. He watched as the old man rummaged inside. He took out the object wrapped in bubble wrap that Pazhman had guarded so carefully. He removed the plastic and examined it. It was a computer circuit board, very fragile, and precious. The old man tossed it to the ground.

"Why have you come here?" the old man spoke loudly and appeared angry and full of energy, almost spitting.

Pazhman did not reply.

There were three men sitting at the far side of the courtyard talking, and when they saw that Pazhman was being questioned, they came over to listen. One had a rifle slung over his shoulder, and Pazhman recognized him as the man who had first discovered him. The other two men had knives under their belts.

Pazhman was exhausted, but he knew he would only grow weaker. If he was going to act, now was the time. In a single motion, Pazhman rocked backwards and swung his bound arms around his feet and stood up, his hands now in front of him. The old man looked at him in surprise. Pazhman quickly hooked the old man's neck in his right arm and broke it with a quick twist of his arm.

Stunned, the man with the rifle began unshouldering his weapon, but he was too slow. As the lifeless body of the old man collapsed at his feet, Pazhman removed the revolver from the dead man's belt, and fired a single shot into the rifleman's head.

He aimed his next shot at a short man seated nearby, but the revolver clicked on an empty chamber. Pazhman pulled the trigger again, but there was no bullet. Without wasting another second he dropped the revolver and slipped his knife from its sheath in the old man's belt, then with a single motion plunged it into the seated man's neck.

Less than five seconds had elapsed. Two remaining tribesmen turned and fled toward the fields. Pazhman picked up the dead man's rifle and shot the first in the back, then watched as the second man hid in terror behind a stone wall. Knife in hand, Pazhman walked slowly across the courtyard to face the man, who had prostrated himself on the ground, begging for his life.

"You are a devil!" the man said.

"Yes," said Pazhman.

# CHAPTER 8

Pazhman recovered his pistol and money, and wiped the blade of his knife on the robe of the old man. He recovered the precious item that had been so carelessly cast aside. He dusted it off, wrapped it in the same piece of plastic and replaced it in his satchel.

The two boys who had thrown stones were nowhere to be seen. They had disappeared. They would tell others, and those others would think twice before they interfered with anyone from Ab Dakar, thought Pazhman.

In the house he found a goat bladder filled with water and drank. He found bread too, and ate that, and also some sweet dates. When he was done he went back outside and surveyed the area. Behind one of the outbuildings he found a rusted old Kawasaki motorcycle. It looked serviceable, and there was air in the tires. He unscrewed the gas cap and smelled inside to see if there was gas, then he threw his leg over the seat and kick-started it. After several tries the motor sputtered to life. Pazhman left it idling while he collected his belongings and the goat bladder, and then got back on the bike and rode away.

The motorcycle made it as far as the River Gul. When the gas ran out Pazhman abandoned it among some rocks by the side of the road and continued on foot. He had trudged along the side of the road for two hours when a truck approached. It was an old Russian Ural 4320, a military transport that had seen better days. In the back of the Ural he saw three men and the motorcycle he had left abandoned.

"Where are you going?" asked the driver, a bald man with a long beard.

"Mardan," replied Pazhman.

"That is a long way."

"Yes."

"Where are you coming from?" asked the driver, who suspected that Pazhman was the one who had abandoned the motorcycle. This could mean he was probably a bandit, because bandits rode motorcycles, though he did not look like a bandit. He had refined features, which meant he was probably Taliban.

"Where I am coming from is no concern of yours. Have you seen any soldiers?"

"Soldiers?" the driver asked. Now he was even more interested in this stranger.

"Americans?" asked Pazhman.

The driver shook his head. "I am going to Jalalabad."

"If I give you ten American dollars, will you take me there?"

"Dollars?"

Pazhman nodded.

"Climb in the back," said the driver.

In the back of the truck, the other men held on to the canopy frame and swung back and forth as the truck lurched along. They were workers on their way to a zinc mine in Ghazni and eyed Pazhman with detached curiosity. Eventually a young man with a foggy white eye said, "Have you seen this motorcycle before?"

Pazhman shook his head.

"It is a very good motorcycle. Kawasaki. Who would leave such a machine by the side of the road?"

Pazhman shrugged. The young man said nothing. One of the men in the truck had a dirty plastic liter bottle of water and some bread. He shared it with Pazhman. Then Pazhman leaned against the back of the cab and slept. But he slept lightly, with his hand on his satchel, ready to kill anyone who tried to rob him. Four hours later the truck arrived at Jalalabad.

Pazhman got out and paid the driver. He was on the outskirts of town and walked toward the main square. There was a safe house in Jalalabad. More important, the city was the gateway to Pakistan, where Professor Al Fariz had a network in place and many friends to help Pazhman on his journey.

Pazhman had never been to the safe house, but it had been described to him, and he had committed the address to memory. It was the home of a follower, whose services had been enlisted for this purpose only. Pazhman found the address without difficulty, first taking a taxi, then walking for more than a mile so the driver would not know where he had gone. The house had a steel gate that opened onto a traditional courtyard with well-tended fruit trees and a well. In the courtyard a fat man with a black beard was repairing the engine of a Toyota pick-up truck.

"Assalaamu alaykum," said Pazhman.

The man looked up from the engine and studied Pazhman. "Waalaikum as-salaam," he replied.

"I have come from far away, seeking a friend of a friend."

"Are you lost?" asked the fat man.

"A true believer is never lost," replied Pazhman.

"What is this friend's name?"

"Omar," replied Pazhman.

"And who is his friend?"

"His name may not be uttered, but they sometimes call him The Lion."

The fat man smiled. "I am Omar, who are you?"

"Pazhman Khan."

The man's smile disappeared.

"From where have you come?"

"Ab Dakar. The Americans attacked."

Omar nodded. He had heard of the recent American raids.

"Come, please be my guest."

Pazhman entered the house, where Omar brought out tea and bread and cheese. After Pazhman had eaten, Omar showed him where he could bathe and after that he gave him clean clothes. Then Pazhman slept.

In the morning, while Pazhman rested, several men came and went, and Pazhman heard hushed conversations. In the early afternoon, one of the men returned behind the wheel of an old Peugeot taxi and Pazhman and Omar were driven across Jalalabad to the oldest part of the city. Here, the streets were very narrow and congested with pedestrians. The taxi stopped in front of a cement block wall. In the wall was a weathered door. They got out of the car and Omar knocked loudly on the door. A young boy opened it. He was dressed in a traditional Afghan white kameez, topped with a fancy embroidered vest. On his head he wore a kufi.

31

The boy nodded and led Omar and Pazhman into a large room with a carpet and pillows on the floor surrounding a brass coffee table. The boy gestured for them to sit. A few moments later a man in a grey suit entered. Omar sprang to his feet and shook the man's hand.

"Greetings, Omar." He turned to Pazhman, who also stood. "You are most welcome here. I am Farrukhzad."

The men sat and the boy brought tea and dried apricots. After pouring the tea Farrukhzad looked at Pazhman and said, "You are the son of Assadullah Khan." It was more a statement than a question.

Pazhman nodded.

"You alone escaped?" he asked.

"I escaped by tunnel."

"And the others?"

Pazhman shook his head.

"Such is the way," said their host. "Some are born to be martyrs, and others, well, others prefer not." He laughed and put an apricot in his mouth.

Farrukhzad was testing him. Pazhman understood and expected this. Their leader, Professor Al Fariz, had to be protected. One had to pass through many layers of security, for there were spies and traitors everywhere, and one could not be too careful.

"Tell me about Ab Dakar," he said, and Pazhman told the story.

"The Americans came for you, and yet you have eluded them."

"Yes."

"If you are caught they will send you to prison."

"I will never be taken."

"That is good. Did you have trouble on your journey?"

"Yes, a little."

"Tell me." He gestured toward the injury on Pazhman's head.

"Some bandits, from Bandar."

"And?"

"They met the same fate as all who stand in our way."

Farrukhzad looked at Pazhman's cold dark eyes. He felt a shiver. He had met many cruel men, he himself was considered a cruel man, but he had seen a look in the man's eyes. There must be a hatred seated deeply within him, he thought, for had he not suffered at the hands of the infidel?

"I knew of your father, many, many years ago. He died fighting the infidel."

"He killed many Russians," said Pazhman.

Farrukhzad nodded as Omar listened intently, his eyes open wide, hanging on every word, surprised at this sudden connection.

"He must have been a very great man," said Omar, eager to inject himself into the conversation.

Farrukhzad ignored him.

"Where do you wish to go?"

"I must see our master."

Farrukhzad shifted his eyes to Omar. He thought for a moment, then nodded.

"In Peshawar, seek out a solicitor named Abdel. You will find yourself among friends."

Then he told him how he should go.

The next morning Omar and Pazhman left for Pakistan. They drove for several hours along the pitted and dusty macadam road, the Toyota's engine wheezed and sputtered. As they approached the border, Omar occasionally craned his neck to look up through the dirty windshield at the sky for American drones, as if he could see anything.

When they neared the border they turned onto a bumpy dirt road. It was a smuggler's route, well known to Omar, which would allow them to avoid the main border crossing. Pazhman had left Afghanistan by a similar route once before, many years earlier. Memories of his early childhood came back to him. Pazhman had been seven when the Hind helicopters first arrived in his valley. The helicopters destroyed two of the nearest villages suspected of harboring resistance fighters.

"You must go to Peshawar, to school. There you will be safe," his father told him.

"Then one day you will return to govern the tribe and care for the family lands, when the infidel Russians are finally vanquished."

So the young Pazhman left the only home he had ever known.

33

He was sent through the Khyber Pass to a school run by a friend of his father's, Professor Al Fariz. Young Pazhman studied sharia law and hadiths, the sayings and deeds of the prophet, but the school was known for its engineering, and much time was spend doing math, physics, chemistry and other sciences.

He was a clever boy, and did well at the school. Pazhman's father had some influence, and so Professor Al Fariz took a special interest in young Pazhman. He noticed that the boy's mind and body showed promise. But intellectual promise was not enough. What was missing was fanaticism. Then one day, when Pazhman was doing his lessons, a messenger arrived at the school. The professor summoned Pazhman.

"Your father is dead," he told the boy.

Tears rolled down Pazhman's cheeks. He felt his throat tighten.

"How?" he asked.

"The Russians."

"And my mother?"

"Oh, she too is dead, and your sister and brother. I will care for you now, as your father wanted. You may grieve today, then tomorrow return to your studies. It is best."

Years passed. Al Fariz saw to it that his studies continued. He promised Pazhman that one day he would avenge his father.

"But how? When?" pressed the young boy.

"When you have learned all you need to know, and when you have learned to be patient, for only through patience will we achieve victory," replied the professor.

Pazhman was sent abroad to a university in New York. There he learned the western ways - how to speak, how to dress, how to behave. He learned how the Americans thought, and what their strengths and weaknesses were. Perhaps most important, he learned that he could move freely among them, make friends with them, without raising suspicions.

When he finally returned to Pakistan, the most difficult training began. It began with physical conditioning in the mountains where the young man joined the other recruits and learned to endure the harshest conditions and the most grueling conditioning. Those who

34

survived learned tradecraft – how to travel without raising suspicion, to send messages, conceal their identity, and alter their appearance. And they learned to kill.

# CHAPTER 9

Now, once again, he was returning to his teacher. The only father he had ever really known. They drove through the night, and in the morning, Omar and Pazhman arrived in Peshawar. Omar pulled over by the side of the road near the Meena Bazaar.

"This is where we part. You know where you are going, I wish you the best of luck," said Omar.

"You will not come with me?"

"My job is to take you as far as this."

So the two men shook hands and Pazhman watched as Omar drove away.

Pazhman followed the directions Farrukhzad had given him. He passed into the old walled city through a series of narrow alleys until he came to a courtyard with a fast moving gurgling stream that passed underneath the buildings and a stone bridge, exactly as Farrukhzad had described it. Pazhman went into a building and up a flight of winding stairs to the third floor. A sign was painted on the wall announcing that it was the office of the solicitor, Abdel Saif. He knocked.

"Yes?" came a tentative voice from the other side of the door.

"Abdel?"

"Yes?"

"I have been sent by a friend in Jalalabad," said Pazhman.

The door opened.

Abdel Saif had a slight build and wore a tattered linen suit. He was in his mid-thirties, had a trimmed beard, and intelligent, worried-looking eyes. He ushered Pazhman into his law office, then looked down the stairs.

"You have not been followed?"

"No."

"Your journey was without difficulty?"

Pazhman shook his head. He noticed that one of Abdel's teeth, a small one in front, on the bottom, was black and rotted.

"That is good," said Abdel. "We will stay here until after

36

afternoon prayers, then we will go."

Once again, Pazhman waited. Abdel paced nervously in his small, cluttered office. He checking his watch frequently and looked out the window at the rooftops below, covered in a tangle of electrical wires and drying laundry. Pazhman drank tea and ate some cakes that Abdel offered.

At 5 o'clock, as the prayers ended, the two men set out through the warren of alleyways in the medina. Twenty minutes later they arrived at a walled enclosure on Charsada Road, a dusty street that smelled of garbage just outside the old city

Abdel knocked on an ancient wooden door.

A peephole slid open and a wrinkled face appeared. Hushed words were exchanged. The door swung open and a smiling toothless man with a beard and an old shotgun slung over his shoulder invited them to enter.

"I will say goodbye here, as-salamu-alaykum," said Abdel, then nervously departed in the direction they had come.


Since leaving the school and joining the struggle, Pazhman had met Professor Al Fariz many times, almost always in a different location: Kandahar, Islamabad, and Yemen. The madrassa had long since been condemned by Pakistani Intelligence and closed down, and the professor had disappeared. Few even knew he existed, and even fewer about the Pachaas Talwaray.

Security was paramount. The professor prided himself on his ability to control events without his communications being intercepted. Al Fariz's commands were passed to a select few, and these trusted servants in turn passed his instructions on to the operators in the field. If captured, no torture could make them reveal the professor's identity because no one knew it; they only knew his most recent location, and they would die before they revealed that. And anyway, none of them had ever been captured.

Pazhman was shown into the room where Al Fariz worked at a computer terminal. He was a slight man with intense blue eyes and white hair cropped short. Pazhman was always honored to be given an audience with the professor. He liked to think he was the only one to be accorded the honor, but he knew there were several

37

others like him.

"My son, you have returned, that is good. Providence shines upon you," said the professor.

Pazhman kissed him on both cheeks. "Babe," he said, which meant "father." "It has been too long."

The professor listened quietly as Pazhman described, in detail, the American attack on the compound.

"Farzad has been killed?" he asked, realizing that Ab Dakar was now a total loss as far as an operating station. Not that it mattered, it had already served its purpose.

"I suspect he may have been."

"But he may have been captured?"

"It is possible."

The professor stroked the tip of his beard and considered this. "You did well to escape, you have done very well. You were not followed?"

"I am certain I have not been."

The professor nodded.

"And so, were you able to bring that which we desire?"

Pazhman closed his eyes and nodded. The professor held out his hand and Pazhman reached into his satchel and removed the dusty plastic-wrapped package.

Al Fariz took the object and unwrapped it. He gave it a cursory examination and snapped his fingers. A young man entered and Al Fariz handed him the circuit board. The young man left without saying anything.

Tea was brought and the two men sat on cushions on the floor. The professor sipped his tea and studied Pazhman. At length he said, "You have done very well, indeed, but you are injured, and you are tired. So now you will rest. Then when it is time you will serve me once more."

"Where?"

"Preparations must be made, there is much to be done over many months. But now is not the time to talk of such things."

Pazhman spent the next weeks resting in the shade of the garden, on cushions spread out beneath a fig tree. The professor's servants fed him well every day: roast lamb, rice and fruit, and a doctor was summoned to attend to the cut on his head. Every afternoon the professor invited him to talk about their struggle. The topics were far ranging and varied: the evils of the West, digital technology, Western banking and economics, vegetarianism, Hindus, the corruption of the infidel, and always, the martyrs, the men who were part of Pazhman's elite class of fighters who had sacrificed themselves.

"The Americans have devious methods which we must counter," he said one day as they sat in the garden. "Their drones have killed many of our friends. More and more every day. The destruction comes without warning."

The professor smiled. "It is not without irony. I spent my youth developing computer programs to control satellites, and now they give me no rest."

Pazhman nodded. He had been told many times of Al Fariz's days as a gifted student at university. In their talks, Al Fariz often spoke of his experiences as a young researcher, and the pioneering work he had done in aerospace before he returned to Pakistan and founded his madrassa.

During their conversations, the professor always watched Pazhman closely, looking for any signs of weakness, but he never saw any. Several weeks later, while drinking lemonade, Professor Al Fariz outlined his plan.

"You will not return to Afghanistan. You are no longer needed there. You will be sent elsewhere, and you may never return."

Pazhman nodded.

"We have spent many years preparing for this, and now you will be my personal emissary, you will be my sword, but first more training and much preparation are needed."

"Where shall I go?"

"America. You know this country well."

"And what will I do there?"

"You will attack them as they have attacked us."

A car arrived later that afternoon and Pazhman went with the professor to a cement-walled warehouse building on the outskirts of

39

town. On the wall was a small sign that read "PDS Group Limited, Data Management Outsource Services" There was a steel door and steel shutters on the windows. As soon as they got out of the car the steel door opened and they stepped inside the building.

"PDS?" Pazhman inquired.

"Peshawar Data Services, just a name I came up with," said the professor with a wave of the hand. "It is a suitable cover."

The building was highly air-conditioned, and Pazhman, unused to the cool air, felt a chill. They were in a small anteroom, where a young man stood with an Uzi submachine gun. The professor brushed past the guard and led the way down a tiled corridor illuminated by a row of fluorescent lights. Pazhman soon discovered the reason for the cold air. The professor opened a door at the end of the corridor where there was a large room. On one side of the room was a huge mainframe computer. On the other were two rectangular tables were a dozen men sat working on computers. Wires ran everywhere along the white vinyl tiled floor.

"It is here I do my mischief," said the professor.

"And these men?"

"Loyal, and very well paid," he smiled. "Come, let me show you."

The professor showed Pazhman into an adjoining room where there was a bank of computer monitors.

"Sit," instructed the professor, directing him to a plastic chair.

Pazhman watched as monitors came on, one by one. Now, for the first time, he fully understood his mission. He realized the value of the cargo he had so carefully protected. The professor truly was a genius, as he had always thought, and now, after all these years, the great plan would be implemented, and the infidel would pay.

For the next six months Pazhman took a car to PDS Group computer center where he completed his advanced training and mastered every aspect of his new assignment. One day, when he returned to the professor's house on Charsada Road, the solicitor, Abdel, was waiting.

He accompanied Pazhman into town to have a haircut, and pick up two suits made by a local tailor. They were Western-style suits, the kind favored by businessmen. They also purchased all the other clothes and shoes he would need. His transformation as an international businessman was complete.  They went to a camera store where Pazhman's photo was taken, and two days later Abdel returned to the house and presented Pazhman with a new passport.

"Your name is Arun Patel now," he said.

"Why Patel?"

"It is a good name, I think."

# CHAPTER 10

*Jacksonville, Florida*

Special Agent Kim Conrad of the FBI Florida Bank Robbery Task Force walked into her supervisor's office in the Federal Building in downtown Jacksonville juggling a sheaf of papers and a laptop. She was fully prepared to make a PowerPoint presentation. She had stayed up until after midnight working on it. Maybe she'd gotten a little carried away with the colored charts, but that was how she operated; she liked to be prepared. It was the level of efficiency that had gotten her accepted to Harvard undergrad and Wharton Business School. It had also landed her a job at the FBI, something she sometimes regretted, as it had meant postings to cities she would just as soon forget. Jacksonville wasn't terrible, but it wasn't Miami.

Kim had a slight frame and delicate features, dark hair, deep brown eyes and lips that tended to turn up slightly at the corners when she found something amusing or ironic or irritating. Even though the agency frowned on it, a cigarette could sometimes be found dangling from those lips.

Frank Monahan was on the phone, saw Kim and gestured for her to come in.

"Put that down anywhere," he said, cupping his hand over the phone.

Monahan had more than 30 years in the bureau and was the ranking agent at the Jacksonville office. Kim placed her files on his coffee table, sat down, and flipped open her laptop. He finished his conversation and hung up the phone.

"What's all this about?" he asked.

Kim adjusted her glasses. "Sir, I've been working on the cowboy case."

"Yes?"

"I think I've got something."

Monahan leaned back in his chair and crossed his arms. "Talk to me."

"Well, I developed an algorithm, based on all the previous robberies, their dates, time of day, location, as many variables as I could find."

"And?"

"I think he's going to rob the First Florida branch on Highway 1 at 2:45 this afternoon."

Monahan considered this for a moment. The so-called Cowboy Robber had robbed 14 banks over the past five months, and had always gotten away clean. He was known as the "Cowboy Robber" simply because he had lately begun wearing a cowboy hat. He was the task force's number one priority.

"The First Florida Bank?" said Monahan.

"Yes, sir," replied Kim.

"At 2:45?"

Kim nodded.

"Not 2:30, not 3 o'clock?"

"2:45 is my best guess, sir. I have a PowerPoint-"

"So this is a guess?" asked Monahan.

"Well, nobody can predict a future event with certainty sir, but I'd put the probability at around 65 percent."

"65 percent?"

"Yes sir."

"At 2:45?"

"We might want to station people an hour before and after that, just in case," she said.

"So how do you figure this?"

"Statistics, sir, and the laws of probability, based on past events."

"You're sure?"

"Like I said, 65 percent sure, with a margin of error of plus or minus 3 percent."

"Give or take 3 percent?"

Kim nodded. "That's the best I could do."

"You based all this on statistics?"

Kim sighed to herself. It was so basic. It was so very boring, really. She spent her days looking for anomalies in bank transfers and statistics that suggested illegal behavior. Lately she had turned

43

her attention to probability studies to gauge the pattern of bank robberies so the bureau could better budget personnel demands.

Numbers spoke to her; she could see patterns and find meaning where others couldn't. As a result, anything involving financial data was assigned to her, which meant all the shady bookkeeping and forensic accounting, spreadsheets and computers, exactly what she'd joined the Bureau to get away from. She rarely went to the pistol range, and she had never once arrested anyone.

"Statistics are all I have to go on, sir. That and the fact that bank robbers have a mean IQ of 92, which implies he will repeat tried and true formulas rather than create new strategies."

"I see." He threw his hands up in the air. "Okay, so stake out First Florida. Put a team together and get over there at about 1:45." He looked at his watch. "You better hurry."

"Sir?"

"Get over there and get set up before this 'cowboy' shows up," said Monahan.

"Me?" asked Kim.

"Why not?"

"Well, that's not really what I do," replied Kim, "I don't spend much time in the field, sir. I'm more a numbers person."

"You went to the academy?"

"Well, yeah, but, it's just that I always work in the office running computer programs. I'm not really a field agent like the others."

"You're current on your marksmanship?"

"Sure, but-"

"Then what's the problem?" he asked.

"It's not a problem, but you just caught me off guard."

"Look, Agent Conrad. You want to put a last minute team in place at First Florida, you're gonna have to call the shots."

Kim didn't know what to say. She fidgeted with her laptop.

"Mean IQ of 92, huh?" asked Monahan.

"Yes, sir."

"Which means half are more intelligent, and half are less intelligent, right?"

"Well, yeah."

"Make sure you bring backup," said Monahan.

# CHAPTER 11

The bank occupied a one-story glass building. The front door opened onto the sidewalk on Route 1, the rear onto a parking lot.

Kim had rushed to cobble together a team. Three of the team members, Lewellyn, Sanderson and Barnes, were investigators who, like Kim, spent their days poring over financial reports looking for phony ledger entries and embezzled funds. To make up for their lack of field experience, she enlisted the help of Art Carmichael, an old hand on the bank robbery task force, and Nancy Davidson, who was in town to attend a meeting of regional supervisors and had some spare time on her hands.

They divided into three teams of two. One team would watch the front door of the bank, one the back, and the third would stand by across the street from the entrance in case things went badly.

The most experienced, Agent Carmichael took the point position at the front entrance. He was joined by Ed Lewellyn, whose specialty was forensic IT, which meant he spent his days in a computer lab deciphering computer hard drives. Lewellyn had to borrow a Sig Sauer 9mm.

Nancy Davidson, being the second most experienced agent, covered the rear door. With her was Jim Sanderson, who worked in auditing with Kim. Kim took the backup spot, across the street from the bank. She waited in the car with Evelyn Barnes, a rookie newly assigned to the Criminal Investigative Division, or CID. Barnes had grown up west of Chicago, been valedictorian of her high school class, achieved summa cum laude at University of Illinois and graduated from the FBI Academy six months earlier.

"So we're looking for a cowboy hat, huh?" asked Barnes.

"He doesn't always wear a hat. Actually he's only worn one 37 percent of the time, but more so lately," said Kim.

"So it's a trend?"

"It is a trend. Sometimes he wears cowboy boots, too. We checked the database for horse owners and ranchers and wranglers or whatever, but no luck," said Kim.

"If you can afford a horse, you'd hardly be robbing banks," said Barnes.

"True. I checked that. You know how much it costs to feed a horse?"

Barnes shook her head.

"Average stable and board in the state of Florida is $463 per month. And there are more that 500,000 horses in Florida, more than Kentucky. Most of the ranches are further north of Tampa, but you get into Palm Beach, Jupiter, it's horse country."

The rookie looked at Kim. "So you don't think he's a real cowboy?"

"Bank clerks described his hands. Said they were soft. I think he just wears the cowboy hat to hide his face from the cameras. I'm guessing the boots mean he doesn't have much fashion sense. But I could be wrong; he could be some kind of cowboy," said Kim.

Kim wasn't at all like the other women special agents Barnes had met in training. For starters she wasn't athletic. At all. She had nails, polished nails, and her hair was cut really well, in a shaggy sort of way. And she had great lips with red lipstick.

"Your skin is really beautiful," said Barnes.

"Thanks."

"I'm sorry."

"That's okay, I don't mind."

Barnes looked at Kim's shoes. French, she thought, the ones with the red soles, she couldn't remember the name. She wanted to ask her where she had gotten them, probably the Bal Harbor Mall, or maybe knock-offs from T.J. Maxx? She decided not to ask; she was new, and didn't want to appear unprofessional.

Kim looked at her watch. They had been sitting in the car for an hour. It was almost 3 o'clock.

"He's not going to show. He's probably robbing some other bank," Kim sounded disappointed. She watched out the window. She was wearing dark Oakleys. It was blindingly hot.

"Be positive, he may show up yet," said Barnes.

"My personal mental outlook might affect my own performance, but it will have no bearing whatsoever on our suspect's behavior. He's never robbed a bank past 3:20, and if we eliminate outliers, the range is 2:15 to 2:45 p.m. He likes to avoid the lunch hour crowd and rush hour," said Kim.

"Yeah, well, there's always the exception," said Barnes.

"But it's statistically unlikely."

"Are you a math whiz or something?"

"I studied advanced mathematics in college, finance in business school," replied Kim.

"Finance?"

Kim nodded.

"So shouldn't you be working in there, with the money, where it's air conditioned, instead of sitting out here in the heat?"

"That was the idea, until I got recruited."

"You were recruited?" asked Barnes.

Kim nodded.

"What made you say yes?" Barnes asked.

"It seemed interesting to me."

"You glad you made that choice?"

Kim thought for a moment.

"For the most part, yeah."

Barnes suddenly shifted in her seat. "Dude in a cowboy hat, across the street," she said. "Holy shit."

Kim raised her binoculars. She saw a man of average height, slight build, walking on the opposite sidewalk toward the entrance of the bank. He had a rucksack on his back, and wore a white straw cowboy hat.

"He bought a new hat," said Kim.

"Not every day you rob a bank," replied Barnes.

They watched as he walked into the lobby of the bank. Kim picked up the radio set. "Suspect just entered the lobby," she said.

She watched as Carmichael and Lewellyn got out of their car and went in after him.

"What should we do?" asked Barnes.

Kim wasn't sure. "Just sit tight, I think."

She looked at her watch. It was 3:05.

Inside the bank, the man with the cowboy hat, who would later be identified as Robert Wade Mitchell, and who had robbed a total

47

of 34 banks stretching from Florida to Arkansas in his career, paused on the terrazzo floor and looked at the tellers' windows. He knew exactly what he was doing. He knew that the window on the right was where commercial customers could make express deposits without waiting in line, and that the commercial teller had more cash. He stepped up to the window and slipped his knapsack off his shoulder. The teller, a middle-aged woman with glasses that dangled from a beaded chain around her neck, smiled. She watched as he reached into the knapsack, and thought at first that he was removing his deposit, though it was strange, because she knew most of the commercial customers. She didn't recognize this man.

"May I help you?' she asked.

"Sure, you can hand over everything you've got in the drawer, except the dye pack, and don't forget to smile."

She looked down and saw that Mitchell was aiming a .38 revolver at her chest.

"Let's make this quick," he continued, smiling.

The teller, Evelyn Pineway, 19 years with the bank, hesitated, then she did as she was instructed. She had been trained to do this by the bank. Don't try to be a hero. Safety first, the money is insured. But still, it galled her. Nervously, she removed bills from her cash drawer and passed them to the cowboy. He quickly inspected them and stuffed them in his knapsack, but shook his head when she tried to pass him a bundle of twenties.

"Unwrap it, please," he said.

She did as she was instructed, fanning the bills to show they didn't conceal a dye pack.

The cowboy stuffed the cash in his knapsack. He smiled at her. "Thank you. Now just sit still until I'm gone, or someone in the bank is gonna end up getting hurt. And you have a real good day."

Carmichael observed the entire transaction while filling out a deposit slip at a stand-up table in the center of the bank. He had watched several of the cowboy's previous robberies, captured by surveillance cameras. This was no different, though he was impressed by how calm and collected the cowboy was, like he was a man with nothing to fear, a routine transaction.

Carmichael and Lewellyn followed the Cowboy out of the bank.

They stepped quickly as they approached the door. They had their weapons drawn as soon as they were on the sidewalk.

"Hold it right there!" shouted Carmichael. "Hands where I can see 'em, down on the ground!"

The Cowboy grimaced and snapped his fingers.

In the debriefing, Kim had trouble remembering exactly what occurred next. It happened so fast. She was about to step out of her car when a white Ford F-150 van pulled up in front of the bank. The van's side door slid open. Llewellyn and Carmichael looked up to see a man in a ski mask holding an AR-15 automatic rifle, like a door gunner in a helicopter gunship. They flattened themselves behind a parked car as the gunman opened fire.

Kim heard the rapid popping of gunfire. She pressed down on the gas and the Crown Vic lurched forward. The tires squealed as she turned sharply, cut across four lanes, and slammed into the side of the van. The force of the impact threw the cowboy and the gunman out of the van onto the sidewalk.

The airbags deployed. Barnes was unconscious. Kim staggered out of the car, pulled her weapon and moved toward the van where the driver sat, momentarily stunned, his window broken. She placed her pistol against the side of his head. He turned and she looked him in the eye, shaking her head.

"Don't make me kill you."

# CHAPTER 12

"So the Sparrow wants to sing?" the embassy man asked as he poured two martinis. The bar was set up on a tiled table under a massive banyan tree in his garden. He dropped three olives into each drink. He knew how his guest liked them.

"So it would seem."

"Do you trust him?"

Rich Moran looked at his host and blinked, like the question didn't make sense. "I don't trust anybody."

Moran took a sip of his drink and raised his eyebrows to complement his friend's martini mixing skill. There were damn few places in Islamabad where you could get a martini, let alone a good one, but Elliot Forrester always seemed to have a supply of good gin and vermouth.

Forrester was the assistant defense attaché at the U.S. Embassy. He was in the business of obtaining intelligence, which meant he was a buyer of information. But good information was hard to come by, because the vendors were, more often than not, unreliable. Often they were outright thieves, or worse. But his job was to weed out the good offers, so he listened carefully.

Officially, Moran was regional vice president, Europe & Asia, of Venture Consulting, Inc., an innocuous sounding organization that represented the interests of American exporters. He told anyone who asked that he was, at the moment, studying the market for a client called Industrial Coatings Corporation of Cleveland, Ohio. Of course, he was doing no such thing. He didn't know anything about industrial coatings, except that it was a fancy name for paint.

"Sounds like a trap," said Forrester.

"They always sound like a trap," said Moran.

"But you believe him?" asked Forrester.

"He hasn't steered us wrong yet."

"And he mentioned Pachaas Talwaray?"

Moran took a sip of his martini. "He did."

"You think there's anything to that?"

"I don't know."

"I thought Pachaas Talwaray had died out. Who was it, some old professor?"

"Al Fariz."

"He still alive?"

Moran shrugged. "Be interesting to find out. Could be better than what we usually get."

Better than what Moran's small network of informants usually provided. They were mostly mid-level Pakistani government officials, a few members of parliament and several Pakistani army officers. They provided information of limited value in return for an equally limited supplement to their meager monthly wages. The usual intel: political currents, which army general supported the commander in chief, which one didn't, maybe Pakistani negotiating strategy in pending arms deals. But when it came to Islamic radicals, the sources dried up.

Then one day Moran found the Sparrow. Or rather the Sparrow found him. Sparrow was the code name Forrester had chosen for him. His real name was never used, no dossier kept except in the deepest electronic recesses of Langley. He was simply the Sparrow. The Sparrow moved silently through the streets of Islamabad and Peshawar, watching and listening, slowly cultivating sources. It was a very dangerous game, and one for which he demanded substantial compensation. Of course, they never paid him what he asked for, you had to be careful not to spoil them.

Moran pressed his hands on his stomach. He had been in Pakistan for 36 months, and was a veteran of Lebanon, Damascus, Cairo, and other Middle East shit holes too numerous to mention, but he still occasionally ate something that blew out his otherwise steel-belted digestive system. The martini hadn't been a good idea.

"The Sparrow's almost too good. Maybe he's working for the other side," said Forrester. It was his job to be skeptical.

"My gut tells me otherwise, and his information has always been spot on," replied Moran.

Forrester considered this. A month earlier The Sparrow had warned Moran of a bomb plot against a police barracks in Karachi. The information, at least a sanitized version of it, had been turned over to the Pakistani Inter-Services Intelligence, or ISI, and the plotters arrested with an impressive cache of explosives. One of those captured had been on the most wanted list. The enemy would not have sacrificed such an operation simply to advance the credibility of a double agent. Therefore the Sparrow wasn't a double agent. Unless... Forrester stood up and paced back and forth along the patio. Unless the Sparrow was playing his own game, playing both sides of the fence. It was moments like this that were the most difficult, but a decision was called for. He downed the martini and turned to Moran.

"Arrange the meeting."

# CHAPTER 13

*FBI Headquarters*
*Washington, DC*

Kim looked up at the poured concrete facade of the J. Edgar Hoover building on Pennsylvania Avenue, the long row of American flags hanging limp in the still morning air. She took a deep breath. *Why couldn't they just tell me over the phone?*

But no, her contact in Human Resources had said they wanted to meet with her first, to have a discussion about her next assignment. It didn't sound good. Kim felt a knot in her stomach.

Two years in El Paso, and Little Rock before that, then Jacksonville – and she was dreading what came next. She'd woken in the middle of the night thinking about Fairbanks, Alaska. Luckily there wasn't a field office there, she had checked. But there was one in Anchorage. Her mind raced. In Alaska, in the winter, it got dark at lunchtime, and Alaska would require an entirely new wardrobe. Snow boots and parkas, and whatever else people wore on the Arctic tundra. She would be cold all the time, deprived of melatonin. She cringed. Calm down, she told herself. Breathe.

Kim had arrived in Washington the day before to find out her fate. Unable to sleep, by five she was running along the Potomac and by seven she was dressed and eating breakfast in her hotel. She got to FBI headquarters ten minutes early. She didn't want to be late. FBI agents were never late.

Andrew Spencer, Deputy Assistant Director of the Human Resources Branch, had a red nose, pale skin, puffy eyes and a persistent sniffle. He dabbed his nose with a wadded up Kleenex as he slowly checked the contents of Kim's file to make sure all her paperwork was in order. She wondered why he didn't blow his nose like a normal person.

Spencer's office was small and tidy. His awards and certificates were neatly hung on the wall, along with the usual collection of grip-and-grins with higher-ups, mid-level government officials and congressmen. They probably don't even know who he is, thought Kim. Sad, in a way, that desire to be superficially associated with power, and yet Andrew Spencer was about to decide her future.

On the credenza was a framed photo of Spencer in a bicycle race, and one of him posing with his team, they were all wearing the same bicycle shirt and shorts. Maybe she should compliment his outfit, she thought, or bullshit about bicycles. But she wasn't a biker, she had nothing to say.

He sniffed again. A long drawn-out sniffle.

*Just blow your nose, for Christ's sake.* "Don't you want a Kleenex?" she asked.

He looked up from the file. "Excuse me?"

"Do you need a Kleenex?" Kim repeated.

He smiled.

"Thanks. I have one."

He discarded the balled up Kleenex in the wastepaper basket, opened his desk drawer and pulled out a fresh tissue which he held to the tip of his nose. He glanced up at her and then returned to her file. Kim watched while he reviewed her report, gingerly turning the pages with his index finger and thumb.

Please don't send me to Alaska, she thought, and don't send me back to Jacksonville. She could imagine it. You've done such a terrific job we want you back there to continue with Operation Such and Such. Not that Jacksonville was the worst place in the world. She had the perfect tan to prove it, and she had learned surfing, or at least taken surfing lessons. From Brett. Brett had certainly made it worthwhile. But Brett was over, and so was Florida. Two years in The Sunshine State was enough. Florida was The Minors. She was ready for The Game.

Finally, Spencer closed the file and looked at Kim.

"So how was Jacksonville, besides hot?" he asked.

"It was a very positive experience; there's a good team there, and we have excellent cooperation from the local law enforcement," she replied.

"And yet you don't like it there?"

"Bit of a backwater, Florida, if you know what I mean," said Kim.

54

"I'm originally from Tampa."

"Oh? It's nice there," she said.

He sniffed again.

"Any issues I should know about?" he asked.

She shook her head.

"How was Carmichael?" Spencer asked.

"He really took me under his wing. Great guy. A real pro," she said.

"He had nothing but good things to say about you. Said you did very well." Spencer picked up her file and tapped it against the desk to straighten the papers. Here it comes, she thought: Springfield, Illinois.

"I want to talk to you about your next assignment."

Her mind was racing. Albuquerque. Though she had never even been there, it was probably very nice. Or Omaha. Did the FBI even have a field office in Omaha? She wasn't sure. But they did have one in Buffalo. She knew that. Oh, God. She smiled and tried to look professional, please not Buffalo.

"How does New York sound?" he asked.

She swallowed, and began shaking her foot.

"Buffalo?" she asked, aware that her foot was shaking.

"No, New York City, we want you in New York."

"New York City?" she repeated.

He smiled. Spencer was starting to grow on her.

"We're beefing up a new joint counter terrorism team there. "Have you heard of Team Omega?" he asked matter-of-factly as he adjusted the position of a box of paper clips on his desk.

She shook her head.

"You're being assigned to it."

"Team Omega?" She felt light-headed.

"One of the new interdepartmental special units, largely independent, idea being to free the agents from certain bureaucratic restraints. There are five so far. Team Alpha, Team Epsilon, Sigma, and Omega and, which one did I forget?" He counted with his fingers, "oh yeah, Lambda."

"Sounds like fraternity row."

"I don't think up the names. But this is a little more serious than college. The teams consist of very highly skilled operatives with a wide ranging capability, operational-wise."

Thoughts fired through her brain. Intelligence operations sounded fine as long as it didn't involve survival training in Nevada, eating ants and drinking water from cactuses, because she wouldn't consider something like that a plus.

"When you get to New York they'll fill you in on the details," said Spencer, smiling.

"Sir, I have limited field experience. If you'll recall, I was brought in to help make sense of the bank transfers."

"You went to the academy, didn't you?"

"Yes, but-"

"And all special agents are trained to be proficient in firearms and field procedures, isn't that right?"

"Well, yeah, but-"

"But what?"

"Nothing sir."

"You'll receive a COLA increase and the standard relocation bonus. We want you there in a week. Can you manage that?"

"I think I can swing it." She didn't tell him that everything from her apartment in Jacksonville was in the trunk of her car in the parking garage. Two suitcases and one box containing some rarely used pots and pans and an iron. Her furniture and a TV and a plastic plant had been rented, and anything else, books mostly, and some beach towels, had been junked or given to the thrift shop in the basement of the Methodist Church around the corner.

"New York's expensive, I don't need to tell you that. A lot of agents don't like to be assigned there. The urban environment isn't conducive to sports and certain recreational activities, like golf, tennis, what have you. Some consider it a hardship."

"I don't play golf or tennis; it's not a problem," said Kim.

"I take it you have family in the area?"

"In Westchester, where I grew up," she said. Kim's father kept a small apartment on East 84th Street. Though she had grown up in Westchester – Bedford – she had dozens of friends who lived in the city, not that she had any illusions about having time for a social life.

She cleared her throat. "Sir, one question, why me? I spent the last two years chasing bank robbers."

"Have a little faith in us Human Resources professionals. We were looking for someone with a very particular skill set, and your name came up. We're concerned that funds are being wired through third parties to fund sleeper cells. Threat indicators are blowing the roof off at NSA and the director's getting heat. So that's the directive, our job is to find out, and you're good with financials."

She thought about that. *Your name came up.* What did that mean? My name came up. How does someone's name come up? She'd spent six years in backwaters tracking down one hick bank robber after another, each more stupid and desperate than the next, and now suddenly she's in New York City, assigned to the counter-terrorism task force. Someone, she didn't know who, must be looking out for her.

# CHAPTER 14

*New York City*

Kim established herself in the Conrad family's Upper East Side apartment. Her father referred to it as a pied-a-terre, but she wouldn't use that term with her colleagues at the bureau, most of who scrambled to locate apartments in the outer boroughs, usually Brooklyn or Queens. Despite the generous housing allowance, finding an apartment in New York was a challenge, and no special agents could afford a pre-war doorman building off Fifth Avenue.

They'd had had the place for years. Kim's father, Benton Conrad Jr., was a senior partner at a Wall Street law firm and could afford to live anywhere he wanted. He used the apartment if he decided to work late in the city, or attend a social function or go to the theater. When Kim told him she had been posted to New York, he had immediately said she could live there for as long as she wanted.

Excited and nervous on the first day of her new assignment, she'd gotten up at 5:30 and gone running in Central Park. She ran because it calmed her nerves, and because all the other FBI agents ran. She returned to the apartment, dressed, and caught the Lexington Avenue downtown express train at 86th Street. She felt giddy about being back in the city.

Half an hour later she arrived at her new office.

Team Omega of the Joint Special Investigations Unit occupied three floors of a tower overlooking New York Harbor. It had been set up there when the government, in an uncharacteristic display of common sense, took advantage of the glut of office space following the financial collapse and secured a low-rent deal.

The location, in the heart of the financial district, was ideal, especially since one of the unit's primary missions was to monitor cyber attacks on the nation's financial network, and to investigate illegal wire transfers flowing through US banks.

Kim passed through lobby security easily enough, but was asked to wait in the reception area when she got to the 16th floor. The receptionist made a phone call and five minutes later a man in a blue suit appeared.

"Special Agent Conrad?" he asked.

She nodded. He smiled.

"I'm Tom Mahan. We weren't expecting you until 8 o'clock. Welcome to Team Omega," he said sarcastically. "Nobody actually calls it that, it's a bit of a joke around here. Looks like we'll be working together. Come on, the boss is waiting."

She sized him up as he led her down the hall. Sporty, yet still formal. He had dark hair and an athletic build. He wore the regulation white shirt and striped tie, but it was the cut of his suit that caught her eye. Baggy enough to conceal his weapon, yet still well tailored. Very well tailored. All in all, a solid package, she thought.

She made a mental note to check the handbook for inter office romance and sexual harassment. She wanted to refresh her memory, and know where the line was before she crossed it.

The boss was Special Agent-in-Charge Neil Gambler. Kim had already researched him. She had determined that he was married and 46 years old. He'd graduated from Hunter College in New York and earned a law degree from St. John's. After ten years or so with the bureau he received an advanced degree from the Kennedy School of Government, and was on his way to becoming a deputy director.

Gambler was on the phone, gazing out the window, when the two agents arrived. He waved them in. His office put Spencer's office in the HR department in Washington to shame. About three times the size, for starters, a stunning view of New York Harbor, and an impressive photo gallery. Kim took it in out of the corner of her eye: senators, the mayor of New York, two presidents, Congressmen, generals. The message was clear: don't mess with me, I know people.

Gambler was a large man, about six-foot-two or three, and slightly rumpled. His tie was loose, not very FBI, and she noticed he had spilled coffee on his white shirt. He put the phone down.

"Special Agent Conrad?"

"Yes sir."

He smiled. "Welcome to the team. I've heard good things about you."

"Thank you, sir."

"Settled in okay?"

"Yes, sir."

"That's good, because I'm going to need you to jump right in. We'll get to know each other in the coming days."

"Jump into what, sir?"

"We think there's a sleeper cell operating. Well, we always think that, but now we're pretty sure. Over the past few weeks NSA has been intercepting more cell phone traffic referencing a transfer of funds, so we're watching the usual conduits. That's what we need you on, mostly forensic accounting and analysis."

"Will I be getting into the field?" She asked.

"We're short-handed so everyone wears more than one hat," replied Gambler. "Any issues?"

"No, sir."

"Good. Mahan can show you around, then fill you in on the details. We don't have a formal on-boarding program here. Questions?"

Sure, nothing but questions. She looked at Mahan, then shook her head.

"So that's it. I'm assigning you two together as partners, okay? Welcome to New York."


"He always that chatty?" asked Kim as she and Mahan walked down the hall from Gambler's office.

"He's got a lot on his mind," said Mahan.

"Like what?"

"Pressure from the brass in DC," Mahan held up his thumb and index finger, "and he's this close to getting tapped for Deputy Director."

Kim looked at Mahan. She wondered what his personal situation was. From his ring, she had already ascertained that he was a graduate of West Point, but there was no wedding band, not that all men wore them.

"When's that supposed to happen?" she asked.

60

"Word is any day now. I'll give you the nickel tour, introduce you to some of the team, then we'll jump right in. You bring your bathing suit?"

He smiled, and Kim found herself smiling too. She could tell right away she was going to enjoy working with Mahan.

"We call where we work 'the Pit,'" said Mahan.

"Sounds nice, why's that?"

Mahan smiled. "Basically, because it is a pit. I'll show you."

He led her into a large open office with cubicles in the center and windows on one side. It might have been the trading department at any one of the Wall Street firms where Kim might have been employed, had she gone that route. There were flat-screen computer monitors and TVs everywhere, providing a continuous stream of video images, news and financial data.

The men and women who worked in the Pit could have been Wall Street bankers, too, or accountants, except their suits were Men's Wearhouse, not Brooks Brothers; T.J. Maxx, not Chanel. They were suits you could run in, or wear while you threw someone against a wall. Inexpensive, and off-the-rack.

On one wall of the Pit there were three large white boards on which were account numbers, bank names, and Arabic script. It looked to Kim like the team was trying to sort out a complex transfer of funds through multiple banks.

"You're probably wondering why you got assigned to this team," said Mahan.

"It did cross my mind. I don't have a background in counter-terrorism, and my tactical experience is limited."

"I read your file," Mahan said, "You went through the academy. You rated top of your class in just about everything. Don't worry about your lack of tactical experience. The fact is they needed someone who knows their way around financial data. Money gets transferred through pretty complicated transactions with offshore corporations."

Kim forced a smile. She had joined the FBI to get away from the grind of financial reports – now she was afraid she would be drowning in them. The minute they found out what you were good at, that was all you ever did. Maybe she should have taken the job

61

at Goldman Sachs, the hours were probably better, and by now she would be earning at least ten times as much, not that she needed the money.

Mahan continued, "One way sleeper cells survive is with money funneled from overseas. That's what we look for."

Mahan stopped in front of two agents who were scanning the boards. One of them had a Magic Marker in her hand.

"Connecting the dots?" Mahan smiled.

A young woman turned to Mahan and smiled back. "Trying to."

Mahan turned to Kim. "These are special agents Sarah Higgins and Neil Baumgartner. Kim Conrad, just transferred up from Jacksonville."

Sarah was about Kim's age, shorter, athletic, with blonde hair cut short. She would have been very cute, thought Kim, if she knew how to dress. She was wearing an FBI windbreaker and a pair of gray trousers with shoes that looked almost orthopedic.

Baumgartner was older, mid-fifties, his hair white, but he still had a youthful face, and appeared to still be in excellent physical condition.

"Heard all about you from my old pal, Art Carmichael. We worked Oklahoma City together," said Baumgartner.

Kim smiled. "Great guy," she said.

If Baumgartner was anything like Carmichael, she knew they would get along well. Carmichael was old school, non-PC, and someone you could always count on in a pinch. He had taken Kim under his wing and showed her the ropes, helped her navigate the internal politics of the Jacksonville field office, and been instrumental, she suspected, in engineering her promotion to New York. Some of these older field agents carried more clout than their rank suggested.

"Why don't you bring Kim up to speed on what we're working on?" said Mahan.

Sarah gestured toward the white board. "Past couple of weeks we've been looking at a company called Global Trust Investments, they get regular wire transfers from the Cayman Islands."

"What's so odd about that?" asked Kim.

"The transfers originate in a bank in Lebanon."

"Where does the money go?"

"Someone named Nabir Azziz, Middle East Gourmet Bakery, here in the city."

"We have it under surveillance. I'll take you there tomorrow, meet the rest of the team," said Mahan.

"Me, on surveillance?"

"Of course, is that a problem?"

"No, I mean, of course not."

Kim spent the rest of the morning familiarizing herself with the computer network and reviewing the files (mostly financial data) of the current caseload. Shortly after noon she paid a visit to her father.

The law office of Smith, Garrick, Conrad and Holderness occupied four floors of prime space two blocks from the New York Stock Exchange. It was a Wall Street institution. When a company went public, or when one corporate behemoth merged with another, chances were pretty good Smith, Garrick played a role. They were Wall Street power brokers, and Benton Conrad called the shots. He occupied a large corner office. It was expected, according to the rigid pecking order followed by the firm's three hundred lawyers, that the top lawyers display the trappings of their position, something tangible the junior lawyers and lowly associates could aspire to; the golden ring, a key component to the competitive atmosphere that was the culture of the firm. Benton Conrad's Calvinistic upbringing was at odds with such ostentatious displays. But those were the rules of the firm, and it would have been unwise, if not impossible, to upset them.

What impressed the young lawyers more than the corner office was that Benton Conrad had three secretaries. Staff assistants, they were called at Smith, Garrick. Most of the other lawyers had one, or shared one. Conrad had three to himself. Chief among them was Mrs. Beadle, his senior assistant, who handled the telephone like a White House switchboard operator. Unflappable, she could anticipate Conrad's every move, and track down corporate CEOs and government ministers around the globe. She was also the gatekeeper. No one, but no one, got in to see Benton Conrad unless Mrs. Beadle allowed them in. And she rarely did.

"Hi, Mrs. Beadle." Kim stood sheepishly at the entrance to her father's suite of offices, as if she were afraid of disturbing him.

"Kim, what a pleasant surprise!"

"I'm not coming at a bad time, am I?"

"Not at all. He's on with the German finance minister but he'll be off in a minute. When did you arrive?"

"Two days ago, late. My office is just around the corner."

"I understand we'll be seeing more of you now. I'm sure he's thrilled."

"It is exciting to be back," replied Kim. "How is he?"

"The same, always very busy around here, you know your Dad."

Kim understood. During election season, her father was always busy bundling money and organizing fundraisers.

Mrs. Beadle lowered her head and put her hand to her mouth.

"I suppose you may have heard, your father is on a very short list for Ambassador to the Court of St. James."

"London?"

Mrs. Beadle nodded. "Don't say anything, he refuses to talk about it. Hang on, I'll just tell your dad you're here."

As if by a sixth sense, Mrs. Beadle knew the phone call was ending, and carried a small stack of papers into her boss's office. She returned a moment later and held the door open. "He's all yours."

Benton Conrad stood and came out from behind his desk to embrace his daughter. "Well, it's about time."

"Hi, Dad."

"Next time tell me you're on your way over, I'd have booked a table for lunch."

"I'm not disturbing you?" asked Kim.

"No," he said, "of course not, Mrs. Beadle will hold my calls."

"What's this about London?" asked Kim.

He waved his hand. "Nothing, it's nothing. So how's the apartment? How's the new assignment? Special Joint Counter Terrorism Task Force, eh? Very impressive."

Her father always seemed to know everything. She wouldn't

have been surprised if he hadn't had lunch or a phone call with the director of the FBI, and secretly found out about her posting, or even arranged it. Of course, that was ridiculous, but it was strange how her father always seemed to know exactly what was going on. It was almost unsettling, as if he subscribed to a secret source of intelligence and was always one step ahead of everyone else.

"I don't have to tell you I'm glad you're here. Why waste your talents in a minor field office somewhere? The government may have its limitations, but talent rises to the top," he said.

Does it, she wondered? What happens to people who don't have fathers with Rolodexes and strings to pull? Kim and her father sat in two leather chairs by a window overlooking the Statue of Liberty.

"How's the firm?" she asked.

Her father shrugged. "It's okay, I guess it's been better. In this economy it's a challenge to keep this whale afloat. We've got some interesting cases, and interesting clients."

"And everything else?"

Ever since the death of her mother, Kim worried about her father. He had found someone else, but Kim suspected his new mate, Barbara, only made things worse. She was a demanding woman, and Kim avoided her whenever possible.

"Everything's just fine. It's all fine. Say, I have an idea. Why don't you come to a party tomorrow tonight."

"Where?"

"The museum. I think you'll enjoy it. Come to think of it, I've invited some clients who don't know many people."

"Dad, I'm not one of your deals."

He smiled. "I'm not asking you to be. I'm asking you to meet a few friends, charm them."

"Ugh, Dad."

"What?"

"Doesn't sound like my scene." She wrinkled her nose.

"One of these guys is very nice."

"He can't make friends on his own?" asked Kim.

"He's new in town, doing business with the firm. I think you'll enjoy him." He looked at his watch. "Sweetie, I have a meeting with the head of the New York Fed and I have to take a call first, I don't have time to chat."

"Of course not." She understood all too well that Mrs. Beadle measured her father's time in six-minute segments, recording every one of them in a computer log. Then clients were charged something like 800 bucks an hour.

"I shouldn't keep this guy waiting," he said.

"I understand."

Mrs. Beadle appeared. Kim wondered if she relied on a hidden camera, or listening device, to time her entrances.

"See you tomorrow night? I'll have a car pick you up at the apartment at 6:30." He winked at her as he picked up the phone.

# CHAPTER 15

Pazhman Khan stood patiently amid the jumble of tired travellers and luggage carts waiting for his turn to clear customs and immigration. Behind him, a Pakistani woman wearing a dupatta, with a mountain of suitcases on her cart, tried to soothe a cranky baby. She rocked it gently in her arms, then passed the baby to her exasperated husband. The line was moving slowly. Pazhman watched the customs agent nearest him question the travelers and carefully scrutinize their passports.

There was a problem. The agent was explaining to a tired young man (Pazhman had seen the man board the plane in Islamabad) that either his passport or visa was not in order. The man tried to explain. The agent looked skeptical. He gestured for the man to follow him through a side door, probably to be interrogated, or sent back, thought Pazhman. He remained calm. I am a successful engineer on business, he told himself.

"Next!"

Pazhman stepped forward.

"What's the nature of your business?" asked the customs agent.

"I'm attending a conference on sustainable water resource management," he replied. His good suit and educated way of speaking supported this claim.

"Where will you be staying?"

"The Hilton."

The customs agent looked at the photo in Pazhman's passport, then compared it to the man standing before him. He handed Pazhman his passport and smiled. "Enjoy your stay, Mr… Patel."

The taxi brought Pazhman through the mid-morning traffic to the main entrance of the Hilton on Sixth Avenue. He paid the driver in cash and, brushing aside the doorman, insisted on carrying his own bag. He walked past the reception desk and exited the hotel by the side entrance on 54th Street. He continued south on 7th Avenue, then turned on West 48th Street. He kept

67

walking until he found a hotel more suited to his needs.

Such hotels had been more common in New York when Pazhman first visited years earlier, before developers began renovating cheap hotels in gentrified neighborhoods, rebranding them as quaint and intimate, "close to all the city has to offer." He found what he was looking for in the Stanford Arms. No doorman, no security, and no questions asked. The lobby consisted of a couch with ripped upholstery and a rack of brochures for discount theater tickets and tour buses. The carpeting was threadbare. A fluorescent light flickered overhead. A clerk in a sweat-stained white shirt sat at the reception desk reading a newspaper.

"I'll only be staying a few nights," said Pazhman.

"Doesn't matter, long as you pay in advance," said the clerk.

Pazhman took a very slow elevator to his room. It was small. There was a television with hand-written instructions taped to the top, explaining how to order a video. The bedspread was filthy, as were the curtains, stained by years of nicotine. The place smelled of cigarette smoke, and he was sure there were bed bugs in the mattress. But he had stayed in worse places, far worse.

He hated to think what the non-believers routinely did in this room. He closed his eyes and cleared his mind of those thoughts. He was on a mission, and would do what had to be done, what was expected of him, even if it meant sleeping in an unclean place. His success, his survival, really, depended on him going unnoticed, even if it meant temporarily adopting the ways of the infidel. It was only a few nights.

Pazhman opened his suitcase on the bed and removed his toilet kit. He took a small pair of scissors from the kit and, in front of the bathroom mirror, cut off as much of his beard as he could, the whiskers dropping into the sink. He wet his face with hot water and shook a can of shaving cream which he slowly worked into the stubble.

Pazhman had had a beard since he was a young man. He had trimmed it prior to his flight, so he would look less radical, but this was the first time in years he had shaved. When he was done he studied himself in the mirror, worried that where his beard had been would be lighter than the rest of his face. He saw a face he had not seen in many years, and that brought back a sudden flood of memories of a time when he had lived like a non-believer. He felt a sudden pang of shame. But had he not lived as he did then, he would not have learned the ways of the infidel, and would not have been of such value to the cause. So everything happens for a reason, he told himself. He rubbed his hand over his smooth face, it was a strange sensation but he was pleased with it. Now he looked more like the people he had come to kill.

The next morning Pazhman rose early, eager to get out of his room. He put on the suit he had had custom made in Peshawar and inspected himself in the mirror. I look like any one of a million businessmen in New York, he thought. He removed a soft canvas briefcase from his suitcase and transferred a few items from the suitcase into the briefcase, and put some cash from his money belt into his wallet. He left the hotel and hailed a taxi.

On Madison Avenue at a men's clothier he purchased three more dress shirts, khaki trousers and a blazer. Though his clothes were made to order in Pakistan, they would not serve him here. He had to wear what Americans wore. Or at least like an Indian who had embraced the uniform of the American businessman. He had met many such conformists at university, and of course he despised them. Now, for the first time, he knew what it was like to look like them. He selected items that would not have to be altered.

"How are you set for socks and shorts?" asked the salesman, his tape measure draped around his neck.

"I'm sorry?"

"Socks and shorts? We have a sale going on. Buy two get one free."

"Excellent," he said.

He selected a half dozen boxers and an equal number of pairs of socks. He would be disguised down to the last detail, he thought.

"Will there be anything else?"

"A hat, and sunglasses."

"It certainly is sunny out, can't be too careful," said the clerk.

Pazhman nodded.

He paid with hundred dollar bills.

The straw fedora stood out, but it was essential.   Without one, facial recognition software could be used to spot him walking past any one of a hundred cameras mounted about the city. He would wear the sunglasses and the hat as often as possible, and perhaps purchase a baseball cap. He had noticed that many men in America wore baseball caps. He would find one that had the local baseball club, the Yankees, stitched on it.

He walked south through Midtown until he passed a shop that sold camping equipment and army surplus gear. There he found a display case filled with hunting knives. He had not dared bring his own knife on the plane, such a move would have been careless and an unnecessary risk to the operation. But he did not feel properly armed unless he had his weapon of choice. He selected one with a curved, sharp blade, an onyx handle and a leather sheath.

"That's one sharp knife, you a hunter?" asked the salesman.

He smiled. "No, I just like knives."

Again, he paid in cash.

Now it was time to awaken the cell.

# CHAPTER 16

Good information was worth money. But good information was hard to come by. The man Forrester called the Sparrow could go days or weeks without turning up anything of value, and then suddenly, one day, a few careless words and choice intelligence dropped into his lap.

But the Sparrow didn't sell everything that came his way. Sometimes it was too valuable to be sold. Sources had to be managed, and protected so they could be harvested year after year. Some information was simply too dangerous to handle. Unless you really needed the money. Today Abdel, the lawyer, a.k.a. the Sparrow, had very good information, for which the Americans would pay.

In the morning Abdel went about his daily routine. He met with two clients, one who was considering changes to a will, and another involved in a minor property transaction. When he was done, he locked up his office and walked the dusty street in the old town through the Bazaar Shah Qabool Olia. He passed the fruit vendors, the carts loaded high with dates and cashews, soaps and deodorant, fly swatters, plastic sandals, radios and anything and everything that anyone could possibly want. It was still as hot as a furnace and the crowd in the square was not as large as it would be later, when the sun went down. At the fountain a group of small boys splashed in the water and he wished he were a boy again and could go in the water. It was that hot. He was perspiring in his linen jacket, thinking he could have worn the traditional Pakistani dress, which was much cooler, but he wanted to look more Western when he went to the Regal Hotel.

He turned onto Khyber Road. Here, the heat was mixed with choking fumes from the perpetual traffic jam, the street filled with pedestrians and cars and auto-rickshaws and a cacophony of horns.

Adbel's shoes were dusty from walking. He would have liked to

71

have them polished before entering the hotel but there wasn't time.

Of course, just as he had thought, the doorman, who wore a tan cotton shirt with gold epaulets, like a ferryboat captain, looked down at his shoes when he opened the door. Abdel walked through without a word. By what right did the doorman at the Regal Hotel look down upon his shoes because they were dusty?

He went through the lobby to the hotel bar. Unchanged since its most recent remodel twenty years earlier (plenty of polished brass and black glass), the tattered upholstery and shabby carpeting were obscured by the dim lighting, which made it ideal, and popular, for business meetings, and the very discrete consumption of alcohol. In Pakistan, such discretion was the dividing line between intolerance and hypocrisy, between repression and freedom. Such discretion eased the friction in a country always on the verge of self-destruction.

Abdel stood in the doorway, trying to not look anxious as he scanned the room looking for a suitable table where the meeting would not be observed, or the conversation overheard. He was relieved that he saw no one he knew, which was absurd. Who, in the bar of the Regal Hotel, would know him?

The bar was nearly full, patrons finding refuge from the searing heat outside. They paid no attention to the solicitor in the wrinkled suit and dirty shoes. He spotted a table for two in the far corner and decided it would best suit his purposes. He ordered a Coca-Cola.

"With ice," he said, though he needn't have because the bar at the Regal Hotel had an ice machine and put plenty of ice in all its drinks.

At exactly 4 o'clock, Moran arrived. He greeted Abdel as if the two were business associates meeting in person for the first time. If anyone recognized Abdel, it would be easy enough to explain that he was assisting Moran in a business transaction. Moran opened his briefcase and took out his company's annual report, to complete the tableau.

Such in-person meetings were rare, but occasionally Abdel's customers had to be convinced of the value and accuracy of his information, and he was a convincing salesperson. He had once sold shoes in the bazaar for his uncle, before he became a solicitor, and had sold more shoes than anyone in his family, more even than his uncle. Not long after that he had decided that he was capable of greater things than being a shoe merchant. He had left home and gone to Peshawar where he had built a profitable business selling small arms and munitions for use by the mujahadeen in Afghanistan, and later to the Taliban, and to whomever else would buy them. But information was a much easier line of work, there was less inventory, and less overhead, and besides, with the Americans it had become increasingly difficult, and dangerous, to find customers for his weapons. The drones patrolled day and night, and his supply routes could no longer be trusted. So he did not object to the meeting, rather he welcomed it, for it was an opportunity to strengthen his relationship with his best client and, after all, what was business all about if not a close relationship between buyer and seller?

"Recently, a man, who is high on your list, I think, passed through," said Abdel.

"Who?" asked Moran.

Abdel smiled.

"Let us begin with where," replied Abdel.

"Okay, from where?" asked Moran.

"He is originally from Ab Dakar."

The name sounded vaguely familiar to Moran. "Where's that?"

"Afghanistan, of course," the solicitor replied.

"What was he doing there, do you suppose?"

Abdel opened his hands and shrugged.

"Taliban?"

Abdel shook his head. "I would not summon you to the Regal Hotel for Taliban."

No, thought Moran, you wouldn't.

"And how do you come by this information?"

Abdel smiled. "I have my sources, carefully cultivated over many years. Many, many years."

Moran wondered if he was also on the payroll of the ISI, Pakistan Intelligence, a useful way to feed CIA unofficial information. Without the protection of the security service, Abdel would be taking a very big risk.

73

"So what have you got?" he asked.

"First there is the question of payment."

*Here we go, let the haggling begin.* "I thought we already agreed," said Moran.

"Yes, we have a usual price, but the information I am about to give you is of greater value."

"Tell us what you have, then we can talk price, but I should warn you, I have very little leeway," said Moran.

Abdel knew how the Americans spent money, how truckloads of hundred dollar bills went missing without a trace in Afghanistan and Iraq. Thousands, millions spent on projects that were never completed. The Americans had an almost unlimited amount of money to spend on what they truly wanted, and they would want what he had to offer.

"There is a man, who, if you knew him, would be very high on your list. Very high," said Abdel.

"You mean he's not even on our list?"

"Oh he may be, but I rather doubt it."

"If he's important we have a file on him."

Abdel shook his head. "I doubt that."

"Why?"

"Because no one knows of him. He is Pachaas Talwaray."

Moran paused.

"Pachaas Talwaray is a myth, it doesn't exist anymore."

Abdel smiled. "Perhaps."

"You want us to pay a premium for some fictitious person no one ever heard of, who doesn't even have a name."

"He has a name, but they call him the Ghost."

"Sounds spooky. The Ghost, huh, you'll have to do better than that. What does this ghost do?"

"He makes bombs."

The CIA officer leaned forward. "Lots of guys make bombs, what kinds of bombs?"

"Many kinds, he is one of the most gifted, and so he teaches the others. You are familiar with the Kabul Police Barracks bombing?"

"What about it?"

"This was a very sophisticated, and powerful device, yes? It was

74

placed in exactly the proper location, was it not?"

Moran knew the bombing well, it had killed nearly 100 police recruits in Kabul. It had been no ordinary car bomb, but a sophisticated series of explosions that had also decimated dozens of rescue workers. The bombs had been remarkable for their power and lethality in a land where powerful bombs were the norm.

"How do we find this Ghost?"

Abdel smiled and shook his head. "First we should agree on a price."

"The regular price."

"The regular price is for regular people."

Moran considered this. He ran a network of agents, twenty or so people. His informants were paid a set amount for information. It was not unusual that they tried to bargain, ask for more. It was unusual that Moran agreed.

"My information is, as I said, of great value," repeated Abdel.

"What are we talking?"

"Thirty thousand rupees."

Moran pretended to choke on his soda. It was convincing, 30,000 was more than he had ever paid. He was authorized to pay such an amount, but he would have to justify it, and he would find himself no longer in the employ of the United States government if they thought he was cheating, or paying too much for information.

"There's no way I can pay that much."

"I will give you the name he is travelling under, and an address in Peshawar, and for this all I ask is 20,000 rupees. It is as low as I will go," said Abdel.

"How do I know I will be pleased after I agree to such a price?"

"Because I have never let you down, and I am telling you."

"That's true. But why so much bargaining all of a sudden?"

Abdel smiled.

"How did you come by his name, anyway?" continued Moran.

"I myself have seen his passport. It came all the way from Islamabad and was delivered to me by special courier."

"To you?"

"Three days ago."

"You waited a long time to tell us."

"To have come any sooner would have been very dangerous. He is traveling to the West."

At this Moran paused. A traveller to the West. Such men were always of great interest.

"Okay, 15,000 rupees," said Moran.

Abdel smiled.

"He is traveling under the name of Arun Patel," continued Abdel.

"Traveling where?"

"New York."

"We'll need a lot more than that. He's probably already switched identities."

Abdel hesitated. "You will find him, if you search hard enough. Also, there is a house, on Charsada Road. There you will find much of interest."

Moran cocked his head to one side.

"What else?"

"This is enough."

# CHAPTER 17

*Peshawar, Pakistan*

Moran sat in his Mercedes sedan and studied the house on Charsada Road. He wanted one last look to make sure the drawings they had created, based on street surveillance and satellite imagery, hadn't left anything out. No unexpected razor wire or security guards. He looked at his watch. It was 2 p.m. In twelve hours, if all went well, the operation would be over.

The house looked empty, which was good. They were there for intel; a major snatch and grab wasn't in the cards. Incursions could be excused in the tribal area, but it was more difficult in Peshawar. Diplomatic relations with Pakistan were at an all-time low. Operations had to take place below the radar, and only then after a risk assessment was reviewed and approved at the top levels in Washington.

But a little poking around never hurt. Moran would rely on his band of thieves: former Pakistani special forces and off-duty police, for the most part ideologically neutral, interested in adventure, and, let's face it, cash.

Moran watched as Ali Lashari, retired Pakistani Army major and former presidential bodyguard, crossed the road and got in the car on the passenger side. Ali was now a contractor and had worked for Moran many times. The two men trusted each other.

"This is not a big problem," said Ali.

"What do you think?"

"I am thinking that after dark we use an aluminium ladder to scale the wall behind the house. You will reimburse me for the ladder."

Moran nodded. Scaling the wall with a ladder had been his thought, too, but he wanted to hear what Ali had to say. He felt reassured that Ali knew what he was doing. Then again, it was Ali who would pay the price if anything went wrong. Any link to US intelligence would be disavowed, a steep price. Ali would likely end up dead at the hands of Islamic radicals, or charged with treason, or burglary and rotting in a Pakistani prison. But he knew the dangers.

"Is anyone in the house?" asked Ali.

Moran shook his head. "We figure everyone's gone now, except maybe a few servants who live there."

"Servants?" Ali looked Moran straight in the eyes.

"I want information, but if anyone tries to stop you, do what you have to do."

Ali nodded and said nothing.

Ali returned with his team in a Toyota Land Cruiser shortly after 1 o'clock the next morning. Ali had selected three men for the operation: a driver, whose name was Irfan, and two operatives, Shani and Ahmad. Irfan turned off Charsada Road, switched off the headlights, and rolled to a stop by the side of the house.

The men moved quickly. Shani removed a ladder from the back of the Land Cruiser and placed it against the wall. Moran watched from his Suzuki Bolan van across the street. He could talk to Ali by radio. If any danger approached from Charsada Road he would warn them.

Ali was the first one over the wall, followed almost immediately by the three others. They didn't hesitate. Ali didn't have to tell them what to do. Irfan and Shani covered the rear courtyard with their pistols while Ahmad, who Ali said was the best entry man in Peshawar, went to work on the lock on the back door. It took him 15 seconds, and the door silently swung open.

Ali left Irfan in the courtyard, for security, and led the others into the house. So far, so good. If anyone was inside, he wanted to catch them asleep. Of course it would have been nice if Moran had lent them night vision goggles, but Moran had flatly refused. He said he didn't want it to look like an "agency operation." It was always that way: Ali was used to being treated like a poor relation.

Ali's plan was simple: tie up anyone they encountered. To do this they carried plastic ties, duct tape to cover their mouths, and cotton sacks to put over their heads. Ali had found that once the hands were bound and the head covered, it wasn't necessary to restrain them any further. Most men usually sat on the floor and waited. Most men.

The garden door opened onto a marble hall that extended to the front door. To one side was a sitting area, with an L-shaped sofa surrounding a large square coffee table. The room was decorated with a gold oriental carpet and an ornate crystal chandelier. On the other side of the vestibule was a modern kitchen. Ali followed Shani through the kitchen while Ahmed stood guard in the hall. Behind the kitchen were the servants' quarters. Shani entered a small bedroom. One of the servants was in bed, asleep. The man's eyes opened wide when he saw the pistol pointed in his face.

"Is there anyone else in the house?" asked Shani.

The servant shook his head.

"You are sure?"

He looked terrified. "Please, I am alone."

Shani bound the sleepy man's hands behind his back. "You must sit on the bed, and not make a noise. If you do that you won't be injured, otherwise...."

Shani tried to place a sack on the servant's head but he twisted his head back and forth. Shani raised his arm to strike a blow.

"Leave him, he's harmless," hissed Ali.

They crept through the hallway to a flight of white marble stairs. This was a very grand house, thought Ali, the interior much finer than one would have expected judging by the crude cement block exterior. The curving stairway gave way to a balcony, off of which were three bedrooms and a bathroom.

Ali hoped the servant had lied, and there was someone upstairs. Then perhaps he would capture one of the men for whom the Americans offered cash prizes. Moran would have a safe house somewhere, and the captive could be smuggled out. Ali could become a rich man.

But what was the use of such dreams, he thought? The Americans paid him well enough for his services. Though, of course, they could pay more. For such a rich country, the Americans could be so stingy. Still, where would he find another client? Nowhere. So he focused his mind on the job at hand. Ali felt for the stun grenade he had in his cargo pocket, always a good idea if things got out of control.

Ali and Shani went room by room. The first was a bedroom, the bed - a simple mattress roll and bedding - was carefully folded and stored above a wardrobe. The second room was an office. Ali scanned the objects in the room. There was a TV, cell phone, a number of books and newspapers, and (prize of prizes!) a laptop computer. Ali's eyes lit up at the sight of it. The Americans paid top dollar for laptops. He would come back to it, but first, they checked the third room. It was a bedroom as well, with the bed rolled out on the tile floor, unmade. Ali knelt down and placed his hand on the mattress. It was warm. He looked up.

"Shani, look out!"

Behind Shani, in the hall leading to the bedroom, Ali saw a barrel-chested man with a beard. He wore a T-shirt and jogging shorts, and carried a PK1 sub-machine gun. The man saw Ali and Shani and hesitated. It was all Ali needed.

"Get down!"

Shani dropped to a crouch as Ali placed two bullets in the man's forehead. As he fell backwards, Shani grabbed the submachine gun, holding it away in case, in a final spasm, he pulled the trigger and sprayed the room. But he was already dead, lying face up, eyes open in shock.

Shani had never seen such skill. A double tap with a silencer delivered from across the room. He looked at Ali, a stunned expression on his face.

"Photo and fingers, quickly, you know the drill!" Ali hissed, shaking his head. Such carelessness - not checking the washroom - is what got men killed.

"Quickly!" he barked.

Shani took a photo of the dead man's face while Ali took his fingerprints, using a smartphone with an app for this purpose. When they were done, the two men returned to the office and began shoveling every book and scrap of paper they could find into a nylon satchel. They checked the other two rooms one more time, stepping over the lifeless body in the hall. The last thing Ali did before leaving the room was to grab the laptop computer and put it under his arm. The operation had lasted less then five minutes.

Irfan was waiting by the back door. The three men moved quickly through the kitchen. Shani was halfway out the door when the servant suddenly appeared behind Ali. The servant's bound hands were now in front of him, and he carried a large kitchen knife. He plunged the knife into Ali's back. Ali shrieked and collapsed on the floor. Shani raised his pistol and fired three silenced shots into the man's chest.

"Good God!" said Ahmad. "Good God!"

He knelt beside Ali and felt for a pulse. There was none. Ali was dead.

Shani took the laptop, which had clattered to the floor, and stuffed it in the satchel. The operatives picked up their team leader's body and left the way they had come.

* * *

Less than twenty-four hours later, Jim Shepley sat at his workbench in the special electronics and computers section at the IOC, the CIA's Information Operations Center in Langley, trying to reconstruct a hard drive, when his boss, Bill DeMarco, walked into the room. DeMarco was accompanied by Angela Williamson, who spoke about six languages, and often worked with their team when things needed translating fast.

DeMarco carried a heavy plastic zip-lock pouch. He placed the pouch on his workbench.

"Priority," he said.

"What is it?"

"Just came in by diplomatic courier from Islamabad. We need to know what's in it."

Shepley unzipped the pouch and pulled out the laptop. It was an IBM T40.

"I assume they checked it for booby traps?"

"Did that before they put it on the plane."

He reached for a power cord and plugged it in, then lifted the top.

"Yuck, what's this?"

On his fingertips was the dried blood of Ali Lashari.

# CHAPTER 18

Kim ran to Fifth Avenue and entered Central Park at 79th Street. She remembered something she'd read at the Academy: "Physical fitness is often the factor that spells the difference between success and failure, even life and death."

Her current fear was of failure. The members of Team Omega were mostly experienced field agents, which she was not. Her marksmanship had been among the lowest in her class at Quantico, and she had struggled to pass the physical fitness tests. The training there had been over the top with endless running, sit-ups, push-ups, lunges. She preferred yoga, maybe once a week. But FBI agents were expected to be fit, so she ran, two miles at the most, one mile was better. None of this five-mile bullshit.

She ended her run on Fifth and 96th Street, then walked down Madison, window-shopping in front of clothing stores. It was still early, just a few dog walkers and janitors hosing off the sidewalks, so she didn't feel self-conscious in her jogging outfit.

"Kim?"

Kim turned from the window of a shoe store. She almost didn't recognize her, then she remembered, Wharton. The woman was wearing a pair of white fitted jeans, Belgian loafers, and a rather gigantic diamond ring. She was pushing a baby carriage.

"Janine?" said Kim.

"My God, it's been forever!"

Kim looked at the baby carriage, one of those blue enamel English models. "Who's this?" she asked.

"He's little Evan, named after his father," said Janine.

"You're married?"

"Well… yeah."

"And a baby?"

"A baby. I left J.P. Morgan a year ago. God, it must be what, five years?" asked Janine. "I think I lost touch after you were, what, didn't you go to work for the FBI or something? How did that work out?"

"I'm still with the Bureau," said Kim.

Janine raised an eyebrow. Kim remembered that at Wharton, when she had turned down an offer at Goldman in favor of the Bureau, some people had been surprised. Shocked really. It was a departure from the standard career trajectory, rejection of a coveted offer.

Kim bent closer and looked at the baby. His head was so big, she wondered if Janine wasn't overfeeding him, but she didn't know much about babies. Better not to say anything.

"So you're on maternity leave?" asked Kim.

"I took two months off for Evan, now I'm back. We have a nanny, but the foreign travel is tough."

"Oh?"

"I spend a lot of time in Paris and London, Zurich too, and Berlin."

"That must be tough."

"It's not bad. Are you here visiting?"

"No, I'm assigned to counter terrorism here in the city."

"Gosh."

"It's not as exciting as you would think."

"You're probably just saying that.

"That's great, we should get together. I'm away next week, but after that perhaps?"

"Sure."

They promised they would call each other and catch up, but Kim had no intention of following through. She walked the rest of the way home. She thought about the path she might have taken. A big salary, marriage, maybe even a baby in a fancy English baby carriage. Had she made a mistake? She was 33 years old, still single with a career that didn't offer much hope of her settling down.

But the FBI recruiter had won her over. They'd shown her videos and a Power Point presentation on the "Life of an FBI Special Agent," and before she knew it she was submitting to background checks and physicals. Within three weeks of graduation, she was enrolled in the FBI Academy in Quantico. The truth was she had wanted to be recruited. The Bureau had dangled a lifeline in front of her, and she had grabbed it.

83

Her father thought she was crazy.

Everyone did.

Kim held a paper bag with a toasted bagel in it in her teeth while she balanced her shoulder bag on her knee looking for her wallet and federal ID card. The attendant at the security checkpoint in the lobby recognized her, but that didn't matter, everyone short of the President, and maybe the Vice President, had to show ID. The security guard gave her a sympathetic smile.

The elevator doors were closing when an arm appeared and forced them open. It was Mahan.

Kim watched the elevator floor indicator, then she turned to look at Mahan and their eyes locked, and Kim turned quickly away. She closed her eyes and took a deep breath, and then the elevator arrived at their floor.

"So surveillance, right?" said Kim.

"I'll stop by your desk in a few. I just have to answer a few emails on the Secret Service Protection Plan for the G20."

"What's that?" she asked.

"Oh, whenever POTUS comes to town it's a freaking nightmare. We have to help with the advance security."

"Isn't that in like two weeks?" asked Kim,

Mahan smiled. "I didn't want to overwhelm you on your first day."

Fifteen minutes later Kim followed Mahan down the hall to the motor services supervisor, Robert Fitzgerald, whom everyone called Fitzy.

"I need a car," said Mahan.

"So take a taxi."

He smiled. "Need a car."

"Who's this?"

"My new partner, Kim Conrad."

Kim extended her hand and smiled. Fitzy brushed his hand on his shirt and shook.

"I just transferred up from Florida," said Kim.

"Why would you do a thing like that?"

She smiled.

"So the car?" said Mahan.

"What's wrong with the subway?"

"It's too dangerous," said Mahan.

"So take a bus."

"We're going on a drive."

"Where?"

"That's classified."

It was always the same deadpan routine with Fitzy. He shuffled among the papers on his white Formica-topped desk and picked up a set of keys which he tossed to Mahan.

"Ford Taurus, it's parked on Centre Street, you know the one. Dark blue with the dent in the rear quarter panel."

"I thought I asked you to get that fixed?"

"Yeah, right, I'm gonna count the dents when you get back, so be careful." He looked at Kim. "Nice to meet you, Special Agent Conrad."

Kim smiled.

On the sidewalk Mahan offered the keys to Kim. She hesitated. The truth was she would have had trouble finding her way to the airport, let alone anywhere else in the outer boroughs. That's what taxis and limousines were for.

"Does this thing have GPS?" she asked.

He shook his head. "Typical New Yorker. I'll drive."

Kim took off her blue suit coat and tossed it on the backseat. She looked up at the sky and smiled. The sun had come out.

"One thing I'll miss about Jacksonville – sunshine twelve months a year," she said.

"Come winter, what I wouldn't give for an assignment in Florida. Miami would be nice," said Mahan.

"So get yourself assigned to the drug task force, they're always hiring."

Mahan shook his head. "New York has its charms."

"So tell me about this Middle East Gourmet Bakery?" she said.

"They make pita bread, distribute it throughout the tri-state area. Small operation, owner's name is Nabir Azzad. We think he may be filtering cash to a sleeper cell here in the US. We check this kind of stuff all the time, it's probably nothing. Baumgartner's setting up surveillance now."

"Where exactly is this bakery?"

"Park Slope."

Kim looked unsure.

"You know, Brooklyn. It's one of the five boroughs. You know. Manhattan, Queens, the Bronx, Staten Island, and... Brooklyn? Very trendy now. On the other side of the East River?"

She made a face. "I've heard of it. Tell me about Baumgartner."

"He's an old hand, real pro. Spends most of his time with the SSG, Special Surveillance Group.

"What's the background on this Nabir Azzad?" she asked.

"Not much. File said he moved here about fifteen years ago. At first he belonged to a group called the Islamic Fraternal Order. The usual website, denouncing American imperialism, immorality, and predicting the ultimate destruction of the infidel. Bla, bla, bla, but looks like he quit about ten years ago. No record."

"Now suddenly he's getting suspect wire transfers from a bank with known links to terrorist groups."

"You got it," said Mahan.

"Could be just a coincidence."

"Yes it could."

"You guys do this a lot?" she asked.

"All the time."

"Anything good come from it?"

"Every once in a while we get lucky."


Mahan parked two blocks away from the surveillance location so they wouldn't be noticed. They walked the rest of the way to the surveillance location, a five-story apartment building, recently renovated, on Bergen Street just off Fifth. The bakery was located in a white brick building on the other side of the street.

They climbed the stairs to the second floor and Mahan knocked on the door to the apartment. A young agent named Nevins unlocked the door and let them in. The surveillance team had chosen a furnished model apartment, a one bedroom with an open

86

living room, kitchen, and eating area. The place still smelled of plaster dust, paint and freshly installed carpet. Black leather chairs and a couch formed a seating area by the window where Baumgartner was looking through a high-powered scope.

Baumgartner stood up when he saw them.

"Nevins, take over, will ya?" he said.

Nevins returned to the window and focused the spotting scope, then double-checked the camera, which was mounted with a long telephoto lens.

"You want coffee?" asked Baumgartner.

"The guy said he didn't want coffee on the carpet," said Nevins. "Doesn't want food or drink anywhere except the kitchen."

"How're you supposed to have a stake-out without coffee?" replied Baumgartner.

"If you spill, he'll charge us."

Baumgartner rolled his eyes.

"Thanks, no coffee for me," said Kim.

Kim looked past the drapes out a half-open sliding glass door that led to a small balcony. She could see the bakery across the street.

"Anything yet?" she asked.

"Azzad showed up about half an hour ago, then also a few employees by the look of it. We took photos. What do you think this guy's up to?" asked Nevins.

Mahan shrugged. "The way our luck's been running, probably nothing. But maybe he is up to something, and maybe he's not so smart and doesn't know he's compromised. Wouldn't that be nice for a change."

Baumgartner moved to the kitchen where he poured himself a cup of coffee from an electric coffeemaker. "It's the dumb ones who are dangerous," he said. "Think they can shoot their way out of a bad situation." He looked at Kim. "You must have run into some interesting characters when you were working bank robbery in Jacksonville."

"You mean like guys who use their mother's car for the getaway?" asked Kim.

He smiled. "You ever run across a smart bank robber?"

"There was one gang, in Tampa. They always picked the right bank, always one step ahead of us. They knew what they were doing, and kept it really simple, but effective. Nine banks, almost $400,000."

"What was their M.O.?"

"Well, they picked small banks, for starters, on the outskirts of town. Always demanded the money unbundled, and they liked to hit banks when it was raining."

"What happened?"

"I developed an algorithm, calculating data about when and where they did their jobs, I got the when, the hard part was the where."

"You figured out an algorithm to catch bank robbers?"

Kim nodded. "It's simply applying the logic of a weighted formula to predict the outcome based on key data. The tricky part is figuring out the weights."

"And did it work?"

"No."

"So much for algorithms," said Baumgartner.

Kim had run into lots of agents like him. Old School. She persisted.

"In this case there were too many variables, but the theory is logical, even if the bank robbers aren't," she added.

"I don't go in for all that computer modeling. Good police work involves intuition." He pointed to his head. "This is the best computer we have. How long you been in the Bureau?"

"I graduated from the academy five years ago. I started off in white collar crime, then I got assigned to bank robbery."

"Whose idea was that?"

"Mine, why?"

"You seem like more of a number cruncher."

"I felt I needed more field experience," said Kim.

"And did you get it?"

"A little, but it wasn't exactly what I expected."

"It never is. But then what do I know? I retire in six months. I'll have to leave you and Nevins here, with your computers and new ways of doing things. Nevins is good at the computer, he even promised to set me up on Facebook.  See anything Nevins?"

"Not yet."

"Well, keep looking."

# CHAPTER 19

Pazhman looked, too. For fifteen minutes he watched the bakery before he decided it was safe to approach.

"Looks like we got another customer," said Nevins, as he snapped a photo.

Baumgartner looked through the scope. "Recognize him?"

Nevins shook his head.

Pazhman entered through the loading bay, where Azzad tallied an order for a customer waiting by a beat-up delivery van. Azzad spoke to his customer in a mix of Urdu and English.

"You bring me the receipt I'll take a look."

"The receipt's wrong. You shorted me on two cases, last week."

"I don't short you on nothing. You ask for ten cases, I send you ten cases."

"And I got eight. You owe me a credit of 42 dollars."

Azzad grew angry. He was about to respond when he saw Pazhman standing in the entrance to the loading bay. His demeanor changed. He was momentarily speechless, then remembered his customer, and finished checking his invoice.

"Whatever, okay, I give you a credit," he said.

His customer looked surprised. It wasn't like Azzad to give in like that. He accepted his victory with a shrug and finished loading the van.

Pazhman approached.

"It has been many years," said Pazhman.

Azzad stared at his visitor a long time. He was stunned. He had suspected something might happen when the cash transfers recently increased. But it was still hard to believe the moment finally come.

The two men knew each other well, which was why Azzad had been chosen as Pazhman's first contact. They had trained together in the mountains near Tirich Mir. Suffered together. Endured together. Sworn their blood oaths together.

"My brother," said Azzad, and the two men embraced. "I have

been expecting you, but I almost didn't recognize you without your beard. Come, where we can talk."

Pazhman followed Azzad into a cluttered office behind a plate glass window in the rear of the bakery.

"May I offer you tea?" Azzad asked. He rarely observed such formalities now, but this was a special event, and respect had to be shown. The tea came from an electric kettle set up on a filing cabinet. Only once it had been served did Pazhman speak.

"Thank you. Is it safe to talk?"

"Of course," said Azzad.

"The professor sends his greeting. He has not forgotten you," said Pazhman.

"I never doubted that."

"I will require a new passport. Have the funds been received?" asked Pazhman.

Azzad nodded.


Baumgartner put the camera down and adjusted the volume of the audio receiver. There was a distorted blend of background noise and a ringing phone, a chair scraping and someone talking in a language he didn't understand. It was all static.

"Where's the bug?" Kim asked.

"No bug, we're picking up the vibration on the long range mike. It's not working that well."

Kim had just poured herself a cup of coffee when Baumgartner looked out the window. Down the street, an NYPD patrolman walked toward the bakery, patrolling his beat.

"What the fuck?" said Baumgartner.

He looked at Nevins. "Did you notify NYPD?"

Nevins hesitated. "I thought you did."

Baumgartner watched with a combination of horror and disbelief as the patrolman stopped in front of the bakery's loading dock.

"What's this prick doing?" he asked.

"He sees something," said Kim, who had joined Baumgartner at the window.

Baumgartner looked again through the camera. "What the fuck

is this numbnuts up to?"

Officer David Kratowski had a knack for spotting stolen cars. He stood on the sidewalk looking at a Ford Escape. Something wasn't right: the rear left window was missing. He noted the license plate and entered it into his handheld ticketing computer. His hunch was right, the vehicle had been reported stolen.

Kratowski peered into the car, then looked around at the nearby buildings. His eyes settled on the bakery. Perhaps someone in the bakery had seen who had parked the car?

"We gotta get him outta there," said Nevins, as the officer headed for the bakery.

"It's too late, let it play out," said Baumgartner.

What played out involved those variables that can't be predicted. Antonio Figeroa, the person who had, in fact, stolen the Ford Escape, was employed by Azzad as a warehouseman. He stole the car because he was drunk on Colt 44 Malt Liquor and it seemed like a fun thing to do at the time. He refused to abandon it on Atlantic Avenue, as his friends had urged. Instead he kept the car and drove it to work because taking the bus would have made him late.

When Figeroa saw the police officer on the loading dock, he lowered his eyes and tried to go unnoticed. Everyone else looked directly at the police officer.

"That your car out there?" asked the patrolman.

Figeroa pointed at his own chest. "Me?"

"Yeah, that your car?"

He couldn't believe that he had been singled out so quickly. How was that possible? But the police officer was stepping toward him. "What car?" he asked, then stupidly added, "that ain't my car."

"What ain't your car?" asked Officer Kratowski.

"I don't drive no car."

"What's your name?

Figeroa hesitated, then, and here again, he was inadequately prepared to accurately predict the string of events that would result. But he was intelligent enough to know that he already had two convictions on his record, and they would throw the book at him for a third. He produced a revolver from the pocket of his overalls. It was a cheap, Saturday-night special that he carried less for protection and more with the misguided idea that it would impress the girls who lived in his housing project. Figeroa fired. The bullet struck Kratowski in the upper leg, severing his femoral artery.

Across the street, Baumgartner turned to the others. "Shot fired," he said "Jesus fucking Christ, shot fired."

Pazhman and Azzad heard the shot too. From the rear office they saw the policeman grab his thigh and collapse to the loading dock floor, wincing in agony.

Azzad had not yet opened the safe to remove the cash he held for Pazhman. He had been serving the tea. Now he watched as Figeroa jumped from the loading dock and sprinted away down the sidewalk.

"What is this?" asked Pazhman.

Azzad shook his head in confusion. "You must leave!" he hissed.

"I have done nothing," replied Pazhman.

"Go!"

Pazhman looked at the officer bleeding on the floor and realized Azzad was right. He began walking toward the open loading dock gate.

Baumgartner was already headed for the stairs, barking orders as he ran.

"Conrad stays with me, Mahan, you and Nevins cover the rear!"

Officer Kratowski's partner, James McBride, who had been writing parking tickets halfway down the block, heard the shot as well, and began running toward the bakery. He radio'd it in as he ran. His short, clipped words, he knew, would bring every officer within miles.

"Shots fired, officer needs help," he said as he drew his weapon.

McBride turned into the bakery's loading dock and saw a tall dark haired man walking quickly toward the exit.

"Stay where you are!" he shouted.

Pazhman froze. The officer's eyes darted nervously from Pazhman toward the inside of the bakery. McBride was a rookie, unsure what to do. Then he saw his partner.

"Dave, you okay?" he asked, holding his weapon on Pazhman.

93

Pazhman took a step.

"On the floor!" McBride shouted. He noticed the other workers, huddled against the side of the bakery. "Everyone get on the ground, hands where I can see 'em!"

Pazhman had no intention of lying on the floor, or, for that matter, of being questioned by the police. He had been questioned twice before, once by Pakistani Intelligence, a routine formality, and once by the CIA in Afghanistan. It had not been a pleasant experience, and he suspected he had narrowly avoided an open-ended stay at Guantanamo Bay. He had been lucky, but would not test his luck again.

"He is hurt," said Pazhman, and knelt down beside Officer Kratowski.

McBride approached his stricken partner.

"Where's the shooter?" he asked.

Kratowski pointed his bloody hand toward the street. McBride looked in that direction.

Pazhman didn't hesitate. He reached under his jacket and removed his knife. McBride never saw it coming. The razor sharp blade stabbed deep into the patrolman's neck. Pazhman pulled it out with an equally quick motion and the officer slumped to the floor, blood pumping onto the concrete floor.

Kim was surprised at the speed of Baumgartner's reaction. Before she had even checked her weapon he was out the door and barreling down the stairs. She caught up with him on the sidewalk between the apartment building and the bakery.

"Stay behind me," he said.

Kim nodded. "Shouldn't we wait for backup?"

"No."

From the loading dock Pazhman saw Baumgartner and Kim rushing down the sidewalk. He cursed to himself and stepped back into the bakery where Azzad stood over the wounded Officer Kratowski.

"Is there another way out?" asked Pazhman.

"No!" replied Azzad.

Officer Kratowski was now sitting up, both hands gripping his thigh, trying to staunch the bleeding. His hands were covered with blood, and his eyes were fixed on the man who had just killed his partner. He felt blood pulsing through his fingers. Kratowski saw his weapon on the floor and reached for it. Pazhman kicked the officer in the leg and wrenched the bloody weapon from his hands as Kratowski screamed in agony. Without missing a beat, Pazhman turned and fired three rapid shots toward Baumgartner, who ducked beneath the loading dock.

Azzad was stunned. He looked at Pazhman.

*What have you brought? For years I have waited, and now this?* He looked at the dead officer and the wounded one and suddenly it was clear to him. These police had not materialized out of nowhere. They had been watching him. His time had come, and he had sworn an oath. He would not be taken alive. He would die a martyr, but perhaps Pazhman could escape.

Azzad did not have a weapon, but he also knew he didn't need one. From his training, those many long difficult months, he had learned that there were weapons everywhere: a rock, a piece of wood, a shard of glass, a stick, a rope, a pencil. It didn't matter. He saw a steel crowbar where the men had been opening a crate. It would do. He saw movement on the sidewalk, and nodded to Pazhman.

Bent low, Baumgartner moved toward the loading platform steps. Kim covered him from behind. At the top of the steps he peeked into the warehouse. He saw the lifeless body of Officer McBride and behind him, Officer Kratowski. Three frightened employees huddled against the far wall. Kratowski, who was on the verge of passing out, lifted his head and looked at Baumgartner, then his eyes shifted to the side, and Baumgartner realized someone was there. It was too late.

Azzad appeared from around a corner. He was a large man, strong, and coming at him. Baumgartner leveled his pistol but Azzad was already swinging the crowbar. It hit the agent's forearm, cracking bone, and Baumgartner dropped his weapon and stumbled backwards toward Kim, his full weight landing on her.

And there was Azzad, charging. Kim shoved Baumgartner

aside, raised her pistol, and fired. The bullet struck Azzad in the neck. He stopped and staggered, but he was in a fury. He raised his arm to strike Kim and she fired again, point blank into his face and he crumpled backwards onto the steps.

As Azzad collapsed, lifeless, Kim saw another man behind him. For an instant, their eyes locked. She marked his penetrating eyes, wavy black hair, dark skin, and then his weapon. She ducked just in time as bullets struck the wall above her head. When she looked up she saw him leaping from the loading platform directly toward her. They both tumbled to the rough concrete floor. Kim brought her knee up as hard as she could. She felt it meet soft tissue and heard Pazhman grunt in pain. Pazhman instinctively reached for his knife. It wasn't there! Then he saw it on the ground.

Kim reached it first and rolled away. She saw Pazhman in front of her and slashed, felt the blade slicing fabric and flesh. She kicked at his ankles as she struggled to get to her feet - and then he was gone. She turned and saw Baumgartner behind her, one arm hanging limp, the other held his weapon.

"You okay?" he asked.

She nodded.

"Then get after him."

Pazhman was halfway down the block before Kim reached the sidewalk. She was running as fast as she could, but he was still faster, how was that possible? Out of breath, she caught sight of Pazhman on the far side of Flatbush Avenue, he was slowing down, trying to meld with the crowd.

She took her eyes off him for a split second while she ran across the street. And he was gone. She scanned the crowd. A hot dog vendor handed a man a can of soda, two businessmen in suits walked briskly toward her on the sidewalk, a gaggle of high school girls talked noisily at a bus stop, yelling and shrieking in laughter, as if challenging the two middle aged women at the same bus stop to say something.

Pazhman walked briskly down Flatbush to Atlantic Avenue, where he saw a taxi. The driver had pulled the cab over and was eating a hot dog.

He opened the back door and got in.

"Didn't ya see the light? I'm off duty."

Pazhman handed the driver a hundred dollar bill. "Drive."

When Kim turned the corner she saw nothing. Pazhman had disappeared. Like a ghost.

\* \* \*

Pazhman felt a sharp pain in his chest - and in his groin. He looked down at his chest. He was bleeding badly. The knife had sliced his shirt clean through, and there was a deep cut across his left nipple. He buttoned his jacket and pressed it against the wound. A thousand thoughts raced through his mind. This was madness! What had just happened? He tried to calm his breathing, aware that he must look like a maniac, his eyes were wide open, and he had sweated through his shirt. Months of preparation, and suddenly police were onto him - and he hadn't done anything yet! He thought about the woman who had chased him, her face clear in his mind. Who was this bitch?

His mind raced. Had he been betrayed? Did the Americans have such good intelligence that they were waiting for him? If that were the case, why hadn't he been arrested at the airport? And if the police had come for him, known who he was, why send a woman? And why had Azzad's employee shot a policeman? He was confused, aware that he was not thinking straight.

Be calm, he told himself, all is not lost. Remember your training, it is your destiny to gain glory in the fight against the non-believer. He took a deep breath. Yes, have faith, all is not lost.

But now the plan he had so carefully prepared lay in ruins. Azzad was to pass on the funds that would be needed to complete their mission. Now what? He would have to improvise, as he had been trained. But how?

He got out of the taxi on Canal Street, easily disappearing among the crowds on the sidewalk. He took the subway to Grand Central and walked from there to the hotel. He kept his coat closed so no one could see the blood. He was sure someone would sound the alarm before he reached the hotel, but no one noticed him.

In his hotel room he stripped off his bloody shirt and examined his wound. It would require stitches, but there was no time for that now. He stepped in the shower and washed, then folded a hand towel over his chest. He put on a fresh shirt and held the towel in place while he went to a drugstore two blocks away where he bought a bottle of hydrogen peroxide, large gauze pads, ace bandages and surgical tape. He returned to his room and bandaged his wound.

# CHAPTER 20

"That was a motherfucking clusterfuck," said Baumgartner when the team convened at Gambler's office after two hours at King's County Hospital. "A royal motherfucking clusterfuck."

Baumgartner had a broken arm. He had been muttering about shit shows and clusterfucks ever since the attack, until Mahan asked him to stop. But he was right, it had been a clusterfuck. A cop was dead and a surveillance operation blown, and they didn't understand why. The only lead was dead, and their suspect had vanished.

Gambler was on the phone when they entered. He finished his conversation and put the phone down.

"That was the deputy director in Washington, he wants to know what the hell's going on." Gambler took a deep breath and looked at the agents. "But I want to know first. Fast. And just so you know, cable news broke the story an hour ago. So far NYPD is saying it's a botched robbery, and that's how we want to keep it for now. No point spooking this guy, whoever he is." He looked at Mahan. "So what are we dealing with?"

"We have to assume we stumbled onto a cell of some kind. NYPD shows and all hell breaks loose."

"This baker, Nabir is dead?" asked Gambler.

"Affirmative," said Mahan.

"So who's this mystery man who got away?"

"We don't know yet," replied Kim.

"Wonderful."

Gambler leaned back in his chair and rubbed his temples.

"I don't suppose I have to remind you that in less than two weeks a G20 meeting is scheduled for Governor's Island."

Mahan understood all too well: leaders from every major economic power converging on New York City, world media, anti-globalist demonstrators, a security nightmare. Was it a coincidence that a terrorist turned up at precisely the same time?

Gambler reached into his pocket and took out a pill bottle. He washed one down with what was left of his coffee, now cold.

Heartburn? Indigestion? Kim wasn't sure. But he was definitely a heart attack waiting to happen, she thought. She guessed he was 45, and wondered if he'd make it to 50.

"Okay, take me though it. Tell me about this Nabir Azzad character, how'd you get to him?" asked Gambler.

"He owned the bakery. We were following a money trail. Nabir's accounts have been on the receiving end of wire transfers, and there are some intermediary accounts linked to some of the banks we've flagged. It didn't add up," said Mahan.

"So you set up surveillance?"

"The usual," said Mahan. "We think officer Kratowski, that's the name of the NYPD officer who was wounded, was investigating a car stolen by one of Nabir's employees. Wrong place, wrong time; nothing to do with our investigation."

"Jesus Christ. So how do we find this mystery man who killed Officer Fernandez?"

"We took his picture when he entered the building, we're checking prints. NYPD is looking," said Baumgartner.

"And that's it?"

"That's all we know right now," said Mahan.

Gambler took a deep breath. "So we've got one dead cop, one in the hospital, a suspect we can't question because special agent Conrad killed him, another suspect we can't question because we don't know who he is, let alone where he is, and the New York Police commissioner on the phone wondering why the fuck no one bothered to pick up the goddamn phone and let the NYPD know we had something in the works!"

"Sir, if we hadn't been there, Officer Kratowski would still be dead, and so would his partner, in my opinion," said Mahan.

"I know, shit happens. But the book says we tell NYPD what we're doing, and if we had, Officer Kratowski would be at the corner bar drinking a beer now."

Gambler understood the political power of the NYPD, and its reach. The department had counterterrorism officers posted around the world, and was larger than most national spy agencies. It was also aggressively protective of its turf. Gambler had been on the phone with them for the past hour. The calls had not gone well.

He looked at Kim. "We need to find out who your mystery man is, and we need something fast."

"My mystery man?" said Kim.

"And since special agent Conrad killed this Nabir character we can't ask him," Gambler said.

"What was I supposed to do?" she asked.

Gambler threw up his hands. "I don't know, shoot him in the leg?"

"He was about to kill me," said Baumgartner, "Special Agent Conrad was watching my back. She had to take the shot."

"She didn't have to shoot him in the face," said Gambler.

"It was a fast moving situation, sir," said Baumgartner.

"Okay, let's set all that aside," replied Gambler. "Given the circumstances, maybe things could have turned out worse, though honestly, I can't see how. No point beating a dead horse."

Phyllis, Gambler's assistant, poked her head in the door.

"There's a Detective Winters here," she said.

Gambler waved him in. "Everybody, I want you to meet Evan Winters, NYPD, he'll be participating in the investigation from here on out. These are Special Agents Conrad, Mahan, and Baumgartner," said Gambler.

Kim turned to see a short, pudgy man with curly black hair who looked like he only grudgingly adhered to the department's dress code for detectives. He was disheveled, and wore a rumpled khaki suit. His shirt collar was open, and his tie (pheasants in mid-flight, a bargain basement buy, perhaps?) was loosely knotted.

"Earned his detective's badge in homicide, spent the last two years in the counterterrorism division," continued Gambler. "He'll be our liaison with the mayor's office. So we don't have any more screw-ups like this morning. I want you to give him a full briefing on everything we know."

The team returned to the Pit where they spent the next 45 minutes going over every detail of the operation, everything Kim could remember. Mahan wrote the key facts and times on the whiteboard. Winters asked a lot of questions.

"I know I'm the new guy, but if you don't mind, can we start at

101

the beginning," said Winters.

"Again?" asked Kim.

"You might have left something out. I need it all for my report."

*We already know all this, thought Kim, now we have to waste time bringing Columbo here up to speed.* She was getting tired. Her body ached, maybe it was the stress, post stress whatever. She needed sleep. She needed a drink.

Mahan cleared his throat. "I suggest we focus on Nabir for now, and then maybe we can figure out who this other guy is, how he's connected, who his friends are, where he lived, who he talked to, the works. This guy has links to radical cells in this country. We need to find out everything there is to know about him."

"Like I said, files are pretty thin," said Baumgartner. "Emigrated to the states from Pakistan in '91. Operated a wholesale restaurant supply business. We pulled him in after 9/11 but nothing turned up."

"And then what?" asked Winters.

"He gets spooked, and the next thing you know it's the shootout at the OK Corral."

Winters turned his attention to Kim.

"What was the other guy like?" he asked.

Kim sighed. "I told you. Five-foot-eight. Dark hair-"

"I don't mean his description, what was he like?"

"Like?" asked Kim.

"You must have picked up a vibe. Saw something in his eyes, in the way he moved. The way he was dressed."

Kim closed her eyes and thought for a moment.

"What was he like?" she asked.

"Yeah."

"He was cool, calm, deliberate. He didn't panic. It was like he was trained to be in a situation like that."

"What kind of training?"

"I don't know. Where does a guy learn to shoot that well?"

"Military?"

Kim shook her head. "It was more like he was, I don't know, a trained assassin or Special Forces type. The way he moved."

"So if he's a terrorist, he's a trained one."

"Maybe. There was something else," said Kim.

"What?"

"He likes to use a knife."

# CHAPTER 21

Lance Dennehy sat in an armchair and watched as Dr. Schiff reviewed his medical file.

"You were wounded in Afghanistan?" asked the psychiatrist.

"Isn't it in the file?"

"Tell me about it."

Dennehy leaned back in the chair. "I don't remember much."

"Start with what you do remember."

Dennehy took a deep breath. "Well, let's see. I remember Lorenzo putting on a field dressing. I remember seeing smoke in the air. After that I remember being inside an operating room somewhere, and that's about it. They flew me out on a C-17 to Landstuhl Medical Center. I remember being there for a while."

"How was Landstuhl?"

Dennehy shrugged. "They told me I had a ruptured ear drum and some internal injuries and that I probably would never be able to run again seeing as how my leg was so fucked up."

"That's a shame, I'm sorry. I see you were an athlete in high school."

"I figured I'd prove them wrong. Be all gung ho and whatnot."

Schiff smiled. "How'd that work out?"

"Not good. The docs were right, pretty much. Been limping ever since. Medical discharge, so much for an Army career."

"So you decided to go into law enforcement." It was more a statement than a question.

Dennehy shifted uncomfortably in his seat. "Yeah, that's right. Seemed to offer the best opportunities. I figured maybe the State Police with my military experience."

The shrink nodded.

Dennehy lowered his head. "Problem is I didn't go to college. Plus I don't think I could meet the physical requirements. So I applied for deputy sheriff with the Woodboro Police. It's

104

temporary, probational."

"That could be a good step," said Schiff,

"It wasn't exactly what I wanted, to be honest, but I thought maybe community college, therapy, I might get that state gig, maybe even a federal job, I don't know."

"It's good to set reasonable goals. You enrolled at the college?"

"Not yet. I guess I let the deadline pass. Maybe next term. I don't know. I've been kind of tired. You're not going to put that in the report, are you?"

"Being tired is normal for someone who is dealing with an injury like yours."

Dennehy didn't expand on it. The truth was that walking, not to mention running, remained difficult. He felt weak, like a runner who was halfway through a race but didn't have the energy to finish. The doctor didn't need to know everything.

"Are you sleeping well? Says here you were having difficulty earlier. Nightmares?"

"That's okay now." Another lie. He did have trouble falling asleep, and when he did fall asleep, the nightmares came.

"Do you drink?"

"The doctors said you shouldn't mix alcohol with the anti-anxiety pills," he said.

"For a reason. They know how strong the medicine is, and what can happen if you mix pills and booze."

I better stop taking the pills, thought Dennehy.


With Dr. Schiff's blessing, and after four weeks at the Ulster County Sheriff's Academy in Kingston, Dennehy reported for duty at the Woodboro Police Department. The police chief, Frank Burke, presided over Dennehy's first morning roll call.

"Listen up, everybody," Chief Burke began, "last night Officer Kendal made a DUI arrest, on Route 4, perp is Bob Kershaw. Again. He's going to be arraigned later this morning. Bill, I'd appreciate it if you see to it and get him to court on time."

"No problemo," said Officer Bill Gastonberry.

The Chief continued. "We'll be beginning our motorcycle safety campaign today, and I want to thank Jane for all the liaison work she did with the community.

Jesus, thought Dennehy. Welcome to my new life.

Jane Simmonds, the clerk, blushed, and then did a sarcastic wave while the officers applauded briefly.

"Please be advised the water department has a crew out on Newell Road again, and we'll need an extra detail there through the rest of the week. Just tell Jane if you're interested in a little OT."

The Chief cleared his throat. "And last, but certainly not least, I want to introduce our newest member, Lance Dennehy. He graduated from the Academy last week and is joining us as a probational officer. Most of us already know him, but please join me in welcoming him and helping me to show him the ropes. That's all I got."

Then Dennehy went on patrol with the chief. The chief drove. Normally, since the department consisted of just eleven full-time officers, patrols were one officer per car, but the Chief liked to spend time with the new recruits, show them the town, explain his law enforcement philosophy.

"I was in the army too, Desert Storm, back in '92," said the Chief, with a note of pride.

Dennehy nodded.

"You guys had it worse. If you ever need to talk...."

"Thanks, Chief," Dennehy smiled as the patrol car pulled onto a quiet Main Street.

"What you'll be doing for the most part is traffic details, crowd control at the fair later this summer, we get a big crowd. After you're not a proby anymore, you'll handle traffic stops, collisions. We get a lot of OUIs, domestics, don't expect anything too exciting. Might be a let down after Afghanistan. But don't try to make it something it isn't."

"I understand."

"Not much goes on, and that's the way I like it. We busted up a meth ring last year, made the city papers. That was pretty big."

Dennehy nodded, as if he knew about it, though he did not.

"You might even find it monotonous at times. Hell, I do, occasionally, but I like the town, I like the people. It's a job, it's a paycheck, it's a pension, which is more than you can say for a lot of

106

people."

If this was a recruiting pitch for Woodboro's Police Department, Chief Burke was doing a pretty shitty job, thought Dennehy.

The Chief turned and looked Dennehy in the eye. "Now you represent the Woodboro Police Department, and I expect you to govern yourself accordingly. You want to get drunk, do it at home. You want to drive drunk, don't even think about it or you'll be flipping burgers at the coffee shop before you know what hit you. Long as you wear that badge, you get no special privileges. In fact, you're held to a higher standard, understand?"

"Yes, sir."

# CHAPTER 22

A brass bell on the front door of the innocuously named Midtown Shoe Repair rang to announce Pazhman's arrival. The proprietor, Hassan Khalifa, was busy behind the counter brushing a pair of suede shoes. His employee, Arthur, who lived off tips from shining shoes, looked up as he rubbed polish on a customer's black brogues. It was a brief, cursory glance, but enough to see if he recognized the customer, and notice what shoes he was wearing. Pazhman's shoes were dirty, dusty and of cheap leather. They didn't match the expensive suit and shirt he wore. Arthur was always amazed at how people neglected their shoes. Hardly worth polishing, he thought.

Wedged between a Greek deli and the service entrance of an office building on West 36th Street, it was a typical shoe repair shop. It smelled of new leather, solvent and shoe polish. The shelves behind the counter held a jumble of shoes to be repaired, shoes of every description, some in brown paper bags and marked with grease pencil waiting to be picked up. A sign warned that shoes left for more than 90 days would be discarded. There was a workbench behind the counter where Hassan worked. It appeared he knew his trade, and the trade must have supported him well enough, judging from the shop's large, cluttered inventory of leather polishes and shoelaces, insoles and galoshes.

Pazhman noted the usual arrangement of three chairs mounted on a raised platform. A young businessman occupied one of the chairs. The businessman read a magazine called Maxim. Pazhman took one of the empty chairs and watched as the attendant, a young man of about 20 in a gray cotton apron, finished polishing the businessman's shoes.

Pazhman placed his feet on the well-worn metal footrests and Arthur acknowledged him with a nod. Without asking, Arthur began washing Pazhman's shoes with a small brush with soapy water, then dried them quickly and applied polish. These shoes need help, he thought. "Emergency surgery," he called it. Some people got their shoes polished even when they didn't need it. Arthur figured maybe this obsessiveness was a way of killing time, a nervous habit. Maybe they had that disease, obsessive disorder, and had to constantly have everything washed and polished. It didn't matter to Arthur. If they sat down in the chair, that meant they got a polish. He charged $4 for a basic polish. When it was busy, he could make $125 in tips per day. It was hard work, but soon he would have enough money to make a deposit on an apartment, or own his own home. He was doing well.

Arthur did the best he could with Pazhman's cheap, dusty shoes. When he was done polishing the shoes he gave a final burst of effort with the rag, pulling it back and forth rapidly, and ending with his trademark flourish. That was how his customers knew he was done. The tips had improved since he began doing that.

Pazhman climbed down and walked slowly to the counter where Hassan, the owner, had begun resoling a pair of shoes.

"You do very good work," said Pazhman.

Hassan looked up at him without responding. He did do good work, he knew, but he was very tired of repairing shoes. He had been doing it for too long, and was, in fact, getting too good at it. But he liked the women who brought him their high-heeled shoes to be repaired. Many of them worked in the office buildings that shadowed over his small shop. They had expensive hairdos and wore makeup, and had long polished fingernails. They could be very rude, very brassy indeed. He considered them no better than whores or harlots, especially the younger ones, who dressed in such skimpy dresses. No doubt they could attract sexual partners at work, or in the bars when they left their offices. What self-respecting man would allow his wife to go into the city dressed as they were, and work for other men? It was, to Hassan, simply another sign of the decadence of the Western world. But still he liked it when they came into his shop, and he smiled, and in the deepest recesses of his mind, he enjoyed repairing their shoes. Sometimes he smelled the insoles of the shoes and sometimes even put the heels in his mouth. He knew such thoughts were wicked, wicked thoughts, and that he must pray for forgiveness. Deep down he knew he was weak in so many ways, but that one day he would

109

make up for it.

"I bring greetings from a friend," Pazhman said in low tones.

Hassan regarded Pazhman silently for a moment.

"What friend?"

"Our old professor," said Pazhman.

Hassan became very still. "And what message?"

"It is time to sharpen our knives."

Arthur glanced at his boss. Hassan suddenly looked worried, the way he did when a customer came in to complain about something, or if a pair of shoes was lost, which happened a lot.

Hassan gestured to the back room with a tip of his head and Pazhman passed behind the counter and followed. Another customer entered the shop and climbed into a seat. Arthur shook his head and started polishing the next pair of shoes. He had never once in the two years he had worked in the shop seen Hassan invite anyone into the tiny back room.

Pazhman and Hassan stood facing each other in the confined space, two feet apart. "My name is Pazhman, Nabir Azzad is dead," said Pazhman.

Hassan's eyes opened wide.

"How? When?"

"He was killed by the police this morning. Have the police been here?"

"No!"

"And you have noticed nothing unusual? No phone calls?"

Hassan shook his head.

"That is good," said Pazhman. "That is very good." For the first time since killing the police officer, he let out a sigh of relief. Perhaps the professor was right. It was his destiny to succeed.

"I need a place to stay," said Pazhman.

Hassan nodded. "Go to Bryant Park, behind the library, it is not far. I will close up and meet you there. You know it?"

Pazhman nodded. "Of course. I will be there in one hour."

Arthur watched Pazhman leave.

"Everything okay boss?" Arthur asked.

"Yeah sure, why not?" Hassan replied, and turned his attention back to resoling shoes.

110

# CHAPTER 23

At 4 o'clock, Hassan abruptly went to the front door and turned the plastic sign around to say "closed," and locked the door.

"I'm sorry, I gotta close early today," Hassan explained.

"Okay, boss," Arthur said.

Arthur had never known Hassan to close early. Usually there was a rush at the end of the day, between four and six, and during this time Arthur collected good tips. But if Hassan wasn't there, it was impossible to stay open. People would arrive hoping to pick up or drop off shoes, and if Arthur was shining shoes, he wouldn't be able to help them.

The two men left together. Hassan made sure the door was locked behind him. Hassan turned left, and Arthur right. Arthur walked a few yards, he turned and, out of curiosity, decided to follow Hassan.

Hassan walked north on Sixth Avenue. Arthur followed. Hassan entered Bryant Park. He glanced about nervously, his gait hesitant and unsure.

Arthur paused at the entrance to the park and watched. Hassan sat on a park bench. A man approached and sat down beside him. It was the same man who had come to the shop earlier. What could that mean, Arthur wondered?

His boss was selling the shop to him, maybe. Didn't he always bitch about the shoe repair business, how he disliked the customers, and didn't he struggle to pay the exorbitant rent? What would selling it mean? Thoughts and questions raced through the young man's mind. Would he still have a job? Could he still shine shoes, somewhere else? Will he have to postpone his engagement to Francesca, move in with his mom?

But he was getting ahead of himself. Maybe Hassan wasn't selling the business. Maybe he owed the other man money, and he had gone to pay it, but if that was the case, why not discuss it in the shop? No, thought Arthur, he's selling his shop, and I won't have a

111

job much longer.

"You have seen the professor?" asked Hassan.

"A week ago."

"And he is well?"

"He sends his greetings."

"Truly?"

Pazhman nodded.

"I suspected someone would come. Over the past two months, Nabir gave me many tasks to perform."

"And you completed these tasks?" asked Pazhman.

Hassan nodded. "Two weeks ago I delivered computer equipment to the farm, and cash, rather a lot, to someone near there. I did not ask any questions, he simply did as I was told."

"That is good. Now you must assemble the others, as you have been taught.

"What do I tell them?"

"Tell them the moment has arrived."

Hassan swallowed hard.

"And the target?"

"You will be informed when the time is right. I will stay at your home. For now, there is much to do. You have a car?"

"Of course."

They drove to Hassan's small apartment in the Woodlawn section of Queens. Pazhman approved of Hassan's car. It was a Toyota Corolla, the most popular model of car in the country, and would not stand out. It also appeared that Hassan kept the vehicle in good running order. A reliable vehicle was a minor point, something easily overlooked, but important nonetheless.

Hassan said little during the drive, he appeared very nervous.

"Relax, my friend, or you will get in an accident," said Pazhman.

"I'm sorry," said Hassan.

"Do not apologize."

"Sorry. I mean, of course.'

"If anyone asks my name is Kamal Noor, and I am your cousin, visiting."

"Visiting from where?"

"Just tell them Cleveland," said Pazhman.

"Cleveland?"

"It will arouse more suspicion if they think I am from Pakistan. You have made the other preparations required of you?"

"Of course."

"You have done well."

"It has been a very difficult wait, very long, and very lonely."

"It has been a difficult struggle for many people. Many people have suffered more than you, you should know that. Have you obtained the weapons?"

"Oh, yes." Hassan said. He did not tell him that it had been surprisingly easy to purchase the automatic weapons.

"And ammunition?" asked Pazhman.

"Plenty."

"Where?"

"They are concealed in my apartment, but what about money? Nabir was entrusted with all the funds."

"Yes, money is now a problem. We will have to make new plans," said Pazhman.

"And the target? When will I know what our target is?" asked Hassan.

Pazhman looked at him sternly.

"You will be informed when the moment is right, and not before."


Hassan's apartment was in a modest, well-kept row of houses with fake brick veneer and a metal railing leading up steps to the entrance on the second floor. There were garages on the ground floor. Hassan carried Pazhman's suitcase and showed him inside. Pazhman sat on a stool in the kitchen and Hassan examined his wound.

"The cut is deep, I may have to stitch it if it will not heal," said Hassan.

He rinsed it with hydrogen peroxide and then applied gauze bandages which he taped in place. Pazhman did not flinch. When he was done Pazhman put on an undershirt and rested on the sofa.

"Where have you concealed the weapons?" Pazhman asked.

Hassan went to the windows in the living room and drew the curtains.

An old trunk served as a coffee table. Hassan removed newspapers and an ashtray from the table and took a key from his pocket. He unlocked the trunk. He opened it and began to remove the weapons, one by one, and show them to Pazhman before placing them on the carpet.

Pazhman stood up and picked up an AR-15. He held it in his hands, then opened the chamber and inspected it.

He smiled. "How did you obtain these?"

"A gun show in Florida, more than a year ago."

"Excellent," said Pazhman, his eyes brightened at a Sig Sauer 9mm pistol. He picked up the handgun and aimed at various targets in the living room. He released the magazine, then opened the chamber and dry fired the weapon.

Pazhman noticed a black plastic case in the trunk and picked it up. He opened it and saw a high-powered rifle, disassembled, the barrel, stock and scope placed into a specially cut out foam pad. He sat down and placed the case on his lap, then quickly and confidently assembled the weapon.

"Is this satisfactory?" asked Hassan.

Pazhman looked at Hassan. Maybe you are not such a fool after all, he thought. Now, if only the others have been as diligent with their responsibilities.

"About this woman, the one who cut you?" said Hassan.

"What of her?"

"How did it come to pass?" Hassan asked.

"The bitch took my knife," said Pazhman. "She was stronger than I expected. I will not make that mistake again."

"Who is this woman?"

"I don't know, but if I find her, I will kill her."

Pazhman looked directly at Hassan and raised his index finger.

"That is a certainty. I will cut her throat."

# CHAPTER 24

"Did time speed up, or slow down?" the researcher asked. Her name was Dr. Catherine Cassidy, and she had an office on Park Avenue South. It was routine. The Bureau was conducting a study on stress and its effect on memory in OIS situations, or officer-involved-shootings.

"It slowed down. I was very focused," replied Kim.

"Interesting."

"Is that normal?"

"Depends how you define normal. For some people it slows down, for some it speeds up. You let me worry about it. What about the auditory response?"

"Huh?"

"Did you hear anything?"

Kim thought for a moment, trying to remember.

"No, everything was quiet. It wasn't quiet, but I wasn't hearing anything. That is, I can't remember hearing anything."

"Auditory lock-out, that's to be expected. Like you said, you were focused."

Kim nodded.

"What else can you remember?"

"I just remember the second guy coming toward me. He had a knife. I remember the knife."

"What about it?"

"It was big, and sharp. And he held it like he knew how to use it, like he was going to use it on me."

"Anything else?"

"Like what?" She was getting annoyed. How many times was she going to ask her if there was anything else?

"What else do you remember?"

"I remember my hand was shaking. I remember struggling for his gun. I remember seeing the policeman, he was screaming something at me, but I don't remember what. He was holding his leg. There was blood."

"And?"

Kim closed her eyes. "I remember Special Agent Baumgartner shouted something, and that's when I ran after the suspect."

"Talk about that."

"I ran down the block. There were some ladies on the corner, waiting for the bus. They looked frightened."

"Did you hear anything?"

"I don't remember. I don't think so," Kim paused. "I ran across the street, I still had my pistol in my hand, then I saw the suspect. He was running. He turned and looked at me, and then he was lost in the crowd."

"And what did you do?"

"I hesitated, I let him go." She shook her head. "I don't remember anything else."

"Have you ever been involved in a shooting before?"

"No, well sort of, not me personally."

"All right, we'll end there. You've been through a very traumatic experience. Your brain and your body will need time to process it. I suggest you take it easy for the next few days. And here, take these." The doctor handed her a small medicine bottle.

"What are they?"

"Lorazepam, they'll help you relax."

Kim rode uptown in a non-air-conditioned taxi that smelled to her like a chicken farm, not that she had ever been to a chicken farm. The driver tried to camouflage it with a sickening pine-scented air freshener, which made it worse. It was hot. They were stuck in traffic. Kim leaned back in her seat and closed her eyes.

Did she really need Lorazepam? She felt fine. A bit tired, maybe, but not traumatized by her brush with death. One thing did bother her, though. She had let him get away.

Suddenly she remembered. Her father. She had agreed to attend her father's benefit, something about someone her father wanted her to meet. She looked at her watch. Shit. It was 6:30, and she had promised to be there at 7:00. She would barely have time to take a quick shower and throw on a dress.

It occurred to her that she could always say that something had come up, that she was stuck at the office, but her Dad would be disappointed. It was a charity that meant a lot to him. Scholarships for inner city children, or was it something else? She couldn't remember. He was on so many charitable boards it was impossible to keep up. He had helped raise millions, and she suspected he was looking forward to having her with him. She had to go.

The taxi pulled up the apartment building and Jimmy, the doorman, looking snappy in his summer tan uniform and white gloves, stepped forward to open the door.

"Good evening Miss Conrad."

"Thanks, Jimmy."

As she stepped into the lobby she considered her free, luxurious digs. Going to the charity event was the very least she could do. She simply had to gather herself, pop a Lorazepam, and go. She took off her business suit as she entered the apartment, letting it drop to the hall floor. Then straight into the shower. As soon as she had dried her hair and thrown on a cocktail dress, the intercom sounded in the front hall.

"Yes?"

"It's Jimmy, Miss Conrad, there's a car here for you."

She rested her forehead against the wall. "Tell him to wait, I'll be right down."

She hung up the intercom, a pre-war Bakelite receiver with a cloth covered wire, and rushed into the bedroom where she put on a pair of shoes, daubed on some lipstick, and strapped her 9mm holster to her inner thigh. It was a custom-made leather holster on an elastic band with Velcro fasteners. She looked in the mirror. Her weapon was completely invisible even in the lightest of summer dresses. She didn't need it, but if the badge allowed her to carry a concealed weapon, why not? It was the rebel in her; maybe she liked being allowed to break the rules. She slipped her FBI badge into her clutch purse.

Time to meet Mr. Wonderful.

The apartment building was old and, despite soaring union labor costs, had never upgraded to push-button automatic elevators. Wally, the evening elevator man, was on duty. He practically touched his forelock when Kim entered.

"Nice to see you, it's been a long time," said Wally.

"Nice to be here, Wally."

"Gonna be staying with us for a while?"

"Looks like it," she said.

"Nice to have someone in 12B after all this time."

"My dad doesn't use it much?"

"Not too often. Sometimes Mrs. Conrad comes in, for a shopping trip."

Mrs. Conrad. She still couldn't get used to that. Well, of course, her mother had been Mrs. Conrad, but she knew Wally was referring to the new Mrs. Conrad. Maybe Wally sensed that.

"We sure miss your mother, she was a really nice lady."

She smiled. "Thanks, Wally."

"Evening out on the town?" he asked.

"Just for a little while. Don't worry, I won't be late." She meant it too. She planned to make an appearance and then leave. One hour. Two tops.

"We'll be here," he said as he slowed and then stopped the elevator, and pulled the metal gate open.

Kim took a glass of champagne from a passing waiter and then wandered through the Met's collection of marble sarcophagi and early Egyptian bronzes. The party was in the Temple of Karnak. After years in the boondocks, she was struck by the glamour. "What have I been missing?" she asked herself.

The band played American standards. The music was vaguely familiar to Kim, she didn't have much of a head for that sort of music. Grunge rock, alternative rock, classic punk were what she had grown up with in high school. Her parents hated it. She had dressed the part: gothic black nail polish, black clothes, multiple ear piercings, most of which had since closed up. As she wandered through the museum she felt like she was leading a double life, that somehow she didn't belong here, in an air-conditioned ancient Egyptian temple among a roomful of well-heeled New York society types fresh from doing battle on Wall Street after she had, well, done battle of an entirely different sort.

She found her father in conversation with a tall, chubby man with dark curly hair, plastic horn-rimmed glasses.

"Kim, glad you could make it," her father said. He turned to the tall man beside him. "This is Bill Davenport, my daughter, Kim."

Davenport wore a Hermes tie, spread collar, and a well-cut grey pinstripe suit. Kim smelled strong cologne, and noticed his nails were manicured. So not my type, she thought. They exchanged autobiographies as her father was drawn away to greet someone else.

"So let me get this straight. You work for the FBI, the Federal Bureau of Investigation?" asked Davenport.

"That's right."

"And you were at Wharton?"

"Right again."

His lower lip extended. "Interesting. I don't suppose you knew… well, I have so many friends who were there, we don't want to play the name game."

"No, we really don't," said Kim.

"I was at Harvard. Well, Harvard undergrad, then Stern. So, I suppose I shouldn't ask, but do you carry a gun and actually apprehend bank robbers and murderers?" He seemed to find the thought amusing.

"Sometimes. So how do you know my Dad?"

"Who doesn't know him? He's doing the legal work for us. A deal we're working on."

Kim said nothing. He wanted to discuss his work. She wouldn't oblige him. Davenport stood there, wondering what to say next. Man, you are seriously challenged, she thought. She almost felt sorry for him, so she decided to throw him a bone. "You're an investment banker?"

She regretted it immediately. He launched into a five-minute explanation of his latest deal, a company that made oil pipes in Louisiana. And he actually thought she was listening. Her father glanced over, raised his eyebrows and smiled as Davenport droned on.

But she couldn't just walk away, not after her father had asked her to be nice to him. Somebody rescue me. Please. Her eyes shifted across the room to a tall slender woman in a cocktail dress. She recognized her, Mimi somebody. Mimi Carlisle. Mimi was listening intently to a dashing man with disheveled hair. He said something and they laughed. The man had rugged good looks and wore a wrinkled shirt and dinner jacket with peaked lapels. There was something interesting about him.

Davenport said something, something about the bond market. She felt a headache coming on. Kim interrupted him. "Will you excuse me, I have to say hello to someone."

She turned before he could reply.

Mimi and Kim had been friends one summer in New York, while Kim was a summer intern for her father. It had been nearly ten years, but she and Mimi had partied hard together until the wee hours, and been regulars at nightclubs all over town. It had been a fun summer. She'd heard Mimi was now a rising star at a bank, she forgot which one.

But who was Mimi's date?

After they had hugged and kissed, and said how great it was to see each other, Mimi introduced Jack Briggs.

"Kim and I go way back, but be careful what you say, she works for the FBI. Oh my God, is it okay to tell people that?"

Kim smiled. "Yeah, it's okay, I'm not in the CIA."

"Thanks for the head's up," said Jack. "But you don't look like an FBI agent." He had a Texas accent.

"We're breaking down stereotypes, but I'll take it as a compliment. And you're visiting from Texas?"

He shook his head.

"You have been away from the city too long, Jack's a columnist for the New York Chronicle," Mimi said.

"But you have a good ear, I am from Texas, originally."

"What do you write about?" asked Kim.

"Local scandals, mostly," Jack replied. "I throw in a little art and culture too."

"I guess you're in the right place," said Kim.

Jack twitched his chin toward Davenport, who was standing alone, flat footed, staring at the crowd. "Who's your friend?"

120

"He's not a friend. Just someone I met tonight. I don't think you'll find a story in him."

"I wouldn't think so, and I'd venture to say the presence of the FBI sounds more promising. So what brings you here?"

"My Dad invited me, that's him over there. But it's been a long day, and I haven't eaten and I'm pretty tired. I probably shouldn't have come."

"Maybe a glass of champagne is what you need," said Jack.

Mimi wandered off and Jack found the champagne. The drink made Kim feel less tired. She and Jack chatted beneath the massive stone Egyptian temple as the sun set through the enormous windows that overlooked Central Park.

The band struck up a tune. "If I weren't so tired I'd want to dance," said Kim.

"I think your Dad is about to give a speech, and this is isn't that kind of party."

"It's just as well. Hey listen, do you want to get out of here?"

"What did you have in mind?" asked Jack.

"I'm starved."

"But your Dad's speech."

They left the party just like that, without saying goodbye. A photographer waited at the entrance. Kim and Jack paused as he took their photo. Kim smiled. She felt light-headed, almost tipsy. They walked east from the museum until they got to Second Avenue where they found a Chinese restaurant.

The waiter at Fujan Gourmet East handed her a menu. There were too many pages, the print was too small.

"I'll eat anything, you order," she said to her companion.

Jack didn't need to refer to the menu. "We'll have General Tso's Chicken and Szechuan beef, and a side of baby bok choy."

"And fried dumplings," added Kim. "And tea. And beer."

"What kinda beer you want?" asked the waiter.

"Tsing Tao," said Jack.

The waiter left with their order.

"I think if I don't eat soon I'll pass out, it's been a long day," Kim said.

"Tell me about it," said Jack. "I'm interested to know what the day is like for an FBI agent."

She smiled. "I don't think I'm supposed to talk to the press."

He smiled. "I'm not the press. I'm someone who you invited to dinner."

"Don't worry, you're not missing any good stories. What I do is not usually all that exciting," she said.

Not usually. She looked at Jack's face and thought about all that had happened that day. She wondered if Jack knew about the shooting. It had been on the local news. The waiter brought the beer and Kim sipped it. She was so hungry she felt faint. When the dumplings arrived she picked up her chopsticks and attacked.

"I suppose we get the wrong picture from all those cop shows," said Jack.

She yawned. "For the most part."

"But if we can't talk about what you do, what can we talk about."

"Tell me how a Texas boy ends up a columnist for the Chronicle."

"Easy. I grew up on my daddy's ranch. Went back east to college, ended up at Columbia J-school."

"And got a job at a newspaper."

He nodded.

"Didn't your Dad want you to be a rancher?"

"No. Town where we're from there are more livestock than people. The nearest town is 20 miles away, and that only has 80 people."

"You visit?"

"As often as I can, helps me keep things in perspective. I like to help my brother around the ranch. It's beautiful. We've got fresh water and prime grazing. Cotton, alfalfa."

"And oil?"

"None of that, unfortunately."

She noticed he had a scar on the back of his hand.

"That where you hurt your hand?"

"You are observant. Got that wrassling with a barbed wire

122

fence."

"Did you say 'wrassling'?"

"What else would you call it when a heifer gets herself all tangled up in the wire?"

"I don't know, I've never come across that. We don't have a lot of barbed wire in New York."

"I wouldn't think so."

"So does this ranch have a name?"

"Of course."

"What is it?"

"BB. It's two B's facing each other, and overlapped. Briggs Brothers. My granddad and his brother."

She picked up his hand in hers and examined the scar.

"I guess we both spent enough time in the boondocks."

She smiled. She wanted to say something amusing, but her fatigue and famine were getting the better of her. Her brain felt woolly and sluggish. She needed to shift gears. She drank some more beer.

Jack said something to her, but it was if through a haze. She started slurring her words, and suddenly feeling sooo tired. For a moment she thought someone had slipped her a mickey, and then she remembered. Lorazepam.

"Jack, I hate to ask you this, but I think you better take me home."

He paid the bill and guided Kim to a cab. In the backseat, her head was tipping back and forth and by the time they arrived he had to carry her into the apartment building. Jimmy unlocked her door and the two men carried her into her apartment. They laid her gently on the couch.

"She forgot she's on medication, made her drowsy," explained Jack.

She was vaguely aware of the two men carrying her into her apartment, looking at her. One was wearing a uniform. The doorman. The other man leaned over. He looked concerned. "You'll be alright, Jimmy will check on you. I'll give you a call tomorrow."

She watched the two men leave as she started to pass out on the

123

couch.

*I'll give you a call.* Shit. She figured the odds were 50-50.

# CHAPTER 25

*CIA Headquarters*
*Langley, Virginia*

CIA technicians Jim Shepley and Angela Williamson worked all day and through the night to unpack data from the laptop's hard drive. Shepley had processed dozens of intercepted hard drives, and had a reputation in the agency as the go-to-man for such procedures. Even without the blood that had gummed up the keyboard, this was a tricky one. He plugged in his cable and dumped all the data into the agency mainframe's decryption and translation program. Then he set to work deciphering it. It took longer than normal. There was the usual encrypted security, and it was in Urdu.

"Are you getting anywhere?" asked Williamson. She didn't know much about computers, but she was an Urdu specialist, and was waiting to have first crack at whatever they found.

"The more you keep asking me, the longer it's going to take. But yes, I am getting somewhere."

"I'm sorry. I'm tired."

But she understood that sleep was not an option. There were only so many Urdo specialists, and time was of the essence. As soon as any terrorist group knew they had been compromised, they would take greater precautions. The element of surprise would be lost.

Shepley began clucking his tongue. Williamson had watched him do this before. He had the nerdy habit of talking to himself, or rather, to the computer, whenever he came up against a particularly vexing problem.

He was getting on her nerves. It didn't help that she thought he had tried to hit on her. He kept asking her questions like "Do you read science fiction novels?" She was afraid he was going to ask her on a date.

"Whoever set it up knew a thing or two about data encryption,"

125

said Shepley.

"Are you going to be able to get it?"

"Oh yeah. Oh, yes in-deedy," he replied, then started talking to the computer again. It was like an imaginary conversation with the person who had programmed the computer he was deciphering, like he was playing a chess match. "You think you can hide from me, but I see what you're doing… what's this? Interesting… kind of a weird way to write code, but okay…"

"Do you have to do that?" asked Williamson.

"Do what?"

"Talk to the computer."

"It helps me think."

"Well, it's annoying."

"Sorry."

He remained silent until ninety minutes later when he said, simply: "I've got you."

Williamson watched him for a moment. "Got what?"

"I got through. Here we go."

With a few keystrokes, computer code began whizzing by on the monitor, and a printer came to life. Williamson picked up the pages as they came out. She scanned them, looking for anything interesting.

"Anything?" asked Shepley.

She nodded as she read.

"Is it good?" he asked.

"Oh, it's very good," she replied.

# CHAPTER 26

Two hours later a preliminary intelligence summary was circulated to the top officials at the agency. The director picked up the phone and called the director of Homeland Security; an item was inserted in the President's daily briefing. By 7 a.m. Saturday, alarm bells were sounding throughout the upper echelons of the entire law enforcement community.

Kim sat at her desk and sipped her second cup of Starbuck's coffee. She still felt groggy. The next time a doctor tried to calm her nerves she'd know better. She was reading the New York Post. There was a story about the party, and there was a photo of her and Jack. She looked at the photo and tried to remember the evening. Mahan appeared in front of her desk.

She took her eyes off the paper and looked at him.

"What's up?"

"Word in from Washington. Our mystery man is setting off all kinds of alarms. We have a briefing."

The secure video link flickered on the big flat screen in the Pit. The team watched and waited, then a man's face appeared.

Gambler introduced him.

"Everybody, this is Lt. Colonel Brad Aronson, U.S. Army Intelligence. He'll be conducting the briefing from the Pentagon."

Aronson was dressed in civilian clothes, but Kim still would have pegged him for an Army officer by his close cropped hair, conservative, off-the-rack blue suit and, of course, the tie. He probably bought it at the PX, thought Kim, (tie, neck, silk, civilian, patterned.)

"Good morning ladies and gentlemen, I'll dispense with the formalities and get on with it. Are you familiar with Pachaas Talwaray?" asked Aronson.

"Should we be?" asked Mahan.

"It's shadowy; we weren't certain it really existed until about six months ago. It's a radical organization, very secretive, specially

127

trained, fundamentalist to the extreme," said Aronson.

"Specially trained?" asked Kim.

"It's a paramilitary organization," said the colonel. "Loosely translated, Fifty Swords, or Fifty Knives, depends who you talk to. Story goes the original group consisted of that many operatives. Most of them are dead now. They're trained in assassinations, explosives, electronics and cyber attacks. We think they're linked to half a dozen attacks in the Middle East, Europe, Africa, and the numbers are growing. We think your man is one of them."

"Why do I get the feeling I'm not going to like this?" said Winters.

"Oh, it gets worse," said the colonel.

A black and white image of Professor Al Fariz appeared on the screen, while the colonel's image shrank to a smaller box inset on the screen. The professor looked younger, and wore a tweed coat and tie, very much the academic.

"This picture's all we've got, it's about 30 years old," said Aronson. "We had good information Pachaas Talwaray was operating a safe house in Peshawar. We hit it, managed to secure a laptop, cost us the life of one of our best men. Stuff we found in the laptop indicates a high profile member of the group entered the US. The timeframe coincides with the increased activity you picked up on."

"Connected to al Quaeda?" asked Kim.

"No, but just as hardcore. More, in a way."

Kim thought of the embassy bombings. "More hardcore?"

"We think he's traveling under the name Arun Patel, a doctor."

Kim wrote the name down in her notebook. Arun Patel.

The colonel continued. "From what little we know, their training emphasizes advanced technology and computers. Their operatives are proficient in foreign languages, advanced weapons training, martial arts, explosives, assassination techniques, you name it, very nasty. We think they're gearing up for a cyber attack at some point, and we've been concerned about sleeper cells from this group for some time. Understand one thing: this group is advanced, technologically. We even suspect they've figured out how to bring down unmanned aerial vehicles. We lost a few last year, including one in an area where we suspect they were operating."

"How would they do that?" asked Kim.

"We don't know."

"Like I said, technology doesn't seem to be a barrier for them. We suspect they're behind several computer viruses, malware, including the Dragon, which you're all aware of, and a few viruses no one's talking about. Their specialty, we think, are root kits," said the colonel.

"Root kit?" asked Kim.

"It's a virus designed to be a sleeper. When it activates it either destroys the computer or begins stealing data. Again, very sophisticated. Their leader, Al Fariz, used to be an electrical engineer, worked for some large defense corporations in Pakistan and Britain back in the '70s and '80s, until the jihadist movement heated up. About 25 years ago he disappeared, then three or four years ago he popped back up on our radar, and we started picking up references to Pachaas Talwaray."

Last year we located one of their training facilities and knocked it out in a drone attack, but we figure over the years they graduated about a hundred fanatics. Let me tell you, these guys have done a lot of damage."

"And you think this Patel, or whatever his name is, is one of them?" asked Mahan.

"We think he was one of their top men. Ended up being an advance operative, suspected of bombings in Iraq, Nigeria, Spain, and then he went to work training others.

"What's this guy's specialty?" asked Mahan.

"He makes bombs," said Aronson.

"His target?"

"Could be anything. We have no intel on that. Subway, the water system, the Statue of Liberty, the airport, Grand Central Station; your guess is as good as mine."

"You're talking about a London-style attack?"

"Could be. Or he could be planning something more... creative. One thing's for sure, they wouldn't send their best bomb maker to New York unless they had something special in mind. Any bozo can strap a few blocks of plastic explosive to his vest. This guy has

129

something else in mind."

Gambler cleared his throat.

"Okay, well, I guess we know what we have to do. We'll concentrate on all suspected sleeper cells in case he tries to make contact, and known sympathizers. Let's check fertilizer supply houses, chemical supply houses, and truck rental companies, the usual."

"He might not even be in New York anymore," said Mahan.

"Are we raising the alert level?" asked Winters.

"Not just yet, we don't want to spook him," replied Gambler. "I'm putting the alert out, but I'm not notifying the media. I'll tell them we're looking for an armed felon, murder suspect, not a terrorist. Meanwhile we'll assume there's an imminent threat. Whoever this mystery man is, we can assume he's not going by the name Arun Patel anymore, we can assume he's gone underground." Gambler looked at his team. "Your job is to find him."

# CHAPTER 27

Kim wrote everything on the white board. It helped her think. Names, addresses, and how they were connected. She used a red marker. At the top was Nabir Azzad, under that she wrote Middle East Gourmet Bakery, Inc. Under that she wrote Arun Patel. It was easier to keep them straight if she spelled them out. She had attended a few PowerPoint presentations on Middle Eastern names and culture, and still found the names a challenge. Often suspects went by more than one name, or names got translated incorrectly, which was why 80-year-old grandmas who had never gone anywhere or done anything suddenly found themselves on the no-fly list.

"So what do we know about Patel?" asked Baumgartner.

"Dr. Arun Patel, born in Karachi, emigrated to the US in '92. He has a green card. Lives in Forest Hills, and works for an NGO, International Health Partners, studying infectious diseases in the developing world," replied Mahan.

He looked up from his computer. "Looks like one Arun Patel flew business class from Islamabad via London to New York two days ago. Entry documents give an address in Forest Hills."

Ten minutes later Winters, Mahan and Kim had wrested a set of car keys from Fitzgibbons and were heading over the Brooklyn Bridge.

"Shouldn't we bring backup?" Winters asked.

"I don't think we'll need it," said Mahan.

"So our guy won't be there?"

Mahan shook his head. "He used Patel's passport because it has a visa. He's got a new identity by now," said Mahan.

Kim sighed as she looked out the window at the passing cars.

"Something bothering you?" asked Mahan.

"It's just that I had him, I fucking had him."

"And you didn't take the shot."

"I did not take the shot."

"Don't feel so bad. I saw the marksmanship report in your file. If it's any consolation, if you had taken the shot, you probably would have missed," said Winters.

Kim turned to him and smiled. "Thank you."

Forty-five minutes later they arrived at a red brick apartment building in Forest Hills. They parked in front of a hydrant outside the entrance and entered the building. Mahan unbuttoned his suit coat and pressed his hand against the holster on his waist, Kim did the same. In the vestibule there was a list of tenants. Patel lived on the third floor. Apartment 3G.

A young woman with a scarf wrapped around her head entered the front door pushing a baby carriage and carrying a bag of groceries. Mahan waited for her to unlock the inner door, then held the door for her while she wheeled the carriage through. Mahan, Winters and Kim followed.

They took the stairs. They had their pistols drawn, Winters on one side of the door, covering one end of the hall, Kim on the other. Mahan knocked on the door.

The door to apartment 3G was ajar. Through the open door they could smell cooking in the kitchen, something ethnic, spicy, and they could hear hushed conversation, occasionally a loud voice, a woman speaking loudly.

Mahan knocked and a young woman in Western clothes came to the door. She was petite and had dark skin.

She saw them and an inquisitive look crossed her face.

"May I help you?" she asked.

Mahan showed her his badge. "We're here to see Dr. Patel."

"You must mean Mrs. Patel?"

"No, Dr. Arun Patel?"

"My uncle is dead. He died of meningitis in Islamabad ten days ago."

"Now what?" asked Kim, in the lobby.

Winters sighed. "We start checking every taxi and limousine that made pick ups at JFK, and hotels."

"How long will that take?" asked Kim.

"You got something else to do?"

* * *

Kim woke early on Saturday and headed into the park for a slow jog. After three days of long hours in the Pit, she'd been given the day off. Time to recharge before the G-20, Gambler said.

She stopped at the reservoir and leaned against the chain link fence looking at the water. Why couldn't she enjoy running the way her friends did? Endorphins were released for them, they said. But never for her. She wanted a cigarette. She walked home. By 9 o'clock she was back at the apartment, and had just filled a glass with tap water. There was a buzzing sound and Kim realized it was the intercom.

"Hello?"

"Miss Conrad?" It was Jimmy, the doorman.

"Yes Jimmy?"

"There's a Mr. Briggs here to see you."

"In the lobby?"

"He's standing right here, Miss Conrad, should I send him up?"

"Yes, I mean no, tell him I'll be right down."

She hung up the receiver, her heartbeat quickening. Suddenly she didn't feel half as tired as she had.

Did we have a date? She'd been so doped up she didn't remember. Is this how they do things in Texas, she wondered, just show up unannounced?

She took a deep breath, then stripped off all her clothes in the living room and jumped in the shower. Fifteen minutes later she found Jack sitting in a reproduction Elizabethan chair in the lobby that no one ever sat in. He stood up when he saw her and smiled.

She wore a pair of white jeans and a black T-shirt, and her hair was still wet, slicked back.

"I'm sorry to make you wait," she wrinkled her nose. "Did we have a date? I'm sorry, I totally forgot, I think I was a bit hammered."

"You were very hammered. You said, 'let's get together again,' and I said, 'sure.'"

"And here you are."

133

He smiled. "Is it okay?"

She smiled. "I'm glad you came. I want a do-over. The last time I saw you I wasn't myself."

"Where should we go?"

"I don't care, let's just walk, I've been staring at a computer screen for days." said Kim as they stepped out onto the sidewalk. It was warm and sunny.

They walked south on Fifth Avenue and when they got to 61st Street Kim remembered Serendipity, the ice cream parlor between Second and Third. It was packed. They waited for a table and then ate hamburgers and split an ice cream sundae.

When lunch was over they walked back uptown. They stopped outside her building. She thought of asking him up, she wanted to, but it was too soon. She looked at his face, putting the clues together, Texas. Rugged rancher background. Journalist. East Coast college. New York. She wanted to figure him out, as she tried to figure everybody out. Figure out if he was for real. But she couldn't. Maybe that was what attracted her to him.

She leaned close to him. Closer. Then it was like two magnets, snapping together. She smiled, thinking about possibilities.

# CHAPTER 28

The Mid Town Shoe Repair had the usual morning traffic, a steady stream of people on their way to work, dropping off and picking up shoes. Arthur helped 14 customers before 11 o'clock. At 11:30, the shop was momentarily empty and Hassan turned the sign in the door to say "closed."

"I have to go out for a while," he announced.

"But boss, it's almost lunch hour rush."

"I have business," he replied.

"What about the bank run?"

"Not today."

Arthur shook his head and watched Hassan leave. He went across the street and bought two hot dogs and a Yoo Hoo from a street vendor and returned to the shop. He had his own key and let himself in. He locked the door behind him and kept the "closed" sign in the window so he could sit behind the counter and eat the hot dogs in peace. He thought about the man who had come into the shop the previous week. For some reason he kept thinking of him, maybe because his boss had been acting nervous and distracted, ever since the stranger had arrived.

Arthur wasn't often in the shop alone, though it wasn't because Hassan didn't trust him around the cash register; he often sent Arthur to the bank with the daily deposit. It was because Arthur couldn't take care of shoe repair customers by himself.

The trip to the bank was usually just after noon, and it was then that Hassan would say his midday prayers. Arthur knew this because he had forgotten his coat once and went back, and he was surprised because he didn't see Hassan. Then he noticed that the door to the tiny storage room behind the counter was ajar and Hassan was on the floor praying. Hassan was a very private, secretive man, thought Arthur. He didn't know very much about him, he didn't even know if he had a family. He knew he wasn't married, at least he didn't think he was. Maybe he had a wife back in his old country, Pakistan. Maybe the man who had come to visit was a relative, a cousin or something, who was in trouble and needed help. Maybe he was about to be deported or some shit like that.

He had noticed that sometimes Hassan rummaged around in a drawer in the storage room and sometimes looked around to see if anyone was looking. He didn't pay much attention to his boss's private work area, though he knew that Hassan kept the key to the drawer under a can of shoe polish on the shelf above his workbench.

Arthur took a quick glance at the front window, then went behind the counter and lifted the can of polish and found the key. He went into the back room, closing the door behind him. He slipped the key into the lock and turned it, then slid the drawer open.

When Hassan entered Bryant Park he was relieved to see Jusef, the young recruit, waiting. Hassan was in a nervous state, and worried things would not go as his visitor demanded. Every day for a week following Pazhman's arrival, he had gone to work as usual. When he returned, his fingernails stained with shoe polish and his clothes smelling of leather solvent, he would find Pazhman lying on the living room sofa with a list of demands (newspapers, cigarettes, fruit). In addition to these petty errands, it fell upon Hassan to change Pazhman's dressings, apply the antibiotic ointment, and prepare the evening meal. Finally, when the wounds were beginning to heal, Pazhman had instructed Hassan to assemble the others.

It was a beautiful day, and the park was filled with office workers enjoying the sunshine, eating lunch outside. Hassan sat next to Jusef. He took a falafel wrapped in foil and a Coke out of a paper bag and began having his own lunch.

"So what's up?" asked Jusef.

Hassan chewed his falafel and took a sip of Coke. "You are to tell the others we must meet. Tomorrow."

Arthur searched the drawer. It was stuffed with miscellaneous paper: a jumble of bank statements and receipts and an instruction

136

book for the credit card machine. He felt foolish for looking in the first place, then angry at himself that he should risk his job for such an impulsive act. But he had come this far. He lowered his head and looked in the back of the drawer. There was a plastic box. He reached in and pulled it out. It felt heavy in his hands. He glanced again at the front door, then opened it.

A .32 caliber revolver rested on a pile of documents. He picked up the revolver. He didn't know much about guns, but he knew it was a revolver, and he could see that it was loaded. Underneath the revolver there was a passport, which he opened. It was British passport, and the photo was of Hassan, but it was not Hassan's name. The name on the passport was Omar Murad. There was also a driver's license, from England, with the same alias. Underneath these documents there was a credit card, and a stack of twenty, fifty and 100 dollar bills held together by a rubber band. How very strange, he thought. Then he looked to the front of the door and was momentarily panicked when he saw a figure through the glass in the front door.

It was a customer. Arthur stepped toward the front door.

"We're closed, can't you see the sign?" he said in a loud voice. The customer looked irritated. He knocked again. But Arthur ignored him. He returned the documents to the box, and the box to the drawer. He slid the drawer shut and locked it before slipping the key back under the can of shoe polish. The customer was still knocking.

"Yo, we're closed dude. Come back later." Then he sat at the counter and finished his lunch.

137

# CHAPTER 29

The cell met in Hassan's apartment.

All the members were present, except Nabir, of course. It was strange without Nabir as he had been the one they looked to for leadership. Now there were just Hassan, Mahmud, Rodney, and Jusef. And Pazhman.

Hassan was in charge of communications. Mahmud was logistics and recruitment; Jusef was the courier; and Rodney was the muscle. Nabir had been in charge of finances.

Rodney was the only American at the gathering. Because of this he was of great value, and Nabir had cautioned the others that he must be protected, and kept at a distance as much as possible. Rodney had been recruited more than two years earlier, and had spent six months in Pakistan, training. Recruiting him had been a great coup. Born in the Bronx, he knew his way around the city, and he spoke and dressed like the native that he was.

Mahmud's job was to recruit Americans. He had specifically been asked to recruit two soldiers at the mosque, he had managed to recruit one. Hassan did not fault him for this. Recruiting people was very difficult and dangerous because there were police and counter-intelligence agents everywhere, especially in the mosque.

Rodney's recruitment had been a long, uncertain process. Mahmud began by flattering him, complimenting him on his strength of character and intelligence, and had predicted that with his new zeal, and his new name, doors would open for him, and bring him stature and prosperity. Then Mahmud had started to open those doors, showing Rodney a world that was largely unknown to him. Mahmud introduced him to several members of his religious circle, which, by design, included no members of the cell, and invited Rodney to join his discussion group, where talk gradually shifted to politics.

The recruitment was built on a foundation of hopelessness and injustice. Every day, Mahmud placed additional bricks on that foundation. It was his specialty. After each meeting, there was always time for discussion, and Rodney asked about Mahmud's experiences with the mujahadeen in Afghanistan, which Mahmud was happy and eager to talk about.

Jusef Wali, the courier, had been recruited in Pakistan, a much easier task. Jusef was a quiet man, young, like Rodney, and devout. He had a job as a copy machine repairman, which allowed him to act as a courier without raising any suspicions. He shared an apartment with Rodney in Fort Lee.

Hassan hated the meetings, and questioned their necessity. The purpose of the meetings was to check on each other, to make sure each was still committed to the cause, that the mission had not been forgotten. But what mission? There was no mission, other than to maintain their false identities, and to perform often inexplicable tasks conveyed to them from afar. And to wait. Hassan had begun to have doubts. He was tired of living in fear, with a knot in his stomach that got tighter and tighter every time the cell gathered.

Now suddenly, Pazhman had arrived. Nabir was dead. The moment had arrived, and he was filled with dread.

Hassan prepared tea in the kitchen. It was a relief to be away from the conversation in his living room. He realized he was avoiding the others.

"Hassan, the tea!" shouted Mahmud. "You are slower than an old woman!"

The others laughed.

"You have seen the papers?" asked Mahmud, his tone becoming serious.

Pazhman nodded.

"The police sketch is good," said Mahmud.

"The woman who chased me remembered me well."

"And there is the photo from the passport," said Mahmud. He sounded worried.

"That is bad, but they do not yet know my name, and that is good."

Mahmud continued. The others did not have the confidence to address Pazhman freely. "The newspapers say only that it was a failed robbery."

139

"The police have released a false story, perhaps to avoid raising an alarm," replied Pazhman. He understood the situation. The cat and mouse game had begun.

Hassan returned with the tea.

"At last! I am parched," said Mahmud, laughing.

Hassan did not like Mahmud. Mahmud pretended friendship, but beneath that lay cruelty and distrust. Hassan had doubts about the others as well: Rodney, who sat silently, his dark eyes shifting back and forth, withdrawn, brooding. Rodney did not look like a foreigner, or a Muslim. Both his parents were Puerto Rican. He wore baggy blue jeans and unlaced basketball sneakers and he wore his New York Giants jacket half falling off his shoulders, almost like a shawl.

"Yo, wazzap?" Mahmud would say. "My brother from 'da hood." It was a common theme, and Mahmud thought it was very funny. Rodney would respond by rolling his eyes and shaking his head. Mahmud would laugh. It was a mean spirited laugh, but Nabir had said it was important to continue to dress that way. Sometimes the joking went on too long, with Mahmud summoning up every ghetto expression he could think of.

And finally there was Jusef, who Hassan suspected was an idiot. Could he be trusted? Of course not. This was amateur hour. They were surely doomed. His life was in the hands of these young misfits. Why was fate so cruel?

If only Nabir was still alive, he thought. Hassan had felt a kinship with him. Nabir had provided advice regarding Hassan's business licenses, his taxes, and bookkeeping. And now Pazhman arrived and three days later Nabir was dead. A police officer was dead, too. When a policeman was shot the newspapers put it on the front page and the police pulled out all the stops until the killer was found. Hassan had seen the news on TV; the mayor had visited the hospital where the wounded policeman was taken. Hassan hoped he survived.

He kept his misgivings to himself and smiled, weakly, and offered his guests fruit juice and tea. He had prepared a plate of dates, also, imported from Morocco.

140

After they had been served Pazhman stood and turned up the volume on Hassan's stereo. It was a radio station playing belly dancing music from Lebanon, perhaps a little too loud. Such music was forbidden where he came from, but Hassan liked it. The neighbor, Mrs. Callahan, an elderly, morbidly obese woman who had worked at the post office, would complain. But he knew Pazhman played the music to cover the conversation, so they wouldn't be overheard. The music was also meant to explain the gathering... they were having a party. Hassan thought it would be better if they were watching a soccer match. In America men watched sporting events on TV together. But no matter, Pazhman had preferred the music. Hassan was sure he would have to speak to Mrs. Callahan.

"Tell us about Nabir," said Mahmud. "The police arrived very quickly, did they not?"

"Yes," Pazhman paused, considering this. "After the first policeman arrived, two others appeared, in civilian clothes."

"Detectives," Mahmud said.

"Coulda been FBI." Rodney spoke for the first time. The others in the room turned to him.

"Coulda been," he said, again.

Jusef's eyes opened wide, then narrowed in a squint of suspicion. "They were watching Nabir."

"There were two, a man and a woman," said Pazhman. "I should have killed the woman, and then she nearly killed me, but she hesitated."

"She is a devil," said Mahmud.

A simple man, thought Hassan, who was prone to such idiotic ways of talking.

Mahmud continued. "I never fully trusted Nabir. He became more interested in his bakery than in serving the cause."

"Perhaps, but he is a martyr now," said Hassan, pouring more mint tea from the metal pot into his glass. "He is a martyr, and we have no funds, and without funds what can we do? We must pay Jemel, and we must pay our other friend."

Pazhman looked sharply at him. "We will obtain the funds we require."

141

"Nabir was to provide us with the money we need," said Hassan.

"Yes," replied Pazhman.

"But without money what can we do?" asked Hassan.

He knew he sounded anxious, he was revealing his doubts, and knew Pazhman would think less of him for it. Suddenly he wished Pazhman would abandon whatever it was he had come to do and return to Pakistan, or Lebanon, or Egypt, or wherever it was he came from.

"The plan must continue," said Pazhman.

"But what is the plan?" asked Mahmud.

"You will be told when the time comes. Have you forgotten your training, do you not understand this?"

Mahmud lowered his eyes. "I do understand."

"And what else did the Professor teach us? That in our struggles there will be unexpected obstacles, but we will overcome them."

"But only Nabir had access to his bank accounts," said Mahmud.

"You are right, as always, Mahmud. You see straight to the most important issue. The necessary funds are essential to our mission, without adequate resources we can do nothing."

"Nothing," agreed Mahmud.

"So we will steal it."

"This is not an easy thing, it will require a special plan," said Mahmud.

"Yes, and your help will be required," said Pazhman.

"Of course," said Mahmud.

"In my outings this week I have noticed that armored cars collect the cash of some businesses."

Hassan became very still. He didn't like where the conversation was going. Pazhman continued.

"The armored cars sometimes have three men, but sometimes only two. Sometimes the guards appear alert and well trained, other times they go about their work in a complacent manner."

"This is true," said Mahmud, always eager to agree.

Pazhman nodded. "We will follow one of the cars, and study its route, and we will decide which is the best time and place to attack."

142

Hassan felt his heart sink. Now his lot was not even to die a martyr's death, but to be killed as a common criminal, a bank robber.

Pazhman continued. "The important thing is that we get the money and deliver it as agreed and on time."

"And when the preparations are in place, what then, what is the target?" asked Hassan.

"It is better that you do not know. You know enough already. If you are captured they could force you to reveal our plans."

Hassan nodded.

Pazhman looked directly at Mahmud.

"You have obtained the vehicle?"

Mahmud closed his eyes and nodded. "All is taken care of."

"And the house?"

"It is exactly as you require. Rodney and I were there just last week."

"Excellent.

# CHAPTER 30

*If I unroll one more carpet I will go out of my mind*, thought Jemel Farzi. A customer, the designer Rafael de Montoya, had arrived with his clients, a young financier and his wife. They had recently purchased a Beaux Arts townhouse on East 92nd Street. The wife had Jemel jumping through hoops. He unrolled one carpet, then she wanted to see another, then another, then back to the first one again. The carpets were so large they had to be rolled and unrolled one on top of another.

The husband was bored, and made business calls on his cell phone until eventually he realized if he didn't take an interest his wife would never make a decision and he would be there all day. Time was money.

"I like this one," he said, pointing to it with his foot. His foot! Jemel ignored the crass behavior. He was ignorant, what could be expected?

The decorator was growing impatient. He finally ended the deliberations by insisting they purchase the most expensive carpet, a Tabriz. (Only $28,000, a steal). He absolutely insisted, and the wife agreed, given that it was the most expensive, and therefore the best, so Jemel had made a killing, since he himself had paid less than six for it.

As soon as he had the check in his pocket he ushered the clients out of the shop and closed and locked the door. It was only three o'clock but he had important business to attend to.

Jemel Farzi was a smuggler. It was the family trade, and a lucrative one at that. His father had been a smuggler, and his grandfather, too. While Jemel's grandfather wore a jalaba and carried his goods (guns mostly, but also gold, spices, carpets) on the backs of camels, Jemel wore the finest English suits and relied on container ships and jumbo jets.

Like his grandfather, Jemel's most important tools were bribery and guile, and, of course, a complete lack of scruples when it came to clients. The dealer knew the world's shipping routes and customs procedures better than any freight expediter. More importantly, he knew the ports, from Asia to Africa to the US, which offered the easiest access. He knew who could be bribed, and how to keep himself well distanced should anything go wrong.

Success required that he trust no one, so there were some jobs he had to do by himself. Jemel dimmed the lights and sat at his desk in the rear of the store to wait. J. Farzi Gallery was open by appointment only, and there were no more appointments in the book. He wanted his gallery to be empty when his visitors arrived.

Across the street, Pazhman and Mahmud watched as the decorator and his clients left. From where they stood in a doorway on the other side of Lexington Avenue, they could see Jemel lock the door from the inside. They saw the lights dim, and walked across the street and knocked on the door.

Mahmud was dressed as a businessman, and might have been just another carpet dealer, with a client in tow. Pazhman, too, had dressed the part: the wealthy customer. He wore a tan double-breasted suit and sunglasses. Jemel recognized Mahmud and greeted him as if he were seeing an old friend.

Pazhman was aware that it was a dangerous moment. Jemel could have been turned by the American authorities, and he could have been walking into a trap. He had thought of sending Mahmud alone, but decided against it. If it was a trap, better to find out now. He carried Hassan's Beretta 9mm in the back of his belt, just in case.

Jemel ushered the men into the back of the gallery where they sat at his antique French Louis XVI desk.

"May I offer you some water, a soft drink, perhaps?"

"No, thank you," said Pazhman.

"I trust all is well." He had read of the shooting, and could put two and two together.

"All is well, I assure you. The shipment has arrived safely?"

Jemel nodded. "I don't mind telling you, this was a challenge."

Jemel took pride in his work, and enjoyed the rare opportunities to discuss it. It was good for business if his clients understood the difficulties. It enhanced his reputation, and ensured more work, and larger payments.

"Tell me," said Pazhman.

"We moved the goods overland to Islamabad, and from there to Singapore, where we consolidated it with a shipment of carpets from a wholesaler I know. The shipment cleared customs in Port Newark with no problems." He waved his hand like a magician.

"And how may we take possession?"

"As long as you have the key to the lock you will gain access to the shipment. It is in a storage facility in Fort Lee. Remove the crates and close the locker when you leave. Throw away the key. The locker is rented under a false name, Universal Printing Supply of Paramus, New Jersey, and paid for one month. You will not need to speak to anyone, provided you arrive during normal business hours, between 8 and 5. I would suggest you arrive after 9 o'clock, and before 3 p.m., to be on the safe side. I will give you a map. All that remains is the payment."

Pazhman made a lopsided smile.

A look of concern crossed Jemel's face. "You have the cash?"

"You will be paid, that is not a concern, but our plans have changed," said Mahmud quickly. He smiled nervously, his eyes shifting to Pazhman.

"How so?" asked Jemel.

"It would seem our friend who handled our money transfers has been killed."

"Nabir. I have heard."

Mahmud nodded.

"But this should not concern you," said Mahmud.

Jemel bit his lower lip and studied his visitor's face. Yes, it did concern him, very much so. Nabir had always been his contact for all payments. Nabir had arranged the transaction, and given him the deposit.

"Then how am I to be paid?" he asked.

Jemel felt his stomach tighten. Jemel had taken a great risk dealing with these men. Now they had arrived with excuses. He hated the excuses his clients brought him. Excuses didn't grease the palms of container ship captains and port officials.

He continued. "This is no small matter, or I wouldn't mention it. But the sum we agreed upon is $50,000. Without full payment you may not have the shipment, you understand," said Jemel.

146

"You will be paid, but you will have to wait, that is all," said Pazhman.

"And why must I wait when I have done all that has been agreed upon?"

"We ask only that you wait a short time, until more money can be transferred. Meanwhile we must have our shipment. It is of the utmost importance," said Mahmud.

"I have no interest in what is important and what is not important. I expect that it is important that I be paid for my end of the bargain."

Mahmud swallowed. If he was unable to convince Jemel, he might lose face in the presence of Pazhman. This was turning out very badly. Very badly indeed.

"You will be paid, in time," said Mahmud, trying to minimize the awkwardness. "But such an approach would not serve our cause."

"Any other approach does not serve mine."

"Perhaps we could make an arrangement? After all, you have already received a substantial deposit to cover your expenses. You know we have the necessary resources," said Mahmud, brightening.

"I know no such thing. I know only that ships and planes and trucks and bribes cost money. I am a businessman who has little interest in politics."

Pazhman cleared his throat. "But you see, we require this package as soon as possible."

Jemel held up his hand, cutting him off. "I am but a humble merchant with a shipping agency on the side, to help make ends meet."

Yes, a merchant who makes his living smuggling weapons, and drugs, and God only knew what else, thought Pazhman. His gaze met Jemel's. Jemel stopped smiling. Suddenly, Jemel had second thoughts.

Pazhman studied Jemel. He was an elegant dresser, he wore expensive Italian loafers and an open-necked English cotton shirt, probably Savile Row. Beneath the polished exterior, Pazhman knew, was a cold-hearted ruthless merchant who would drive a hard bargain. Jemel was not interested in the slightest in their cause, only in profiting from it, which meant today there would be a problem. Jemel smiled uneasily and wondered. *What evil do you have planned?*

"Will you grant us a week to deliver the funds?"    asked Pazhman.

Jemel sighed. "A week, yes."

"And the shipment is secure?" asked Pazhman.

"Of course."

"And we will have it when the balance is paid?"

"Payment in full."

Pazhman felt his face flush. *I could kill you now, he thought, and perhaps I should.* He imagined how he might do this, he certainly knew how, and Jemel certainly deserved to die. But Jemel had what they needed.

# CHAPTER 31

At 2 o'clock Tuesday afternoon, NYPD Detective Ernesto Rivera walked into the lobby of The Stanford Arms Hotel. Over the past 36 hours, police had been systematically checking every hotel in the city. The manager was hunched over his desk behind the inch-thick Plexi-glass window, reading the Daily News. He ignored the detective.

Rivera rapped on the Plexi-glass.

The manager looked up from the paper. "Can I help you?"

Rivera flipped open his badge. "I'd like to ask a few questions."

"Give me a break. I run a hotel, that's all it is, and I pay my taxes. A guy wants to bring a girl in here on his lunch hour that ain't against the law, least I ain't done nothing wrong."

"Relax, will ya?  You're not in any trouble. Just take a look at this."

The detective held up the black & white print of Arun Patel's passport photo. The manager frowned and shook his head.

"Yeah, I remember him," said the manager.

"What?"

"Checked in over a week ago."

"You sure?" asked Rivera.

"I'm pretty good with faces."

"He here now?"

"He checked out."

"Got a registration slip?"

"Probably around here somewhere."

The manager sighed, folded his paper, and stood up. He rummaged through some papers behind the desk and eventually produced a small slip of paper that Pazhman had signed when he checked in.

The detective read the slip.  He'd checked in as Arun Patel, and had paid cash.  He had checked out the next day.  The number 408 was written in ballpoint pen on the corner of the slip.

"This his room number?"

"What's this all about? What'd this guy do?"

"Is anyone in the room now?

The manager shook his head.

Twenty minutes later the lobby of the hotel was crawling with police and CSIs. Forty minutes later Kim, Mahan, and Winters arrived. The manager was a nervous wreck.

"I run a discrete establishment, you're gonna kill my business," he said to anyone who came close enough to hear.

Kim was looking at the registration form. "Relax, we'll only be here a few hours."

"A few hours?" He practically cried.

"How did this Mr. Patel pay for the room?" asked Kim.

"I told you already, cash. Lotsa people don't like to use credit cards."

"And the cash is where?"

"In the bank. We make a deposit every morning, first thing."

"How many people stayed in the room since he checked out?"

"I don't know, three or four."

"What about the keys?"

"What about them? I have two keys for each room, plus a master I keep myself." Kim noted they were the old-fashioned standard keys, as opposed to magnetic cards. Each key had a green, diamond shaped plastic key chain with the room number on it. The two keys for Room 408 had already been bagged as evidence.

"I'm gonna need those back, you know," said the manager.

"We'll give them back to you," Kim assured him. "So did you notice anything strange about this guy?"

"What strange? He checked in, he checked out. I don't think he spoke two words to me. He wasn't a regular client, no one I'd seen before."

"How was he dressed?"

"Coat and tie, I think. Jesus, when are you gonna stop asking questions and give me my hotel back?"

Mahan approached. He was talking to someone on his cell phone, and snapped it shut. "You done here?" he asked.

"I think so, why?" replied Kim.

"They're ready for us upstairs."

They rode the elevator to the fourth floor where two uniformed police stood guard outside the tiny room. Inside, technicians were searching for evidence.

"Booties," said one of the policemen. He handed the two agents paper shoe covers, which they put on before entering the room.

One of the technicians was on his hands and knees on the bathroom floor. He looked up as the agents entered.

"What do we got?" asked Mahan.

The technician shook his head. "We might have some prints, and this." He held up a pair of tweezers.

"What is it?" asked Kim.

"Housekeeping isn't so good here. This is hair, I had to guess, this dude shaved off his beard, and check this out."

He pointed to the tile behind the sink. Kim bent over and looked closely.

"That look like blood to you?" she asked.

Mahan examined it.

"Yes it does."

"Funny," said the crime tech, "I thought so too."

They were finished at the crime scene by early evening. Mahan looked at his watch.

"No one would accuse us of slacking off if we didn't get back to the office," he said as they left the hotel.

"Rush hour traffic, what would be the point," said Kim.

"How about dinner?" asked Mahan.

"Huh?"

"Would you like to eat dinner with me?"

"Tonight?"

"My treat. I don't know, I thought it would be nice."

Kim "Normally I'd say 'sure, I'd love to,' it's just that I made other plans."

Mahan smiled. "Oh, well, another time," said Mahan.

The other plans were with Jack. She'd exchanged text messages with him, and agreed to meet at an art opening on 52nd Street, then go on to dinner. Kim saw a taxi and hailed it. She left Mahan standing on the sidewalk.

It was an artsy crowd, and very casual. She took a turn around the gallery, looking at abstract landscapes, then found Jack speaking to a clutch of artists and writers. As soon as he saw her he broke free.

"I made a reservation at a French restaurant I like, how does that sound?" he asked.

"It sounds great, but I've been on my feet all day since 6 o'clock."

"You're really on a big case?"

She nodded.

"You can't talk about it?"

She shook her head.

"Would you mind if we went to my place and ordered pizza? Maybe watched a movie. I know that sounds lame."

"No, it sounds perfect."

Twenty minutes later they were back at her apartment.

She kicked off her shoes and sat on the couch, handing Jack a refrigerator magnet that had the number of the pizzeria. "You call it in."

"Pepperoni and onion?"

"Mmm."

"Greek salad?"

She nodded.

He pulled out his cell phone and called in the order. She curled up beside him, touching his ear as he tried to order, and as he completed the order, she kissed him on the mouth.

"You're not spending the night, you know," she said.

"No, that would be bad."

"That would be bad."

"And we don't want to be bad."

She couldn't pull away. "And it would be wrong."

"So wrong. So very wrong."

"And bad," she corrected him, her tongue exploring his lips.

"Very bad."

He kissed her on her neck. "Wouldn't want to do this."

She put her hand on his leg. "Or this."

"No, definitely not that."

152

Their kisses took on an urgency, and suddenly Kim was groping, pulling at his shirt. She embraced him, rocked her head back and laughed, intoxicated by what was to come.

# CHAPTER 32

*Newark, New Jersey*

The four men sat in a stolen Ford Explorer parked on a quiet commercial street flanked by large warehouses. The few windows on the street were either bricked up or covered by metal grates, and the walls were covered in graffiti. Newark.

They watched the entrance to a building halfway down the block on the other side of the street. A sign above the door read "Saltieri Bros. Construction and Demolition." But the Saltieri Brothers hadn't constructed anything in years. Their specialty was knocking buildings down: big buildings, tall buildings, buildings that often stood just yards from other buildings where people lived. If all went well, the idea was that the other buildings wouldn't be damaged.

For this expertise, the Saltieri Brothers commanded a fee in the millions of dollars. The fee was well-earned. Both Joe and Victor Saltieri had advanced degrees in structural engineering and combustibles, and months went into the planning and preparation for their large contracts. They had demolished more than 300 buildings around the world, and had never suffered a major injury or fatality. The company employed 40 full-time employees, most of whom were, at any given time, on a job site somewhere.

The door to Saltieri Brothers opened and a woman in sandals and a tight dress stepped out onto the sidewalk. She waited on the sidewalk while a man in a tan janitor's shirt and trousers behind her locked the door. The man helped her into her car, a silver Mustang parked in front, and she drove off. The janitor walked away.

"That's Gloria, the receptionist. She's always the last to leave, and then this Frank dude locks up," said Rodney.

"Are you sure?" asked Mahmud.

"What do you mean?" asked Rodney.

"Are you sure they have locked for the night?"

"Pretty sure."

"So you're not certain. There could still be someone," said

154

Mahmud.

Rodney sighed. "Could be, anything could be. Everyone always punches out at 5 o'clock, unless they're working on a deadline. I'm just telling you what I know, what do you want?"

"Are you certain your keys will work?" asked Mahmud. It wasn't the first time he had asked.

"How can I be sure of anything? Yeah, they could've changed the locks. We'll find out soon enough, right?"

"If the keys do not work, then what?" asked Mahmud.

"Then I guess we go home, I mean, what the fuck?"

Mahmud looked at Hassan. "I'm just wanting to make sure," he said.

"Look, there's no guarantees, but there's no way they can tell I stole copies of the keys, and they had no reason to change the locks. Gloria's always the last to leave, and then Frank locks up, and no one stays after 5 o'clock," said Rodney.

Pazhman shook his head. Where he came from women wouldn't work in offices with strange men. He would never understand the ways of the West. *If I had a wife, and if she dressed like Gloria, I would beat her*, he thought.

"And the camera?" asked Mahmud.

"What about it?"

"You are certain it's not working?"

"Like I said, it's just for show. Unless they fixed it, but I doubt that."

They had discussed the plan many times, more often and in greater detail than was necessary, thought Rodney, who knew a thing or two about breaking into buildings. "Are we going to do this or what?" he asked.

"We will wait, to see if anyone else is there," said Mahmud.

Rodney sighed again, and shook his head. "So, if there's anyone in there when we go in you just do your Kung Fu shit on them."

Hassan laughed and immediately regretted it. Mahmud did not have a sense of humor. Not a good one, anyway, thought Hassan. He laughed at cruelty, at the stupidity of the infidel, and when the infidel suffered, or was destroyed. In the martial arts class they took together Hassan had noticed a sadistic side to Mahmud. He struck with more force than the others, even though it was practice. He didn't play by the rules, either, delivering low blows, and hitting after the instructor had told him to stop.

No one in the class liked Mahmud.

Pazhman turned to the others. "If anyone is inside it will change the plan. Don't hesitate to kill."

Mahmud nodded.

Rodney took a deep breath and wiggled in the driver's seat. He decided not to talk to Mahmud anymore. Mahmud never engaged in pleasant conversation. But he didn't mind talking to Hassan. Hassan liked to talk about Islam, and the Koran, and he spoke for a long time about it. He sometimes spoke of his home in Aden, and a place he liked where the desert met the sea. He also spoke of how he had come close to being caught when he smuggled himself into Saudi Arabia, and how he had been imprisoned in Rijad, and how he had survived there.

Mahmud sat tense, watching for any movement. When he thought he saw something he tensed up, moving his face closer to the windshield, then he relaxed when he realized it was simply a pedestrian walking on the sidewalk. Hassan shook his head. Mahmud wanted to be a commander, but he was just a soldier. He had only the most basic training they had all received in Pakistan, and thought too highly of himself.

Ten minutes passed, there were no signs of activity.

"Okay, we go," said Pazhman.

The men pulled on leather gloves and fleece ski masks. Hassan removed a rucksack from the back seat and got out of the car. Rodney followed. They walked fast toward a fenced courtyard between the office and the warehouse. Rodney quickly unlocked the padlock with a copy of one of the keys he had stolen when he first took a job at Saltieri Brothers. That had been his greatest contribution so far.

Hassan put the padlock back on the chain but did not lock it. They passed through the yard to the warehouse entrance. It was a heavy steel door, and again, Rodney inserted a key into the lock and, to his relief, the lock opened. Too easy. He took a deep breath and felt his heart racing.

Rodney had explained that the explosives they sought were stored in a locked room within the warehouse. The warehouse was filled with shadows, the late afternoon light coming in through the few barred windows on one wall. Hassan led the way through the workroom, where the demolition charges were prepared, to the locked room in the back. It was a similar steel door, just as he had described it. Rodney selected a second key from his key chain and looked at Hassan. He kissed the key and inserted it into the lock. He turned the key, then pressed his shoulder against the door. It swung open.

Everything was still there, just as Rodney remembered it. Carefully stacked packages of TNT, C-4, and spools and spools of detonation cord. There were also boxes of detonators. The men knew what they needed and quickly loaded their bags.

They had discussed whether they should detonate the remaining explosives, so it would look like an accident, and so no one would know that anything had been stolen, but decided against this, fearing it would draw too much attention.

They went out as they had entered, careful to lock the gate behind them. Hassan's shirt was wet with perspiration, and he was breathing deeply as he placed the heavy duffel bag in the back of the Explorer and climbed in. Rodney started the engine and they slowly pulled away.

"See, nothing to it," said Rodney, "you just gotta be cool."

Mahmud smiled. Pazhman was very pleased.

157

# CHAPTER 33

*Manhattan*

A bell sounded. Kim lay sprawled on the bed, naked, the sheets in a twist by her feet. Beside her, asleep on his stomach, was Jack. He felt so good there, so right. Kim opened her eyes, she'd been sound asleep for just four hours. She slid her foot under his leg and yawned. She looked at Jack, his eyes closed, breathing gently, mouth open, then she heard the bell again. She raised herself up on her elbows and shook her head.

What was that? She thought as her head dropped back onto the pillow and she closed her eyes.

The bell was followed several minutes later by an urgent knocking at the door. Kim slid off the mattress, found a robe and put it on, then fumbled with the combination of dead bolt and lock, locking and unlocking the door several times before it would open. Mahan stood in the hallway. Jimmy, the elevator man, was behind him, watching from the open elevator.

"Didn't you hear the intercom?"

She shook her head. "I was asleep."

"I tried your cell phone too."

"I must have set it to vibrate," she said.

Mahan took in what he could of the room behind her, but Kim blocked his view with the door.

"This is your apartment?" he asked.

"It belongs to my father."

"You gonna invite me in?"

"I can't right now. What's up?" said Kim.

"We got a DNA match from the hotel and ID'd our guy."

"Great!"

"That's not all. We're on our way to New Jersey, thought you might like to join us."

"What's in Jersey?"

"Well, there used to be about 250 pounds of C-4."

158

"Give me five minutes."

Mahan nodded. "I'll wait in the lobby." He made one last effort to peek past the door, but Kim pressed it closed.

She dressed in a hurry, with just time to brush her teeth, and take a two-minute shower. Then she allowed herself a minute to lean over and kiss Jack. She smiled when he woke up.

"I have to go to work," she said.

He yawned. "When are you coming back?"

"Don't wait."

"I'll be at the newspaper."

"Call me."

Mahan was waiting in the lobby, sitting in the same Elizabethan chair and looking up at a tapestry depicting a medieval hunting scene. A deer was jumping over a hedge and several horsemen were following it. They got into the waiting car. Winters was in the backseat.

"Nice place," Winters said. "Sublet?"

"It's my dad's, he uses it as a pied-a-terre," replied Kim.

"Huh?"

"When he has to stay late in the city."

"Oh."

"He said I could stay there while I'm posted to New York," explained Kim.

"Rent free? Nice."

"Yes, it is. So what happened?" asked Kim.

"Someone ripped off 250 pounds of high explosive last night in Jersey, C-4. They discovered it early this morning," replied Winters.

It wasn't her expertise, but Kim remembered enough of what she'd learned about explosives at Quantico to know what that meant.

Anyone could make a bomb. Car bombs or truck bombs required just a few hundred pounds of ammonium nitrite, available easily enough at any farm supply store; C-4 was something else. It was made of RDX, military grade explosive, and conjured up any numbers of scenarios involving small, easy to conceal bombs, or suicide vests.

"Where?" she asked.

"Construction demolition company in Newark."

"Our guy?" she whispered.

Mahan shrugged.

"So tell me about him," said Kim.

"He's an Afghan."

Winters reached from the back seat and handed Kim a photo. It looked like an enlarged copy of a yearbook photo, about 20 years old.

"Recognize him?" he asked.

"I can't be sure."

He handed her a second photo, watching her face for a reaction. The photo was of a man, taken from a distance with a telephoto lens: a man in suit walking across a crowded city street.

"That was taken in Sana'a, Yemen, about three years ago. Now you recognize him?"

"Sorry."

"Well, it's him. They think his name is Pazhman Khan."

Kim looked at the photo.

"It looks like a yearbook photo."

"State University at New Paltz," said Winters.

"He went to college in the US?"

"Under an assumed name. Not much of a record, except he studied electrical engineering, even had a government grant to pay part of the tuition."

"Jesus."

"Yeah, this prick really did a number on us," said Winters.

"Here's another one. The Brits captured this surveillance photo two years ago in Yemen. It's not a great photo, but computer says it's a match," said Mahan.

Kim studied the photo. It showed a man at a bank counter talking to a teller.

"The Brits were keeping tabs on him, at least trying to. They said he likes to make bombs."

"They must have more if they think that."

"Very little. It's like the guy never used a cell phone. He's old school, well-trained, good tradecraft. The Brits had a nickname for him. They called him 'The Ghost.'"

160

Half an hour later they arrived at Saltieri Brothers. Gambler was waiting in the office, talking to a heavy-set man in a blue suit who Kim didn't recognize. Gambler introduced him as Sean Ryan, New Jersey State Police.

"Apparently I know a thing or two about explosives, anyway, that's what they pay me for," said Ryan as he shook hands with new arrivals.

"So what do we have here?" asked Winters.

Ryan answered. "These guys handle projects all over the Eastern seaboard, big outfit, first class all the way. The explosives were all locked up, according to regulations, so we think this was an inside job. Someone had to know how to get into the storage vault. Whoever got in had keys and knew exactly where the explosives were secured. They knew the office schedule and the guard's routine. We're still double-checking inventory, but it looks like 250 pounds of C-4, plus detonators, fuses, the works. Not what we want to have unaccounted for."

"What could they do with it?" asked Gambler.

Ryan nodded. "Let your imagination run wild. Could be we're talking car bomb, which means any high profile target in the city... the UN, Wall Street, Midtown, Times Square, places where there's surface congestion. Then you've got bridges and tunnels, or they could pack it in bags and attack buses, trains and the subway."

"Jesus," said Gambler.

"Jesus is right," replied Ryan. "And from the look of it, they have everything they need to get started right away."

Gambler looked at the team. "We have to assume this ghost character, Khan, is part of this. It's too close to be a coincidence, He may have been sent to trigger multiple attacks when the G-20 is here. Coordinate with NYPD and keep checking your leads. If this was an inside job, we need a list of all current employees, plus anyone who's worked here in the past twelve months, and that includes repairmen, contractors, consultants, deliverymen, you name it. I want a lead. Today. Questions or comments?"

Mahan nodded.

"What about the press?" Kim asked.

Gambler shook his head. "Not yet. Let's hold our cards close to the chest for the time being. We don't want to spook him now."

Vince Saltieri had greying hair trimmed short and muscular arms. Kim guessed he was on the other side of 60. He wore cargo pants and a t-shirt with the name of the company printed on it. He looked worried, and Kim figured it was because he knew as well as anyone what the stolen high explosives could do.

"You always have that much explosives on hand?" asked Mahan.

"Only when we're staging for a job," replied Saltieri as he sat at his desk. "We're getting set to knock down a hotel in Atlantic City. We were supposed to take it down next week. I've had crews there for a month doing the prep work."

"A hotel?" asked Kim, exchanging a glance with Mahan.

"Fourteen stories, and casino," he replied. He saw the look on her face and added. "Two-hundred-fifty pounds of C-4 plus TNT can do the job, if you know what you're doing. But you've got to set the charges just right to bring down a building that size."

"How many people know how to do that?"

"Not many. Requires a specially trained engineer, but only if you're gonna do it right. You don't care what kind of damage you cause, any asshole can do it."

"How many of your employees have keys?" asked Mahan.

"About six of us. Me, my brother, and about three other guys, managers, plus a couple guys on the cleaning crew."

"The cleaning crew comes and goes at night?"

Saltieri nodded, "But all the combustibles are locked up separately."

"Can we see?"

They followed him through the office and into the warehouse to the storage room. The door was more formidable than the front door. It would have taken an explosive charge to open.

Unless you had the key.

"No one has a key except me, my brother, and Herb Meyers."

"Who's Herb Meyers?"

"Our chief engineer. He's away on a job in Baltimore."

"And he has his key with him?"

"I talked to him two hours ago. He checked, he said he has it with him on his keychain."

"So how did someone get in here?" asked Mahan.

Saltieri shook his head. "I don't know. Nobody has access, unless..." He paused, thinking things through.

"Unless what?" asked Kim.

"Unless they made a copy of the master key."

"There's a master key?" asked Mahan.

"Well, yeah."

"Where?"

"In a key locker in my office."

"Show us," said Mahan.

The Achilles heel of Saltieri Brothers Demolition was a lightweight steel key organizer mounted on the wall under the owner's desk. It contained a copy of every key to every lock possessed by the firm, and was itself secured by a lock that could have been picked by a paperclip.

"When was the last time the locks were changed?" asked Kim, looking at the keys hanging in the box.

"I don't know, maybe three years ago?"

"Then we need all your personnel records and vendor records for anyone who had access to the facility - maintenance men, repairmen, you name it, going back three years."

Kim and Mahan sat at the conference table in Saltieri's office going through the personnel files. They typed each name into a laptop so it could be quickly matched against bureau databases and watch lists. The personnel files were handwritten forms, so the process was slow. Sometimes social security numbers were missing, and names were misspelled.

"No Middle Eastern names, Pakistanis, nothing that stands out," Kim said after they had finished with the last of the personnel files.

"So?"

"So we're dealing with someone who's homegrown. If this is a sleeper cell, they've been recruiting."

# CHAPTER 34

Gambler was furious. He held a newspaper in his hand and read aloud. "Manhunt! Authorities suspect terrorist cell operating in New York!"

It was early, and Kim hadn't had her coffee yet. She listened quietly as he sputtered through selected portions of the story. The article cited the shooting in Brooklyn and the manhunt and suggested there was a sleeper cell. Evasive comments from an NYPD spokesman seemed to confirm the story.

"Dammit, how'd this get out?" said Gambler.

"Sir, there are thousands of police in this city who know something's going on. The press was bound to catch wind of it eventually," said Mahan.

"Bullshit!" said Gambler. He threw the paper on his desk. It was the morning's Chronicle.

Kim felt a chill. Jack worked at the Chronicle. She remembered she had left papers out in her bedroom, while she slept. Was it possible? Could he have overheard a conversation with Mahan.

Gambler continued. "We'll find the leak as soon as I personally put the heat on the editors, and the reporter. Meanwhile, the cat's out of the bag. Pazhman knows we're connecting the dots. We may as well issue the composite sketches to all media. Jesus Christ, get ready, this city is going to go berserk."

As soon as the meeting was over, Kim dialed Jack. The call went to voice mail so she texted him. He replied, and suggested they meet for a drink that evening.

* * *

Woodboro was three hours north of the city, in Ulster County, surrounded by hundreds of thousands of acres of state forest. Discovered by New Yorkers in the early 1980s, it was just do-able for a weekend getaway, and cheaper than anything in Connecticut or Long Island. That meant that in addition to the generally prosperous farms, there were weekend houses, and with those came small businesses in the village of Woodboro that catered to them. Jane's Gourmet Grocery, The Woodboro Organic Cheese Co., and more than a dozen shops that sold antiques, art and home goods.

There were plenty of bars and restaurants, too, but the locals went to Clyde's. Lance Dennehy went to Clyde's. They knew him there, and would call a taxi, or a friend, if he needed one.

Clyde was doing inventory behind the bar, getting ready to phone in an order with his distributor when Jill arrived. It was 10 a.m., the bar was closed to customers, but the door was open to allow for deliveries. He could tell from the look on her face it was serious, and he knew what it was about.

"Got a minute?" she asked, standing in the door.

"Of course, come on in." He picked up a towel and started wiping the bar. "You want a cup of coffee?"

"Sure. Thanks."

He poured two cups and placed one in front of her as she pulled out a stool. Then he put out a glass bowl of sugar packets and a small pitcher of milk.

"This about Lance?" asked Clyde.

She nodded. "I think he has PTSD. Actually I don't think it, I know it. I've looked it up on the Internet. He's got all the symptoms, you can tick 'em off. He's depressed, anxious, seems disconnected from his work, his friends... me."

"Very normal for a returning vet," said Clyde.

"Is it normal to wake up in a sweat, nightmares, your muscles all tense?" She looked at Clyde. Jill had a pretty face, even when she had a worried look on it. "Before he left, we talked about getting married, but he doesn't want to talk about that anymore."

Clyde sighed. Why is it always me, he wondered? He'd wrestled his own demons, and conquered them, licked booze, drugs and thoughts of suicide, and now everyone turned to him for help.

"Has he talked to anyone about it?" asked Clyde.

"He says he won't talk to any more Army shrinks. I know he was diagnosed, I saw his disability papers, but he won't do anything about it. I'm worried it's worse that they think," Jill replied.

Clyde rubbed his forehead. He'd seen too many vets whose lives fell apart after they got home. Clyde's own war had ended with the battle at Kham Duc, when he was 18.

Jill continued. "He's trying to hide it, but it's like his mind's in shock. He seems so disconnected, sometimes I can't even talk to him. It's like he's not there. Last weekend he just lay on the couch all day, and didn't say a word."

"What about his job?"

"Says all he does is direct traffic around the work crews. Just standing there all day. I asked him why they have him doing that and he said 'I guess that's all I'm good for.'"

"He said that?"

She nodded.

"I don't know what to do. I don't want to leave him, but I can't stand by and let him do this to himself." She looked at Clyde. There was a pleading expression in her eyes. "Can you help him? You went through a lot, right?"

Yes, he had. Somehow Clyde had survived his war. Gradually, the nightmares had subsided, but the memories still haunted him.

"I guess I could talk to him," said Clyde.

"Would you?" Jill brightened with relief.

He smiled. He had always looked after his men. He figured he always would.

"Sure."

* * *

At the end of the day, Kim hurried to get to the restaurant Jack had suggested. Café Roma was a casual Italian place on East 62nd Street. She wore a T-shirt and a short summer skirt, with sandals. He hadn't arrived yet, so she took a seat at the bar to wait. She ordered a glass of Prosecco. Fifteen minutes passed. The bar at the restaurant was filling up, a lively scene. A man and a woman entered, laughing, having a good time, and she gave up the stool she was saving for Jack. She checked her iPhone. No messages, so she sent one herself.

"I'm here where r u?"

166

There was no reply. Had she misunderstood? Did she have the date, or the time and place wrong? Ten minutes later she sent another. "Didn't we have a date??"

What was going on, she wondered. Had he abandoned her, gotten hit by a car? Or was she getting ahead of herself? But they always did leave her, right? Her analytical mind went to work. So why was that? She caught a glimpse of herself in the mirror. Was she so different from the other women at the bar? She had gone through half a dozen relationships over the past three years. She had calculated and measured them in her mind dozens of times. How long they had lasted, how many dates, how many times they had had sex. But they had all ended. And what was the common denominator?

Me.

Is it the cigarettes she smoked in bed after sex? She wondered. Is my nose funny looking?

"Did you want another Prosecco?"

She turned. It was the bartender.

"Uh, I don't know."

"Are you meeting someone?"

She shook her head. "No, and yes, I will have another."

# CHAPTER 35

All week, Hassan went to work at the shoe repair, as usual. Every morning, Pazhman left the house with him, then disappeared. Pazhman always wore dark glasses and a straw hat, which looked ridiculous but he said they served a purpose. The city has cameras that no one knew about, of that he was certain, though it wasn't as bad as London. He suspected the cameras were connected to the powerful computers that could measure a man's face and know who he was. Hassan did not know where Pazhman went or what he did, but when Hassan returned after a day at the shoe repair, Pazhman was always waiting in the apartment.

One day Hassan arrived home to find the members of the cell looking at a map spread out on the kitchen table. Hassan was tired, and upset to have the others in his kitchen without him having invited them. It was as if it was no longer his apartment, but Pazhman's, and he was merely a guest, and an unimportant one at that.

"We have been waiting," said Pazhman.

"I have been at work, I have a business to run," replied Hassan, realizing at once the absurdities of his words.

"That is good, but we will not have need for the business any longer," said Pazhman.

So the moment had come, thought Hassan. Now he would learn what Pazhman had been doing on his daily outings, and he would understand, fully, what was to become of him.

They listened as Pazhman explained his plan.

"An armored car delivers cash to check-cashing businesses in Corona, Queens, and then collects cash from two small banks and a mall in Long Island City where there is a discount liquor store. The liquor store is called Gotham Super Liquor," he said.

Hassan knew the liquor store. He had shopped there.

There were two floors of liquor, bottle after bottle, every type of wine and spirit that you could imagine.

"The armored car has the most cash after the liquor store,

168

therefore, we will attack it here," said Pazhman, pointing to a spot on the map. Mahmud and Rodney leaned forward to study the map.

"We will attack an armored car?" asked Hassan.

"I have visited this place. It is quiet. It is the shortest distance between the liquor store and the expressway, it is the route the driver takes." Pazhman had taken photos with Hassan's digital camera. He used the camera to show the photos to the others.

It was a desolate street, near the expressway. On one side of the street was a discount clothing store with very few customers. On the other side was a locked warehouse. On the corner was a bodega. Pazhman explained as the others looked at the images.

"This is the best location, because it is a quiet street, but the van must turn here after leaving the bank in order to get on the expressway. This is where we will intercept it," said Pazhman.

"How will we do that?" asked Hassan.

"You will block the street with a car."

"And if we do stop it, how will we get inside?" Hassan continued.

"We will blow it up," said Pazhman.

Hassan's eyes open wide.

"An armored car? How?"

Pazhman dismissed Hassan's concerns with a wave of his hand.

"I have experience in such things."

That was all he said. He could have told them that he had destroyed vehicles larger and heavier and stronger than an armored car. He had destroyed armored personnel carriers, and even a tank, an M1 Abrams tank. But they did not need to know this. He did not have to convince them. They had only to obey. It was simpler that way.

They spent the rest of the evening eating pizza, drinking soda, and discussing the plan.

Hassan paced the apartment. He questioned why he had ever decided to get involved. Yes, he had once been a believer in jihad, he still believed, but he no longer wanted to be a soldier. He did not want to die. Was that so wrong?

Mahmud, on the other hand, was calm and collected, at

peace, smoking cigarettes and drinking tea and watching TV. He smiled in a relaxed manner when they discussed the plan, examining it from every angle.

"Hassan, you are behaving like an old woman," said Pazhman. "So why don't you go into the kitchen and make some tea?"

He would have suggested that Hassan drink some whiskey to calm his nerves, but he knew that would make him even more upset, and he needed Hassan. Besides, despite his nerves, Hassan had done well in his duties. He could be forgiven for his nervousness, as long as it ended soon, before the real work that was to be done.

# CHAPTER 36

Benton Conrad didn't go in much for power lunches at the Four Seasons or the Palm. At lunchtime he could usually be found at his desk, eating a turkey sandwich from a deli on Rector Street. When he absolutely had to use a restaurant, he went to Fraunces Tavern on Pearl Street. It was where George Washington had said goodbye to his officers, and the menu was probably as unpretentious now as it was then: fish and chips, strip steak, and shepherd's pie.

He was waiting on the sidewalk when Kim arrived. She noticed immediately that he was looking at his watch. He wasn't smiling.

"Am I late?" asked Kim.

"No, right on time," her father replied.

"Is everything alright?"

"Just one of those days."

"Dad, if this isn't convenient, we can do lunch another time."

Kim wasn't much of a lunch eater, either, and if her dad liked a turkey sandwich from the deli, she was happy with a container of cottage cheese and an apple. They were cut from the same cloth, both forcing themselves to a lunch neither of them wanted. But Kim had been in town for two weeks and had barely spoken to her father.

He smiled. "Come on, let's eat."

As they were shown to the small table for two near the window in the colonial-era wood paneled room, her father was greeted or at least acknowledged by half a dozen Wall Street honchos. He was a mover and shaker, and his arrival always caused a ripple. Kim didn't go unnoticed either.

He ordered his lunch as soon as the waiter arrived. Benton Conrad's life was fractionalized into six minute increments, and he had a pretty good idea how many of them he needed for the rest of the day. He wasn't about to waste any of them choosing lunch. Kim rushed to study the menu as her dad ordered a corned beef sandwich. She didn't have time to read all of it. She saw green salad, and asked for it.

"With chicken?" asked the waiter.

"Sure, thanks."

She sat back and took a deep breath.

Her dad looked distracted. He was staring out the window.

"You must be working one hell of a deal, Dad."

He shook his head. "I'm sorry sweetie. These past few weeks have been tough."

"How so?"

Benton Conrad looked pained, like he wanted to tell her something, but didn't know how.

"It doesn't matter. I didn't get a chance to talk to you at the museum. Tell me about what you're up to."

"You know I can't, all I can say is I'm attached to an inter-agency team here in the city. We're involved in counterterrorism, and let's leave it at that."

She didn't want to tell her father about Brooklyn, about the fieldwork she had suddenly been plunged into. She didn't want him worrying, and besides, it was strictly classified.

But he wasn't listening. He seemed distracted, worried. Why had he asked her to lunch? Was it about the ambassadorship? Was he hiding something? A health problem? Was it Barbara, his new wife?

"Is something wrong, Dad?"

Her father took a deep breath.

"I've been a lawyer for more than forty years." He shook his head. "We had six partners when I started the firm."

It wasn't like her Dad to get nostalgic. She crossed her arms and put her elbows on the table, leaning forward. "Is there a problem at the firm?"

Benton Conrad nodded. "I'm afraid it's rather serious."

He scratched his ear, then ran his fingers though the hair on the side of his head. "We had a client, rather big client, involved in a foreign banking transaction. I probably shouldn't be telling you all this. There were… regulations were violated."

"Dad!"

"Nothing that I knew about. That is, nothing I knew about at first. The problem is, we arranged the underwriting on the deal. It's all coming to pieces now. There are sure to be lawsuits."

172

"So you'll handle them," Kim said with confidence.

"It's a serious situation. I think it's best if I don't tell you too much. I need a lawyer. I'm getting Marvin involved."

"Dad, what are we talking about here?"

"The firm's been losing money. The last two years have been lean, and well, you can imagine what our Wall Street and Midtown rents are like, not to mention what we pay our associates and paralegals. I'm a rainmaker, I have to bring in the business. There's something else... and this affects you..."

He paused. Kim saw the color drain from his face. He grimaced in pain. Then he winced again and slid off the chair. Benton Conrad lay on floor gasping for air. Kim turned to the man at the next table.

"Call an ambulance!"

# CHAPTER 37

*Long Island City, New York*

Ernie Padilla worked his way through the traffic on Queens Boulevard. It was roasting hot. He was sweating badly. The a/c was running full blast, but it wasn't enough, something was wrong with the unit. Maybe it was low on freon, and with so many stops, it was impossible to keep the truck cool. He turned, as he always did, on Van Dam Street, thinking that he really should vary the route. Maybe next time. That's what they had been taught: don't get into a familiar pattern. But it was easier this way, the shortest distance to the expressway.

Padilla looked over at Chuck Henderson, who was sitting in the seat opposite him, removing a slice of cold pizza out of a bag. Henderson was a tall, lanky man who had worked for Cross-City Security for 14 years. The first five he had been assigned to the lobby of a bank in midtown, then he transferred to the armored car division, which he preferred. He had been "riding bitch," as they called it, for Padilla for two years.

"What are you doing?" asked Padilla.

"Eatin' my pizza?" replied Henderson.

"You fill out the log?"

"Yeah."

"How can you eat that shit?"

"What do you mean?" asked Henderson.

"For starters, it's loaded with cheese, you know what processed cheese does to your fuckin' arteries? And the fuckin' thing's dripping with grease," said Padilla.

"What are you, my doctor?"

Padilla had watched Henderson eat an egg-McMuffin earlier in the day, then delve into a sack of doughnuts as they made their rounds to the ATM machines.

"Where'd you get that, anyway? Padilla asked."

"I had it from yesterday."

"It's cold?"

"You never ate cold pizza?" asked Henderson.

"You ought to have your cholesterol tested," said Padilla. He turned his attention back to his driving as a 2005 Oldsmobile Cutlass suddenly pulled into the intersection.

Padilla pressed with both feet on the brakes, but it was too late. The armored car wasn't moving fast, but it was heavy. It hit the Cutlass's passenger side near the rear, crushing the rear quarter panel, tearing off the bumper and spinning the Cutlass around.

Henderson wasn't wearing his seatbelt. He slid off his seat and was pressed against the dashboard, the pizza smeared on his shirt.

"Ah Jesus!" he said. "Mother fucker!"

"You okay?" asked Padilla.

"Yeah, I'm fine," he said, as he looked at the tomato sauce on his hands and on his uniform. He wiped his hand on his shirt and started to open the door.

Padilla stopped him. "Nuh-uh. We wait for the cops, that's the rules."

"Shouldn't we see if anyone's hurt?" asked Henderson.

"Unless we're on fire, we stay put. Rules." He looked at the Cutlass, it didn't look too bad. Then, glancing in the side view mirror, he saw two men walking quickly from the corner toward the back of the van. It was their purposeful movement that concerned him. They weren't running to see if anyone was hurt in the van, they weren't curiously investigating the accident. They were making a move.

"We got company," Henderson said.

"Where?"

"Two guys, on my right."

Henderson unclipped his seatbelt and climbed into the back of the van. He looked through the Plexiglas window in the rear door.

"The fuck?"

"What is it?" asked Padilla.

"I lost them."

"What do you mean you lost them?"

"They were here and now they're not," said Henderson.

Henderson had his revolver out now, ready to fire through the

175

gun port, but he didn't want to slide the gun hatch open until he saw a target.

Padilla checked the side view mirror. He saw two men hunched near the rear wheel well. One of them reached around the van and placed something on the rear door.

"They put something on the door!" shrieked Padilla.

Henderson turned to him. "What?"

"They put something on the fucking door! Move!"

Before Henderson could react, Pazhman had rushed to the front of the van, fast, so the guards had no shot. He had a second bomb in his hands, and was pulling the fuse as he ran. He swung his left arm around and the explosive stuck to the front windshield. Then he ducked down in front of the van. Padilla looked at the object on the windshield in front of him. It was the last thing he ever saw. The shaped charge detonated, hurling flames and bits of glass and Plexiglas like grape shot through the interior of the armored car.

Moments later, the second bomb detonated, blowing the rear door off its hinges. Pazhman stepped though the smoke. On the floor of the van, he saw Henderson, wiping blood from his face with both hands.

Pazhman fired three shots quickly, then emerged from the van carrying two canvas and leather bags of cash. The entire attack had taken less than 45 seconds.

# CHAPTER 38

"Both the guards are dead. High explosives," said Mahan.

Kim slipped under the police tape as technicians from CSI pored over the armored car and the totaled Cutlass.

"You ever see anything like this before?" she asked.

"Yeah, but not here," said Mahan. "Any word on your Dad?"

"He's in the hospital. Heavily sedated. They say he'll be okay, but..."

"But what?" asked Mahan.

"Nothing. Thanks for asking," replied Kim.

She wore her FBI baseball cap and had her badge around her neck as she always did on crime scenes. She saw Winters standing next to a crime tech in a Tyvek suit and walked over to him.

"How long before we get a detailed ID on the explosive?" she asked.

The crime tech was short, pudgy and sweating in the suit, perspiration dripping down his cheeks.

"Looks like there were two charges. One on the door, one on the windshield. Guys inside never had a chance. Give me about an hour," he said.

Kim looked at the armored car. When she'd been on the bank robbery task force in Florida, she'd handled an armored car attack, but not one like this. On that one, the robbers had waited for the armored car driver to walk out of the bank, then shot him. This was different.

"Sometimes there's a video camera on the roof of these things," said Kim.

Winters shook his head.

"Old model. Didn't have that."

"What's the story on the car?" she asked.

"Reported stolen in Brooklyn six hours ago. They switched the plates, probably right before the job, I'm guessing. We're dusting it, but the driver wore gloves, nothing on the wheel," replied Winters.

"Ballistics?"

"From the looks of it, the shooter fired three rounds. Two in the chest, one in the forehead."

Kim turned to the crime tech. "Very professional."

"I'd say. Not your typical street heist, specially not with the C-4. That why the Feds are involved?"

Kim nodded. "We're looking for someone, can't tell you more than that. Sorry."

"Well, I sure as hell hope you find him soon."

The crime tech returned to the stolen car, where two technicians were swabbing the front seat to collect any fibers that might have been left. Kim turned her attention back to the surrounding buildings, looking for a security camera that might have captured the crime. She found what she was looking for at the end of the block, on the corner of a warehouse building. The building was brick with steel mesh covering blacked-out windows, like the other warehouses that lined the street. A sign above a pair of double doors read Webber Plastics. On one side of the sign was a camera. Maybe, just maybe, thought Kim.

"Sure, they work," said the dispatcher at Webber Plastics. She had curly red hair and long nails with a design painted on them, accented by baby rhinestones. She studied Kim's badge.

"You're with the FBI?"

"That's right," said Kim.

"My cousin's a cop, in Jersey. You have to go to college for that, right?"

"You do," said Kim.

"I got two years community college, sixteen credits."

Kim smiled. "So you say the cameras are working?"

"Oh, yeah, sure."

"Can we look at the tape?"

"It's digital. It gets backed up in the mainframe in Manhattan, but I know how to look at it here, too."

"What's your name?" asked Kim.

"Yvonne."

"Can you show me?"

Kim watched as Yvonne logged onto the security program and

accessed the digital recording, her long nails slicking against the keyboard. Kim had been right, one of the cameras on the roof was angled in just such a way that the robbery and murders had been captured in the background.

"Go back about an hour, say around 1:15 p.m.," she said.

Yvonne adjusted the time using the mouse, and after a few minutes searching the grainy black and white imagery they saw the armored car and the Cutlass enter the screen and collide silently. A man got out of the car and sat down in the street, then they saw two men walk purposefully toward the truck, and moments later the screen was over-exposed with a white flash, quickly followed by another.

"Holy shit," said Yvonne.

A few seconds after that they could make out one of the attackers stepping down from the back of the truck carrying two bags.

"Can you freeze it?" asked Kim.

Yvonne clicked "pause," and Kim and Mahan looked closely at the image.

"I hate it when they wear ski masks," said Mahan.

"Yeah, and they know that," said Kim.

"So how do we know they're our guys," said Mahan. "Maybe whoever stole the explosives are just bank robbers."

Kim looked at Yvonne. "Go back, would you?"

Yvonne clicked "reverse" and the image began running backwards. They watched as the men went to the van, then came out again, moving backwards. They placed the bomb on the windshield where it seemed to stick.

"Hold it there," said Kim. "Hit 'Play.'"

They watched as the bomb on the windshield exploded. They watched it again.

"I'd say that qualifies as advanced bomb making. These guys aren't bank robbers," said Mahan.

"So why are they knocking off an armored car?" asked Kim.

* * *

Kim was quiet as they drove back to Manhattan.

179

"What are you thinking?" asked Mahan.

"Assuming, for the moment, that Pazhman hit the armored car, why send an operative here without enough pocket money?" said Kim.

Mahan shrugged.

"You wouldn't, so follow the logic. Nabir was the money man, he was on the receiving end of the wire transfers, and the cash is still in his accounts, and in his safe."

"So they have no cash," said Mahan.

"So they hit the armored car," added Kim.

"Which means he's improvising, and he's good at it," said Mahan. "You think he knocked off explosives like that just so he can do a hit on the armored car?"

"No, maybe he just used the explosives because that's what he's good at," replied Kim.

Mahan considered this for a moment. "Which means he now has cash, and at least 200 pounds of high explosives, give or take. You thinking the G20?" he asked.

"We have to assume he might," said Kim.

"He won't get within ten miles."

"He could paralyze the city. Just think of all the UN missions, and the ancillary events. Not to mention this would be a total embarrassment. They're going to have to brief 20 different intelligence services that there's a major threat in the city."

"Which is why the NYPD Intel division is going ape shit," said Mahan.

Kim nodded. "We invited them here and now we have to tell them it's not safe."

They pulled to a stop at a red light on Grand Street. "Ever read Sun Szu?" she asked

"'The Art of War?' Sure, I guess."

"A successful general always adapts and improvises, that much we've already seen him do."

"Okay...."

"And a successful general always practices the art of deception. Makes his enemy think he's attacking one place, then strikes somewhere else. Causes him to deploy his resources in a

180

disadvantageous way."

"So maybe the G20 isn't the target?" asked Mahan.

"Maybe not. Look, he arrives a few weeks before the event, knowing we're bound to reach that conclusion. We spend all our resources defending foreign leaders, and he strikes somewhere else, something wide open. It's a feint."

"Great idea. Let's call the Secret Service and tell them to stay in Washington."

Kim frowned.

"It's just a theory."

"And not a bad one, but there's one problem."

"What's that?"

"If we hadn't stumbled across him in the first place this whole confusing-the-enemy strategy wouldn't be necessary."

"So then what is he up to?"

Mahan looked over at Kim and smiled. "I don't know. But I like the way you're thinking outside the box."

# CHAPTER 39

*Poughkeepsie, NY*

Everything depended on Doppelman.

The computer programmer sat in the Riverway Diner and waited. Mahmud always took his meetings with Doppelman in the same coffee shop. The familiarity helped build a sense of safety, and trust.

The relationship had begun innocently enough: a conversation on the Internet among gamers. (Doppelman's favorite was a futuristic strategy game called Global Domination.) Doppelman had struck up a friendship with another player, someone called Miles, who, he thought, lived outside Sacramento. In fact Miles was a loyal follower of Professor Al Fariz, and lived in Peshawar, in the same computer center that Pazhman had visited, weeks earlier. An online friendship slowly developed.

Miles learned that Doppelman was worried about money (child support, a difficult ex-wife), and frustrated with his superiors in the IT department where he worked. Doppelman lacked the social skills to network for a better job. Miles commiserated, advised, and then offered some freelance programming work, which Doppelman readily accepted. The work was done (a rudimentary security protocol for a wholesale shoe manufacturer) and money was paid. More money than he was worth.

More work followed. ("Would you be interested in additional assignments? I have overseas clients who need good programmers.")

Doppelman knew he was a good programmer, but he had never fully realized his true value. Miles sent more clients his way. They were relatively simple assignments: mobile apps, security portals for websites, databases. Nothing extravagant but they paid well.

Then came the tricky part.

Could Doppelman help with a geo-synchronous program to reach consumers on their mobile phones?

*But of course, that's my specialty.*

One evening, during a break from their ongoing game of Global Domination, Miles messaged Doppelman:

"You should meet my client face to face, he's based in Albany. Very cool guy, works for an Indian computer programming company."

And so the meetings with Mahmud began. Mahmud always dressed the part, short-sleeved shirt with tie, ill-fitting khaki pants, black shoes. He was a computer programmer, which wasn't much of a stretch, since he had trained to write code as a young man, before he joined the cause.

"The client is very impressed with your geo-synchronous marketing software, Mahmud told him, and another similar assignment followed. At their second lunch meeting, Mahmud asked, "You work at Yorke Aerospace, right?"

Doppelman chewed on his hamburger and nodded.

"That's interesting, because I have another client in India in the aeronautics field. I should really connect you."

"I'm open to all the business I can get."

Doppelman was retained on a consulting basis to advise the client on encrypted communications programs. It was restricted technology, proprietary. Doppelman was breaking the law, and he knew it.

On their last visit, Mahmud said, "It would be really helpful if you agreed to provide the passwords into the Yorke Aerospace network. They would pay you a great deal of money."

Mahmud ate his sandwich and watched Doppelman's fat face as he waited for an answer.

"How much are we talking?" asked Doppelman.

"$25,000."

"What exactly do you need?

# CHAPTER 40

*Manhattan*

Pazhman sat in a velvet armchair and surveyed the room. It was a grand room that took up most of the townhouse's first floor, with French doors that opened onto a patio facing the inner courtyard. The furnishings were opulent, with a Moroccan theme, a mix of east and west: oriental carpets, richly upholstered furniture and a gaudy polished brass sculpture of a lion. Above the fireplace a reference to his host's past: a large oil painting depicting a caravan of camels in the desert, a turbaned man in the lead, trading with an Afghan tribesman.

Jemel sat on the sofa across from Pazhman. He was dressed in a blue double-breasted suit with a purple scarf in the pocket.

"Business is good," said Pazhman. It was more an observation than a question.

Jemel turned his palms up. "It gets more difficult every day. I truly don't know how much longer I can survive. But, I do what I can. I manage."

Pazhman smiled. He was seated on the plush sofa, drinking tea. I'm sure you do, he thought.

Jemel was anxious to conclude the deal. This was not the usual exchange of corporate espionage which was his bread and butter. That much he knew, though he hadn't asked what was in the shipment. All he knew was that it was advanced electronics. What it would be used for, he didn't know. He preferred not to. Not that it would bother his conscience, but if he were caught, he could always plead ignorance.

He knew something dangerous was afoot. He had good intuition when it came to people, it was something that had served him well in his shadowy dealing – counterfeit watches, stolen jewelry, industrial secrets, pirated software – it didn't matter to him, and yet something told him that Pazhman was a man to fear, a man to steer clear of from now on. He wished he had not agreed to let Pazhman meet in his house.

"You have the shipment?" asked Pazhman.

"Of course. Your car is nearby?" he asked.

Pazhman nodded. Mahmud was double parked outside, by a fire hydrant.

"And the money?"

Pazhman opened his briefcase and removed two large stacks of bills, bundled with rubber bands, which he placed on the Moroccan mosaic coffee table. $50,000, all twenties, from the armored car. Jemel's mood brightened when he saw the money. *Maybe this wasn't such a bad deal after all.*

Jemel removed a key from his jacket pocket and walked across the room to a closet door. He inserted the key and opened the door. In the closet were four cardboard boxes. He placed these on the dining table.

"They are as I received them," he said.

Pazhman peeled back the tape from the first box. He saw that they were still exactly as he himself had wrapped them in Peshawar. He opened all four, just to make sure.

"I have a handcart," said Jemel, anxious to conclude the transaction. "Come, I will help you."

Jemel left the room and returned with a small metal handtruck on which he placed three boxes, which was all that would fit.

"I will help you to the car," said Jemel.

"That won't be necessary," replied Pazhman. "You have been most useful enough."

Pazhman hadn't survived this long without trusting his instincts, and those instincts now told him that Jemel would think nothing of betraying Pazhman to the authorities if it would save himself.

He had thought it through a dozen times. Jemel had been paid with cash stolen from the armored car. There was a good possibility that the police knew some of the stolen currency's serial numbers. When Jemel circulated the cash, which he inevitably would, and it was deposited in the bank, it would be identified and traced back to Jemel. Then Jemel would almost certainly crack under the questioning.

Pazhman was sure of that.

185

"There is one thing," said Pazhman.
"Yes?
Once again, Pazhman relied on the knife.

# CHAPTER 41

Kim dropped her briefcase and bagel on her desk. Mahan stared at her.

"What? I'm ten minutes late," she said.

"I tried to call you."

"Oh shit, my phone. I forgot to charge it." She cringed. It was an unofficial rule. FBI agents didn't make excuses about their cell phones. "What did I miss?" she asked as she took the bagel out of the bag.

"Homicide. Yesterday. Jemel Farzi, fairly well known rug dealer."

Kim sipped an iced coffee and read. The maid found the body and a preliminary autopsy report revealed death by knife wound to the carotid artery.

"Don't you think it's strange?" asked Mahan.

"Don't I think what's strange?"

"All of it."

"Meaning?"

"Well-known oriental carpet guy, murdered in his own home, motive unclear, Middle Eastern, and he was killed with a knife."

"Lots of people are killed with knives."

"Not nearly as many as are killed with guns," he said.

"True."

"And like you said, Pazhman had a knife," said Mahan, "Pachaas Talwaray, Fifty Knives."

"Swords."

"Whatever."

"Where's this Jemel Farzi dude from?" asked Kim.

"Paper says he's of Pakistani origin."

"You know how many Pakistani Americans there are in New York?" she asked.

"A lot?"

Kim nodded. "We should check it out."

The crime scene was still active. There was yellow police tape across the oak front door, and a uniformed police officer stood watch. The lead homicide detective was named Snyder, mid-forties, grey suit, striped tie.

"Lotta blood, sliced the jugular," said Snyder, as the two agents looked down at the carpet where the body had been.

"Any signs of a struggle?" asked Kim.

Synder shook his head. "Just the one cut. Looked to me like a plunging wound. The murderer knew what he was doing."

"He?" said Mahan.

"Picked up a partial bloody footprint, on the carpet in the hall. Definitely a man's shoe," said Snyder.

"What else?"

He shook his head. "We have fiber samples, but I don't think they'll link us to the perp. Like I said, there doesn't appear to have been a struggle."

"So he knew his killer?" said Kim.

The detective nodded. "Most likely. No sign of forced entry."

"Prints?" asked Kim, covering all the bases.

He shrugged. "We did find some hair samples on the couch."

"We should compare those to the sample we got at the hotel, see if it's a match," said Kim.

Mahan looked at the detective. "What about the victim's friends and family, business associates?"

"He had lots of e-mail and cell phone contacts in his phone," the detective replied.

"The guys we're looking for don't use cell phones, or e-mail. Did he have a notebook, diary?" asked Kim.

Kim stood behind the antique desk and surveyed the room's furnishings. There was a leather blotter and antique silver pen and ink set, as well as an arrangement of ancient stone carvings, not Greek or Roman, more Mesopotamian, she thought.

"So what else do we know?" she asked.

"From what I understand, this guy charged top dollar. We're talking ten, twenty grand for a single rug. I guess he imported them from wherever rugs come from. He has a Manhattan gallery, and one on the Island," said the detective.

"Sounds like a big operation," said Mahan. "But who's dropping that kind of cash for carpeting these days?"

The detective shrugged.

Kim picked up a silver framed photo from the desk. It showed Jemel, tanned and smiling, standing between an elegant man and a woman aboard a large yacht. "This guy lives large," she said, showing the photo to Mahan.

Her eyes moved back across the desk to the corner of the blotter. There was a business card stuck in it, almost completely concealed. She removed it. Midtown Shoe Repair, 36th Street.

"Strange," she said.

"What's that?" asked the detective.

"Just that I noticed a shoe repair place right around the corner. So why would he go down to 36th Street?"

# CHAPTER 42

Benton Conrad may have been, until a few days ago, one of the most respected and powerful attorneys, a deal maker, on Wall Street. But when he had a problem, a mess that really needed sorting out, he turned to his own lawyer, Marvin Wasserman.

Wasserman had been his roommate at Harvard, and ran a small private office. You wouldn't have known it by looking at him. No Dunhill suits or Turnbull and Asser shirts. Marvin Wasserman was more likely to be seen trudging up Lexington Avenue in a loose-fitting, wrinkled suit, rumpled shirt, orthopedic walking shoes, with a legal file clutched under his arm. His office was a mess (he was just shy of being diagnosed as a hoarder) with legal files everywhere, journals, correspondence, and newspapers going back months, much to the consternation of the building's fire warden. His secretary, Dorothy (he called her Dot), had long since given up trying to keep it tidy, but she could locate files and missing correspondence with remarkable speed, much like someone playing Concentration, remembering where an overturned card is.

Wasserman looked down at the couch, scratched his head, then decided to transfer the papers piled there to the coffee table so Kim could sit down.

"I tried to reach your Dad in the hospital, I couldn't get through," he said.

"He's not taking any calls, he's still very groggy and confused," answered Kim, shaking her head.

"What's the prognosis?"

Kim sighed. "They don't know. It was a minor heart attack, but he also had some kind of mental breakdown."

It was the first time she said it, and the words seemed to hang out there over the coffee table. It was hard to believe. Benton Conrad, mental breakdown. Benton Conrad… the legal mind that engineered Wall Street take-overs, who calculated ways to win boardroom battles, merge huge corporations; the man she had looked to for guidance for so many years. A mental breakdown?

190

"That might help us, if we can establish non compos mentus," said Wasserman.

"Help us?"

"I spoke to a contact at the Justice Department, he wouldn't give me all the details. Your father is the subject of a criminal investigation."

"Jesus Christ, Marvin, what are you talking about?"

"I'm saying your Dad will likely be charged with a felony."

Kim felt like she had been punched in the stomach. A Justice Department investigation? Kim knew what that meant. The ambassador's nomination would be off the table, her dad would be crushed.

"Your Dad put together an investment group south of the border to finance construction of a number of new hotels."

"Hotels?"

"Word is the money belonged to a Mexican billionaire named Miguel Despinosa. Heard of him?"

Of course she had, he was one of the richest men in Mexico. She nodded.

Wasserman continued. "Despinosa was arrested in Mexico City yesterday on corruption charges. I'd venture to say his entire empire, or at least a sizeable portion of it, is built on drug money. Looks like your Dad unknowingly entered into business with him to scrub the cartel's money. But it's drug money, no two ways about it."

"Dad can't have known," said Kim.

"If your father has to make a deposition, I can probably delay until we sort it out. This may lead to lawsuits from other clients, and I imagine your father, and the other partners, may be charged with violating SEC laws; either way we need to lawyer up."

"But he didn't do anything," said Kim.

Wasserman waffled his hand. "Things aren't so clear cut. We're dealing with very complex regulations here governing foreign transactions. It's a mess. He could conceivably face a heavy fine."

"How costly?"

"Millions. This is a tough spot, Kim. Any time you go up against the government. Well, you should know as well as anyone."

"So what do we do?"

"We'll cross that bridge when we come to it. One step at a time."

Kim took off her glasses and rubbed her temples.

"It gets worse."

She looked up at Wasserman.

"I don't know how he's going to pay for all this," he said.

"Can't the firm pay?"

"The firm is broke. Your Dad's been keeping it afloat with his own resources, and this also concerns you. He's dipped into the trust."

"My trust?"

Wasserman nodded.

"When you say dipped in, what does that mean?"

"The way it was set up, he was allowed to borrow against it, and that's what he did. Technically, the trust now consists of your father's personal IOUs."

"How much?"

"All of it."

All of it! She was stunned. That was her money, set aside by her grandfather. It had supplemented her government salary, meaning she never had to worry about money, could shop Madison Avenue, go on vacations….

"Oh Jesus," she said.

"Frankly, you don't have the resources to attract the kind of legal team that's needed here."

She took a deep breath.

"So what happens?"

"I don't know."

"How bad is it?

He looked at her. "It's not so easy to say, but you never want to be in a position where you're fighting a criminal case with the government. Either way, he's screwed. The firm will have to close." He threw his hands up in the air. "We're gonna have to end up cutting a deal, how good a deal, I don't know."

The next day the stories broke in the tabloids.

"Financial scandal sinks top firm," read one tabloid headline,

"Partners in crime," read another. Splashed on the front page was a picture of Benton Conrad at the museum gala, and standing next to him was Kim.

Pazhman read the papers every day. He had been trained to, not so much to check police updates, but to immerse himself in the city, and be better able to blend in. He recognized Kim immediately. At first he assumed she was a detective protecting a VIP, and he was surprised when a closer reading identified herself as the daughter of this troubled lawyer.

I have found you.

# CHAPTER 43

Arthur rode the No. 6 train downtown. He didn't want his mother to know he was out of work, even if his unemployment was temporary. He didn't want her to worry. Two days earlier, he had received a phone call from Hassan, who said he was sorry, but something had come up. The shop would be closed for a few weeks. That was all he said.

So every morning, Arthur rode the train to the shop, where the sign in the window read "closed." He sat in the park until it was time to go home.

That Saturday, his mother celebrated her 50th birthday in the family's apartment in Alphabet City in the Bronx. Arthur's cousin Hector, with his wife and son, drove in from Parsippany, and so did Arthur's Uncle Manny.

Hector was a patrolman with the Transit Authority Police, and everyone in the family looked up to him because he had graduated from college, and owned his own freestanding house in New Jersey.

Hector joined Arthur in the small kitchen while Arthur handed his cousin a tall-neck bottle of Budweiser. Hector poked his cousin on the arm.

"When are you gonna schedule that interview I got you with the Port Authority?" asked Hector.

"Why are you always pushing that on me?"

"I told you, they're looking for people, mechanical engineers. It's an opportunity. I got you the in with HR."

"I plan to, just been real busy."

"Too busy shining shoes to get a real job?"

Arthur looked over sharply, a frown on his face. Hector put both his hands up. "All right, that's all I'm gonna say."

Despite his occasional criticism of Arthur, Hector was very affable, and the two cousins were close, and confided in each other. Hector had buckteeth, a big belly and short curly hair. Not at all like Arthur, who was tall, skinny, and had long wavy hair. They both had dark complexions, their Puerto Rican heritage. Hector was like an older brother to Arthur, in some ways like a father to him.

"Something I want to ask you about," said Arthur.

"What is it bro?"

"You know the dude I work for, Hassan?"

"Yeah?" In fact Hector had never met Hassan, but Arthur had described him before.

"Well, I ain't been shining no shoes. Boss closed the shop."

"When did this happen?"

"This past week. He's been acting kinda strange."

"What kind of strange?" asked Hector, taking a sip of his beer.

"Some dude came in, another camel jockey."

"Dude, that ain't cool. You ain't supposed to call them that," Hector raised an eyebrow.

"You know what I mean."

Hector was married to a Muslim, and didn't like it when Arthur used terms like camel jockey and diaper head. He said it was disrespectful.

"Go on, what about him?"

"Hassan kinda freaked out. He closed the shop, skipped his prayers, which I never seen him do before. I seen him meet with this dude in the park, I figure something's going on," said Arthur.

Hector pointed at him with his open beer. "So you get the job at Port Authority and you don't care what boss man is up to."

"Lemme finish."

"Go ahead."

"I go back to work and decide to look through where he keeps his stuff. He's got this drawer he always keeps locked."

"Yo, why are you rummaging through someone else's personal shit? You're gonna need a written recommendation from this dude, and you don't want him to have you arrested and have a record, dude."

"Well, I didn't get arrested. Will you just let me finish?"

Hector's wife called in from the other room. "What are you guys doing, having a private party?"

"Just a minute, baby," said Hector. "Talking to bro."

Arthur took a deep breath and let it out, shaking his head.

"I look in the drawer, and he's got a gun, for starters."

195

"Long as he got a permit."

"I also find a phony passport and driver's license, says his name is Omar or some shit. And he's got a stack of cash about this thick." He held his thumb and index finger an inch apart.

"Get the fuck outta here."

"I'm telling you."

"So what do you think?' asked Hector.

Arthur rubbed his chin. "I don't know what to think. Money, passport, gun, and this weird dude shows up. It's like maybe he's ready in case he gotta run away. I don't wanna lose my job, but it seems fucked up," said Arthur.

"I hear you, bro. Let me think about it, maybe run the names, on the sly, just so we know what's up. Meanwhile don't go looking in any more drawers."

# CHAPTER 44

Lance Dennehy and his girlfriend Jill found two seats at the crowded bar.

Marcus, the bartender at Clyde's, recognized them and ignored the others who were waiting to get his attention.

"Pabst Blue Ribbon, said Lance. "Add a shot to that, will you?"

Jill looked at Lance. She didn't like him ordering the shot. He had promised to drink less, and to stop mixing pills.

"What are you having?" Lance asked.

"Club soda, I'll be the designated driver."

Jill saw Clyde standing in the door to the kitchen. She knew Clyde never touched a drop, which was strange, since he owned a popular bar. And he rarely poured the drinks, he ran the kitchen and he let his nephew, Marcus work the bar.

Jill knew Lance was going to get drunk again. No one ordered the shot unless they wanted to get drunk. Her heart sank. Sometimes Lance was in a good mood when he drank but, more often than not, he became remote, unwilling to have a conversation with Jill.

Jill watched Lance down the first shot of whiskey, then noticed a friend of hers, Gwen, at the end of the bar. Gwen worked with her at Yorke Aerospace, where Jill had been ever since graduating from Syracuse. It was a good job, and Yorke was considered the best place to work in Woodboro. Gwen was with some other people Jill knew. Without saying anything she moved to the other end of the bar to say hello.

Lance pushed his shot glass toward Marcus.

"I'll have another," he said.

Marcus flipped his white bar towel over his shoulder and took Lance's glass.

Lance saw a man he didn't recognize talking to Gwen and Jill. The man was telling a story and Jill was laughing. He was wearing khaki shorts and a T-shirt that read "Ski Breckenridge." Jill seemed to know him, and he thought perhaps he worked with Jill at the plant. Another man who looked like he might be from the same group leaned over the bar near Lance, blocking his view of Jill. The man turned his back to Lance, talking to several other people.

Lance took a gulp of beer. The crowd behind him was laughing and getting louder. Getting bigger too, crowding Lance. An errant elbow prodded him and Lance prodded back. Beer spilled.

"Dude!" It was a man in a dark blue polo shirt.

"Do you mind?" asked Lance.

"Yeah, you just spilled my beer," said the man in the polo shirt.

"Then maybe it's time to move somewhere else."

"Maybe it's time you did, asshole."

Lance stood up. He reached back and was about to shove the other man when he felt a hand on his shoulder. It was Clyde, pulling him back.

"Talk to you for a minute? Guys, this is over," said Clyde.

Clyde pushed Lance back toward the rear of the bar, where the kitchen was and Clyde kept a small office. He opened the door and gestured with his index finger for Lance to go in.

"Time to talk, Lance."

"About what?" said Lance.

Clyde pointed to a chair. "Sit down."

As Lance sat, Clyde noticed he had to adjust something in the small of his back.

"Jesus fucking Christ, you're packing," said Clyde.

"I have a license," said Lance.

"Not for a fucking bar, you don't, not in my bar. Gimme it."

Lance stared expressionlessly at Clyde.

"Either shoot me or give me the fucking piece," said Clyde.

Lance let out a breath and unclipped the holster. He handed it, with the pistol, to Clyde.

"I am a deputy," said Lance.

"You're a probie, you ain't shit."

Clyde looked at Lance and frowned, shaking his head. He pressed the release on the side of the pistol and let the magazine drop into his hand, then he pulled back the slide and locked it in the

198

open position, checking the chamber to make sure it was empty.

With his thumb, he pushed the bullets out of the magazine. They tumbled onto the desk.

"Don't take this the wrong way, but you seeing a doctor?" asked Clyde.

Lance took his time before answering.

"I saw one, yeah."

"I'm not talking about the shrink who talks to everyone when you get home from your tour. You talking to anyone now?"

"I'm taking pills."

"You have PTSD you know that, right?"

"Everyone gets it. Soon as the paperwork comes through, it's worth 400 bucks a month," he smiled.

"No, I mean, you really have it. Trouble sleeping, irritability, flashbacks."

"Like I said, they give me pills."

"Pills are one thing, you gotta see a shrink. I did, only wish I'd done it sooner. Woulda saved a lot of time, and heartbreak. When I got back from 'Nam they didn't even know what it was. Took me a good eight to 10 years to deal with it. You keep this bullshit up you're gonna lose something a lot more valuable than the full use of that leg, and she's sitting out there at that bar."

"I don't need a shrink," said Lance.

Clyde unlocked his desk drawer and put the pistol in it, then slid it shut and locked it. He gathered up the bullets in his hand and stuffed them in his pocket.

"The hell you don't. If you don't like the guys at the VA you can talk to my guy. He's a vet, like us. Airborne." He wrote a name and phone number down on a piece of notepaper and slid it over to Lance. "I'm not asking you I'm telling ya. And I want you to call me tomorrow after you make the appointment. Roger that?"

Lance looked straight at Clyde, their eyes locking.

"Roger."

# CHAPTER 45

"Talk to me," said Kim as she and Mahan got into the car outside the office.

"Winters ran all the names of people who worked at Saltieri Demolition, we got a hit on someone named Rodney Williamson."

"What kind of hit?"

"He listed Nabir Azzad, our baker, as a reference when he applied for the job."

"That was careless of him."

"Address is in Fort Lee. From what we can tell, he shares an apartment with someone named Yusuf Wali."

"We know anything about Wali?" asked Kim.

"No arrests, no watch lists, no known contacts we're worried about. Emigrated to the US two years ago. He has a green card. But he went back to Pakistan about six months ago, stayed two months. The surveillance group has been there all night."

Winters and Baumgartner sat in an unmarked van. Winters wore headphones and occasionally looked through the telephoto lens of the camera. Baumgartner sat in a small swivel chair in the rear of the van reading a novel.

"What are you reading, anyway?" asked Winters, as he adjusted the focus on the camera.

"Stephen King," said Baumgartner.

"Which one?"

"'The Dark Tower.'"

"Which volume?"

"Three, 'The Wastelands.' You like Stephen King?" asked Baumgartner.

"Yeah."

Baumgartner didn't look up from his book. He always brought a book with him on surveillance because surveillance was long and boring, and you never knew how long, and how boring. Sometimes there were two men in the van, which meant you could rotate the task of surveillance.

"How many pages?" asked Winters.

Baumgartner looked up from the book at Winters. Then he flipped to the back of the book. "448."

"At this rate, you'll probably finish it before anything happens."

"I won't if you don't stop asking me questions."

"You mind if I read it when you're done?"

Baumgartner made a sarcastic smile. "Sure. We'll form a book club. I'll bake cookies. Now let me read."

They watched the apartment until 9 a.m., when Kim and Mahan arrived. Baumgartner pulled the van away and Mahan took his parking space. The Bureau liked to use a variety of cars when they did surveillance. Mahan was driving a Ford Expedition with tinted windows.

"I don't think this car is working for us," said Kim examining the interior.

"Why not?"

"We don't look like crack dealers, for starters."

She was right. Mahan had noticed the custom hubcaps and chrome trim.

"Fitzy must be messing with us. But it doesn't matter, we're not the lead vehicle."

"Who else we got?"

Mahan gestured with his chin toward a black man setting up a folding table on the corner. "See the guy with the counterfeit watches?"

"Yeah."

"He's from the special surveillance group."

"That's it?" asked Kim.

He shook his head. "We're surveillance team Bravo. There's two others, Alpha and Charlie. When this dude moves, we're on him."

Kim had some, not much, experience in vehicle surveillance, most of it from Quantico. She also knew that New York City, with its traffic and streetlights, had its own set of rules.

"Where are Alpha and Charlie?"

"Alpha is around the corner. If Williamson moves, he'll lead him. And Charlie should be down the block in case he goes that way."

"And what do we do?"

"We watch. And we wait."

Kim settled in to wait. She studied Mahan. On the surface, anyway, Mahan was the model FBI special agent, but was there more to him than met the eye? Some of her colleagues could be so dull, like a weird hybrid: secret agent meets insurance salesman. She wondered what he did when he wasn't being an FBI agent. She didn't even know if he had a girlfriend. She had never asked him, and she didn't really care. She was just trying to figure him out. Trying to strip him down and see who he really was.

"You seem lost in thought, what are you thinking?" Mahan asked.

"Oh, nothing."

"You sure?"

"Yeah."

"Your Dad?"

"No, it's nothing. Want coffee?" asked Kim.

"You see a men's room anywhere near here?"

She shook her head.

"Then no."

Kim smiled and closed her eyes. She was tired, hadn't slept well, so she decided she would let Mahan watch the building. He seemed so intent, anyway. And how many people did it take to watch a building, really?

She and Mahan sat in the Ford for more than two hours. It was hot, but Mahan said they couldn't run the a/c. Wasted gas, he said. And then they wouldn't have gas when they needed it. Besides, it drew attention for a car to sit for hours with the engine idling. Bad for the environment, too, he said. She rolled her eyes.

"You don't believe in the environment?" asked Mahan.

"I believe in not sweating my ass off. In Florida we ran the a/c."

"Good. We're not in Florida anymore."

"I noticed."

"Go ahead, get out and stretch your legs. You can keep an eye on things from the sidewalk. No rule says you have to stay in the car," said Mahan.

"What about you?" she asked.

"I don't mind sitting."

"I gotta stretch," she said.

"Don't go too far."

"Do you want anything?" she asked.

"Like what?"

"I don't know, a hot dog, a bottle of water?"

"Maybe. Sure." He reached into his pocket.

"My treat."

Kim got out of the car and walked to the corner. She took her time, letting someone else go in front of her. When it was her turn, she ordered two dogs and two bottles of water. She assumed Mahan wanted mustard and sauerkraut. If he didn't, too bad.

Jusef Wali said his morning prayers near his neatly made bed. Rodney never made his bed, which, like Jusef's, was a mattress on the floor of their shared studio apartment. He never washed his clothes, either, and he left food out. He was a pig. According to the holy teachings a man must keep his body clean. But not Rodney, and it annoyed Jusef. There was friction between them in the apartment. It was bad enough that he wasted hours every day delivering messages all over town because Pazhman and the others forbade the use of cell phones, but to have to share his apartment with someone like Rodney was too much. Rodney was sullen and moody, he never spoke, and he wore a knit cap even though it was summer. He was a very strange person, Jusef thought.

But as long as Mahmud paid for Jusef's apartment and living expenses, he could say nothing. Anyway, Jusef had been told he would be returning upstate soon. It couldn't be soon enough. At 9:30 Jusef left the apartment.

Kim saw a Middle Eastern-looking man leave the apartment building while she was paying for the hot dogs and water. She ran back to the car. Mahan had shifted to the passenger seat.

"That him?"

"I'd say so. You drive," he said. Kim tossed the bag of hot dogs on the dashboard and got in. She started the engine as they watched Jusef walk down the sidewalk and get into a gypsy cab. "I want to be ready to hop out," explained Mahan.

Like honeybees outside the hive, the surveillance vehicles maneuvered around in a well-choreographed, mysterious dance as Jusef's cab headed toward the bridge. One car took the lead only to be silently replaced by a second, switching with a third chase car a few minutes later. That was the idea, anyway. Mahan directed her as she followed the gypsy cab. She clenched the wheel tightly. She wasn't used to city driving.

"You look tense," said Mahan. "Relax, but stay close."

"For your information, we have traffic in Florida, too."

"But not gridlock."

"You wanna drive?" she asked.

"No, you're doing fine."

"Thank you."

"Look out," he said.

A yellow light turned red. Kim pressed down on the accelerator and punched through the final intersection in downtown Fort Lee. Mahan looked out the rear window.

"Shit, we lost the other units. It's just us now." He turned to Kim.

"No pressure."

They trailed the taxi through the Holland Tunnel. Once in Manhattan, the taxi headed uptown. Kim squeaked through another red light on Eighth Avenue as Mahan squirmed in his seat. They drove north through midtown, Kim switching lanes and occasionally braking to avoid getting too close. They turned east on 59th Street and pulled over when the taxi stopped to discharge Jusef in front of the Plaza Hotel.

"I'll get out here," said Mahan. "Park the car."

Kim watched Jusef cross the street toward Central Park. Mahan followed at a cautious distance. She left the car amid a tangle of taxis, horse-drawn carriages and limousines. There was nowhere to park the car. She got out and phoned Winters.

"Where are you?" he asked.

"Central Park, southeast entrance, it's probably a meeting," she said. "We might have him boxed in. He's on foot now. Bring backup, but no sirens."

Kim ran to catch up with Mahan at the entrance to the zoo. Mahan showed his badge and the attendant let them through without paying.

She remembered visiting the zoo as a child, before it was redesigned. In the center of the plaza the sea lions were still there, but the pool had been spiffed up, and the Delacorte Clock was as she remembered it.

"You call for back-up?" asked Mahan

"They're on their way. Where is he?" asked Kim.

Mahan gestured with his head toward the penguin house.

She remembered the building that now housed the penguins had been the monkey house. The large cage with dozens of different monkeys shrieking, their voices reverberating off the glazed cinder block walls, the urine running in long yellow streams across the cement floor to the drains. Now there were more humane enclosures that resembled natural habitats.

Mahan put his finger to his ear and spoke into a microphone bud in his sleeve. "This is Mahan, do you copy?"

He listened for a moment. "Shit."

"Nothing?" Kim asked.

He shook his head. "If anything happens, I'll stick with him, you handle whoever else shows up. We'll have the rest of the team handle the exits."

Mahan moved toward the south wall of the sea lion pool, then stopped when he saw their subject. He leaned his elbow against the brick wall and pulled Kim closer to him.

"What are you doing?" asked Kim.

"We look like cops," he said.

"Speak for yourself."

"Pretend we're lovers."

Kim let herself be pulled closer, her eyes opened wide. "This is

205

bordering on sexual harassment, you know," she said.

"Don't make it feel weird," she said in his ear as they embraced.

He turned, so her head looked to his left.

"What's he doing now?" asked Mahan.

"He's walking toward the cafeteria."

"Let's hold hands and follow."

"I have a better idea, why don't we pretend we're having a lover's quarrel?"

He clutched her hand and winked. "Because it would draw too much attention. Besides, we make a great couple."

"Oh, Jesus."

Jusef moved quickly past a school group watching a pair of monkeys grooming each other on some rocks. He carried a satchel under his arm, like a football. Ignoring the monkeys, he stopped at the entrance to the rain forest building and checked his watch.

Mahan pressed Kim against the wall, looking right at her. She could see Jusef out of the corner of her eye.

"What's he doing?" Mahan asked.

"He's just standing there. You sure do take surveillance seriously. How long are we supposed to stay like this?"

"Until he does something. That's the beauty of it."

Kim almost lost herself in the warmth of the embrace. She felt confused, too. Should she be enjoying this? Because she was. But was Mahan? Suddenly, she tensed.

"What is it?" she asked.

"I think he sees someone."

Kim saw him too. A man at the turnstile entrance to the zoo, paying for a ticket. Despite his hat, she recognized him immediately.


Pazhman carried a nylon sports bag. Inside was a small explosive device he had quickly constructed the night before. He could have planted it himself, but why take the risk on a secondary target, when he had someone who was expendable, like Jusef?

The Afghan pretended to watch the sea lions being fed. He scanned the crowd, saw the two lovers, noticed the zookeeper throwing herring to the sea lions, and several mothers and nannies and baby carriages. Then his eyes came to rest on the nervous Wali, who waited by the tropical rainforest exhibit.

Pazhman moved slowly. Patience, methodical caution was part of his tradecraft. The others of the original 50 were mostly dead now, yet he survived, and he credited that to his superior skills, and luck, of course, and perhaps Divine intervention, for what else could it be?

"He might recognize me," said Kim, as Pazhman moved closer. "Kiss me," she said.

"What?" said Mahan.

She pressed her lips to his. She reached her arms around his neck and held him. She felt a jolt of excitement, a spark. She looked at his face, then kissed him again.

Mahan opened one eye and watched as Pazhman entered the rain forest building.

"Let's go," he said.

Kim pressed her index finger up to her earpiece. "The team's not in position," she reported.

"We gotta go."

Kim and Mahan moved quickly across the zoo courtyard and through the double doors into the hot humid interior of the rain forest exhibit. Tropical birds squawked. Kim spotted Pazhman.

"He's heading upstairs," said Kim. She had an arm around Mahan's waist, and nuzzled his neck.

Pazhman climbed to the balcony where Jusef waited. The two men stood side by side and looked at the exhibit.

Pazhman wasted no time. He passed his bag to Jusef.

"You are to take this and deliver it to the address written inside. Do you think you can do that?"

"Of course," said Jusef.

A small bird flew overhead and Pazhman instinctively turned to look at it. In that instant he saw Kim turn her head away. He knew at once it was a trap. Jusef, you fool! In a split second, his mind calculated the variables. He reached into his breast pocket and withdrew a Glock 9mm. Jusef started to say something as Pazhman fired three shots into his chest. Dozens of screeching birds took flight in unison. A woman screamed. Pazhman saw the two special agents begin to move toward him. He turned the opposite direction and disappeared behind a group of tourists frozen in fear.

Pazhman sprinted across the zoo's courtyard. Kim heard more gunshots as she emerged outside, Mahan right behind her. A police officer lay on the ground. He wasn't moving. She saw Pazhman momentarily entangled in an overturned baby carriage, the mother reaching for the toddler. Then he was in the clear, no civilians in her line of sight. It was all she needed. Kim leveled her weapon.

At that moment, Pazhman turned to her, then ducked to one side as Kim fired. A woman screamed. Pazhman vaulted over the turnstile. Kim raced after him toward the street as he disappeared into the crowd.

"Split up," shouted Mahan, and he plunged into the crowd.

Kim headed for the exit. She paused on the sidewalk outside the park and scanned the street. She saw a flash of movement down the block, and there was Pazhman, running west on 59th Street, partially concealed by the row of horse-drawn carriages.

She rushed down the sidewalk, then cut into the street between two carriages. The driver pulled back on the reins as Kim lost her footing on wet cobblestones and fell to the ground. The horse reared. She scrambled to her feet and scanned the crowd on the other side of the street.

He was gone. Again.

Like a ghost.

# CHAPTER 46

*Fort Lee, New Jersey*

Mahan and Kim drove back to Jusef Wali's apartment. His building was cordoned off by the FBI Evidence Response Team. They found Special Agent Baumgartner, who was in charge of the crime scene, in the apartment. The place smelled of tobacco, dirty laundry, and a mix of Pakistani spices.

"Anything?" asked Mahan.

"A few pistols, ammo, but nothing else yet. Looks like he got them at a gun show in Virginia. Didn't have a computer. We're bagging the evidence now. Guy next door said mostly he was a good neighbor."

"What a surprise. Prints?"

"Plenty. We're gonna need help packing this shit up."

He gestured toward the bookcase and the desk. "It's all going."

Kim pulled on a pair of latex gloves and began removing books from the shelves, one by one. She leafed through them before placing them in an evidence box. Everything had to be saved. Printed texts could be used for otherwise unbreakable book codes. It wasn't beyond the realm of possibility, and all possibilities had to be considered.

She found English/Pakistani phrase books and dictionaries, as well as several books on shoe repair and leather care, and a Consumer Reports guide to purchasing a used car. More curious, perhaps, were a few dozen erotic romance novels. Unusual, as she thought these were read primarily by women. They were well-thumbed, and the sub-genres ranged from gothic to vampire. On the same shelf as the erotic literature were porn magazines, a sizeable collection. Raunchy. Bondage. Leather. Kim was glad she was wearing latex gloves as she flipped through the pages.

"Anything?" asked Mahan.

"This guy was really into porn."

"What else?"

"A few guidebooks, the United States, the Northeast, the Mid-Atlantic states. Maybe he was planning a trip, what about you?"

"Checkbooks, bank statements," said Mahan, who was going through the contents of the desk drawers. "Nothing unusual so far."

Kim thumbed through a stack of road maps. One was of New Jersey, another all of New England. But most were for New York State. One had not been folded correctly, suggesting that whoever used it had travelled upstate to Ulster County. Kim knew the area, it wasn't too far from where her family had a summer home. She opened each map and looked for any marks.

There was a stack of tourist brochures, too. It looked like Wali had raided the brochure display at the local tourist office.

She placed the maps and the brochures in a cardboard box and began helping Mahan with the documents in the desk. About an hour later they did a final walk-through of the apartment. They loaded the boxes in the back of an FBI Ford Explorer and drove back to Manhattan. Mahan's cell phone rang. It was Gambler. Mahan spoke for a few moments, then turned to Kim.

"He wants us back at the office. ASAP."

Gambler sat at his desk and shook his head. Kim felt exhausted. The adrenaline had worn off and she was crashing.

"You had him. You should have had him. What the hell happened?" asked Gambler.

"He got away," Kim said.

"Obviously. Why not wait until Winters had his guys in position? This is a team, remember? For God's sake he shot a cop right in front of you!"

"As I explained, events unfolded very rapidly, sir," said Mahan.

"Obviously."

"We were planning to hold back, but he spotted us," said Kim.

"He spotted you?" Gambler repeated. The way he emphasized "spotted" suggested he didn't think highly of her surveillance skills.

"Yes sir," said Mahan.

"And where exactly were you when he spotted you?"

"We were in the tropical zone, we had him under surveillance.

We were posing as lovers."

"Lovers? Excuse me while I experience a warm and fuzzy moment here." Gambler sat back and looked up at the ceiling, then looked back down at the two agents. "It's just that I don't remember impersonating lovers in the field manuals."

"We were trying to blend in," said Kim.

"Yeah? Well I just got off the phone with someone from the Zoological Society. She says someone shot a seal."

Kim cleared her throat. "That must be me, sir, my shot did go a tad wide."

"A tad wide?" He repeated her words, pausing after each word. "Yes, without looking at the ballistics report, I'd venture to say it went a tad wide."

"The subject was moving fast sir, and taking evasive action."

"Remind me, Special Agent Conrad, you did pass the marksmanship exam at Quantico?"

It was an unfair question, he knew most agents never fired their weapons in the line of duty. She doubted Gambler had. No test could prepare you for that. Besides, he was the one who had pushed her into the field.

"I did score proficient at the Academy, sir."

"Not proficient enough to avoid wounding a seal. And incidentally, you violated the Marine Mammals Protection Act. I'll have to place a letter of reprimand in your file."

"Sir, if you didn't want me in the field you shouldn't have chosen me."

Gambler sighed. "I hope you know this is a PR disaster, not to mention a major embarrassment given that we have the G-20 coming to town with this suspect on the loose, and it seems the FBI's special agents can't shoot straight. I have headquarters breathing down my neck, the director is briefing Congressional leaders as we speak, the Mayor and the Chief of Police want to know what the fuck went wrong, and Mrs. Wentworth whatshername from the board of trustees of the zoo wants to know why we shot her fucking seal! He had a name for Christ's sake."

"What was his name?" asked Kim.

"What?"

"The seal's name? And it's a sea lion, not a seal."

"The fuck do I know? Mona, or Moana, or something."

The veins in his neck were bulging. Kim knew that it was not a healthy way to cope with stress. She could imagine him having a heart attack, or maybe a blood vessel in the back of his brain would burst and he would collapse on his desk. Vinyasa yoga would probably help, and meditation, but she figured now was not a good time to suggest it.

"And that's not all. We worked our sources in the newsroom at the Chronicle. Seems one of their roving editors, Jack Briggs, is the one who first caught wind of this story. Special Agent Conrad, would I be correct in understanding you have a personal relationship with said editor?"

Mahan looked at her in surprise.

"No sir, not anymore."

"I see."

"To be honest, I have no idea how he pieced the story together, and I'm not in touch with him anymore."

Gambler looked at her, and nodded. "Well, I'd prefer not to open an investigation, and I don't need to tell you what the policy is regarding leaks. If you do see him, ask him how he did it. That's all I'll say on the matter."

"Both of you are officially on notice, there will be an internal investigation regarding the incident at the zoo. I may reassign you pending the review. Anything else?"

"I did get a good look at him sir," said Kim. "He's changed his appearance slightly, shaved, cut his hair. I'd say he doesn't look at all like the old photo."

"Wonderful." He said with more than a touch of sarcasm. "We'll get the sketch artist to work on it. What else?"

She shook her head.

# CHAPTER 47

Mahan slumped against the back wall of the elevator as the door closed. "That actually went worse that I thought it would, if that's possible."

"What should we do?" asked Kim.

"Do? I know a good bar, I think we should go there."

"I don't need a drink," said Kim.

"You just shot an endangered marine mammal, trust me, you need a drink."

"I don't think sea lions are endangered. They're just protected."

"Some protection," said Mahan.

"So where's this bar?"

The bar was actually an Italian restaurant on Sullivan Street. Kim pointed that out when they got out of the taxi.

"They serve booze. I need to eat, you need to eat. When I'm upset about something, Italian food makes me feel better, and if you eat more, you can drink more. You don't have to join me."

"This is a side of you I haven't seen. I'm intrigued."

She looked at her watch.

"You have other plans?" asked Mahan.

"It's just that I don't usually eat at 6 o'clock."

"So we'll have a cocktail first, and an antipasto, then it'll be 7:30 and then we'll eat."

"By then I'll be drunk," replied Kim.

"You catch on quick."

They found a small table by the bar. The restaurant was mostly empty, the waiters were still setting the tables. Mahan ordered a single malt whiskey, and Kim said she'd have the same, with ice.

Mahan raised his glass. "Tomorrow we'll start picking up the pieces, assuming we still have a job. I hope you didn't have plans for the weekend."

"We worked weekends in Jacksonville, too. Bank robbers don't take Saturday and Sunday off."

"Your ghost won't."

"So what's next?" asked Kim.

"I was thinking we'll start going through every contact we have for this magic carpet man, Jemel Farzi, and work from there. But I don't want to think about it now. For now, I want to think about drinking this."

"I'm not really a whiskey drinker," said Kim.

"Now's as good a time as any to start."

He smiled as he watched her take her first tentative sip. She looked as if she were expecting to gag, but she raised her eyebrows.

"This is good," said Kim.

"Yes it is."

She felt a warm feeling returning, the feeling she had first experienced at the zoo with Mahan. "I always thought whiskey was too strong, maybe that's because I remember tasting it as a child."

"I take it you don't drink?"

"I drink white wine, and champagne. You know the bureau frowns on the excessive consumption of alcohol?" said Kim.

"The bureau frowns on a lot of things, and since when did you go by the book?"


"So where does this leave us?" asked Kim.

"Us?" replied Mahan.

A look of confusion momentarily crossed Kim's face. "Our investigation."

"Oh. I don't know. I guess the NYPD checks every mosque, every truck rental office, every hotel, you name it."

"And they won't find him," said Kim.

"Why do you say that?"

"Because he's too good. You saw the way he spotted us, fired on the run."

Mahan raised his glass. "It's been my experience that good police work usually pays off."

"This guy isn't your usual suspect. He's not going to sit on his C-4 forever. Meanwhile we're here drinking whiskey."

"Why don't we let the NYPD do its job, and we'll do ours, which right now is having a second round of these, and then ordering dinner. They do a Tuscan steak here that I highly recommend."

"Why do I keep thinking we're missing something?" asked Kim.

"Why do you care so much?"

"Because it's my job."

"Correction, it was your job. We're probably going to be reassigned, remember?"

"He didn't say that."

"Inductive logic. We screwed up. People who screw up get fired. Therefore we will get fired."

"I think that's deductive."

"Does it matter?"

She slumped in her chair and looked Mahan in the eyes. "You think I screwed up?"

"No," said Mahan.

"We screwed up?"

"We were on our own, we made the call."

"And we got it wrong. We should have waited until everybody was in place," said Kim.

"How long would that have taken?"

"Now he's spooked," said Kim. "He'll never resurface."

"Can we not do this?" Mahan said suddenly.

"Not do what?"

"Talk shop?"

She let out a deep breath. "Sorry, what do you want to talk about?"

Mahan shrugged. "I don't know. How about what do you in your spare time?"

"Huh?"

"What do you like to do?"

Kim thought for a moment. "Well, I run, but I hate it, does that count?"

"Not really, you probably go to the gym, too. What else?"

"I read," she said, sounding hopeful.

"There you go, what do you read?"

"The Economist."

"Anything else?"

"I just finished 'Predictive Analytics,' by Eric Siegel. It's actually the second time I've read it."

"I mean fiction, not math textbooks."

"I don't read much fiction."

"Oh."

Kim smiled. "What about you?"

"I like to hike."

"Where?"

"The Appalachian Trail."

"Really? A real country boy."

"Yep."

"Born and bred in Bayside," said Kim.

"Very good," replied Mahan, sipping his whiskey.

They were drinking on empty stomachs, Mahan ordered calamari. The waiter asked if they wanted to see the wine list.

"Nothing more for me," said Kim, "I'm a lightweight." She was still nursing her first whiskey. Mahan was 190 pounds, Kim weighed in at 110. She calculated that if she drank the second drink, she would be drunk. And she was not interested in eating squid. She sat back and looked at Mahan. She thought of them at the zoo, and shook her head. She felt light headed, that was for sure, a combination of the hunger and the drink.

"So I hope I'm not being too bold, but is there a special someone in Special Agent Kim Conrad's life?" asked Mahan.

"I thought we weren't supposed to delve into each other's personal lives?"

"We are partners. It's going to come up."

"It will if we keep drinking these," said Kim. "And no, there isn't." She felt sad saying it. "I don't think there is. But I have a question for you, Mr. Mahan, Special Agent Mahan."

"Yes?"

"Why the FBI?"

"I joined because they recruited me after the Army, I was in Intel. My mother always told me government jobs are the way to go, guaranteed employment and a secure retirement. I have no regrets. Do you?"

She looked at Mahan, raised an eyebrow. She thought of the

men at the investment bank where she'd interned, who were so unlike Mahan, and the never-ending spreadsheets, number crunching, income statements, balance sheets, and legal contracts. She thought of her friend and her baby in the fancy English baby carriage.

"No, I don't."

# CHAPTER 48

Hassan couldn't sleep. He lay on the pull-out sofa in the living room, it was hot and very humid, the air still. He remembered as a child, in Aden, when it was this hot they soaked the sheets and slept on the rooftops. That was so long ago; so much had changed. The living room windows were open, and he listened to the sounds of the city, horns, traffic, someone talking on the sidewalk. He waited for the sound of footsteps, sirens, the police.

There had been a time when he had looked forward to this day. He had believed in the cause with a fervor which made no sense to him now. He made all the preparations asked of him. He received a monthly stipend from Nabir, after all, extra money that was a big help to his family in Aden, and he had sworn an oath of obedience.

Be patient, he was told, you will likely wait for years, and when the time comes, you will strike. He built a small business. His parents, if they could have seen him, would have been so proud. He never dreamed he would be so successful. He dared not say it, but it was true what they said about America. And so gradually, over the years, he came to dread the call to action, hoping, almost convincing himself, that he would be forgotten. With Pazhman's arrival his heart sank.

Ever since Pazhman had arrived he had felt his blood pressure rise. Could such a thing be felt? He thought so. The Americans paid a great deal of attention to their blood pressure, Hassan knew. His own doctor had disapproved when Hassan told him that he smoked a pack of cigarettes every day. He was proud that he could afford to buy so many cigarettes, but the doctor has responded by clucking his tongue and saying that he must stop, so Hassan had not told him about the water pipe he smoked after dinner.

Thinking of his doctor reminded him that he had a dentist's appointment coming up. I will cancel it, he thought. What is the point as I will be dead soon enough. But how would it come to pass, he wondered?

Perhaps there is a way, he thought. Perhaps if I go to the police, and tell them who I am, and betray the others, I will be spared. This new idea turned in his mind. But what then of my family, my mother and father, and my brothers and sisters and nieces and nephews? What would become of them?

He closed his eyes and took a deep breath. It seemed hopeless, but he must find a way out. Somehow.

Hassan remembered how Pazhman had behaved when he returned from the zoo that afternoon, his eyes bulging, furious. "I will kill the bitch," he said. "The woman stands in our way. So she must die, and then we will proceed with what we must do."

Hassan watched Pazhman's mouth curled in smile and he realized that Pazhman, the man they had waited for all these years, was insane.

* * *

The next day, Rodney watched as Pazhman carefully prepared the device. First he removed a hot water bottle from its cardboard box. He discarded the bottle and inserted the explosive, with its complicated fuse, into the empty box. It fit perfectly. Then he replaced the box inside the white paper bag from the pharmacy where the hot water bottle had been purchased. On the outside of the bag he wrote the name and address for the delivery.

"This is the address, and this is the woman," said Pazhman. He showed Rodney the newspaper article with the photo of Kim and her father.

Ninety minutes later Rodney stood in front of the heavy glass and wrought iron door until the doorman opened it. He handed the bag to the doorman. The doorman looked at the name printed on the side of the bag, noticed the logo of the drugstore, and retreated into the lobby with the bag. That was it.

Rodney carried a newspaper under his arm, which he unfolded and pretended to read while he sat on a bench by the granite wall surrounding Central Park.

He didn't have to wait long. Just before 7 p.m., Kim returned. He watched as she approached from Madison Avenue, she had a tote bag under her arm, and was wearing a blue skirt and suit coat, but also sneakers, which allowed her to walk briskly. The doorman opened the door for her and in she went.

The doorman would hand her the delivery, Pazhman had said. She would be confused, because she hadn't ordered anything from the pharmacy, and perhaps she would look inside the shopping bag, maybe even open the box. Maybe she would immediately suspect something, but it would be too late. Pazhman had considered telling Rodney to wait, perhaps detonating the device when he thought she was in the elevator, where the blast would be more lethal, but the cellular connection might not be possible once the bomb was in the elevator. He had decided Rodney should wait 30 seconds, then detonate it. That would give the doorman ample time to fetch the shopping bag from the small storage room near the front door.

"Thanks Jimmy, how are you today?" asked Kim.

"Very good, Miss Conrad, and you?"

"Not too bad," she smiled, without breaking her stride as she headed across the black and white marble checkerboard floor toward the elevator.

Jimmy watched her as she crossed the lobby and stepped into the elevator where Wally, the elevator man, was waiting. Then he remembered the package.

"Miss Conrad, wait, you have a package -"

Jimmy stepped quickly toward the mailroom just as Rodney pressed the final number on his cellphone. Kim was in the elevator when the bomb exploded.

She rushed into the smoke-filled lobby. Jimmy was on the floor, leaning against the wall. He looked unhurt. The mailroom wall had shielded him. Jimmy put his fingers in his ears and shook his head. Kim coughed, then dialed 911.

# CHAPTER 49

"We're taking you off the team," said Gambler, once the others had left the emergency morning meeting.

Her mind raced. Her cover was blown. She would be lucky to be reassigned as a postal inspector in Nebraska.

"I think that's a mistake, sir."

"You said it yourself, this isn't what you do. And besides, it's getting too dangerous. Pazhman has taken a personal interest in you, he knows your face. I have to take steps to protect you."

"I don't need protection," said Kim.

He put his elbows on the desk and clapped his hands together as if in prayer.

"The thing is, I have a job to do, and I don't need to be distracted by worrying about one of my agents."

"Would you say that if it was Mahan, or Baumgartner?"

"They wouldn't be in this situation."

"What does that mean?" asked Kim.

"It means if it was Mahan, or Baumgartner, Pazhman would probably be dead by now. There, I said it."

Kim was speechless. She didn't know how to reply. His words stung, and it showed on her face.

"I'm sorry, that was a cheap shot." Gambler took a deep breath and looked at her. "You're entitled to a security detail, you know."

"Thanks, but I'll pass."

"Might be better if you got out of the city for a while, at least until we figure out what's going on. You got somewhere you can go?"

So that was it, she realized. He had never thought much of her, and now he was using the bombing as an excuse to get rid of her. He'd already decided she was unsuited for fieldwork, but she was confused, hadn't he been the one to push her into it in the first place?

If only I'd taken the shot when I had the chance, she thought.

221

Now she would be reassigned. End up doing what she had been hired to do originally, forensic accounting. Assigned to a cubicle somewhere, probably in a windowless basement office in Virginia.

"Got anywhere you can go? Out of the city?" asked Gambler.

"My family has a farm upstate, I could go there," she heard herself saying. She felt lightheaded, unfocused, her mind drifting.

"Why don't you? And we'll be in touch. A few days off will do you good."

"This is bullshit," she said.

"It is what it is," he replied.

She smiled. Next time, she thought, if there is a next time and she had him in her sights, she'd kill the son of a bitch.

# CHAPTER 50

Dennehy spent the morning watching a utility crew dig a hole in the road. It was his third day with the same crew. They were working on a gas line. Every once in a while a car approached, and Dennehy waved it past, then he went back to watching the men work in the hole. He had gotten to know them, since there were long intervals when no cars passed.

The men told him they would be digging a lot of holes. The project was scheduled to take months.

*Great, just what I signed on for when I joined the police. Now I can expect to be directing traffic and watching work crews dig holes for the rest of my life. It'll get even better when winter sets in*, he thought to himself.

He had a terrible hangover, which didn't help, and his bad leg made his back hurt when he stood for long periods. Those weren't the only reasons for his present funk. Jill hadn't called him in a week, and no e-mails or text messages. She'd unfriended him on Facebook.

He hadn't tried to contact her either. He was trying to send a message, but what message? He would have to ask his shrink, if he ever went to see him again. He had a pretty good idea what he would say. Lance Dennehy, former platoon sergeant with the 75th Rangers, was feeling sorry for himself, and wanted the world to know.

"Hey why don't you take your thumb out of your ass and hand me my Thermos?"

Dennehy looked over at the crew chief, MacFarland, who was standing in the hole. They called him Mac.

"It's not like you're doing anything," said Mac. His insults reminded Dennehy of Don Rickles.

"In the front seat of my pickup," he said.

Dennehy crossed the road to the pick-up and returned with the Thermos and handed it down to Mac. "Don't worry, I used my

223

other hand."

"Hey, that's good," said Mac.

Dennehy watched as Mac twisted the plastic cup off the top of the Thermos and poured coffee into it. Mac sipped the coffee, then spoke to one of the other men in the ditch. "I didn't tell you to stop working."

He looked up at Dennehy. "How long were you in the service?"

"How'd you know I was in the service?"

"'Cause I'm observant. You still got an Army haircut. You know you can let it grow now, or didn't they tell you that?"

"I like it short," said Dennehy.

"Where'd you hurt your leg?"

"Afghanistan."

"Doesn't seem to slow you down, if you don't mind my saying so."

Denneny didn't mind. Most people were too uneasy talking about it. "I get around okay."

"That's good. How old are you?" asked Mac.

"Twenty-three."

"You got your whole life ahead of you. So you decided to join the police department, huh?"

"There was an opening," said Dennehy, then he added, "but I was thinking I might apply to the State Police eventually. So this project's gonna be a few months?"

Mac sipped his coffee. "At least. Beefing up the gas lines for a new development. New housing's going in for Yorke Aerospace. They're really ramping up, big defense contract, that means we gotta build infrastructure, too."

Dennehy had heard about it from Jill. But it was a secretive company, and she never could tell him details.

A car approached. Dennehy waved it by. Such a lightly trafficked road, a few orange cones would have done the trick, but rules required that the utility crew pay a police detail. Most of the guys jumped at the chance for well-paying overtime, but with his disability payments and salary, Dennehy already had more money than he could spend. Extra money only got him into trouble.

A white Toyota Corolla slowed as it approached the construction area. The driver, a young man with dark hair and a beard, looked uncertain at the bright orange detour sign. He's probably lost, thought Dennehy. Woodboro was a small town, Dennehy recognized many of the cars that passed, but not this one.

A police officer looking at him made Mahmud nervous.

"Keep going, don't stop," said Pazhman. "It's just road work."

But it was too late, he was almost at a full stop. Mahmud had also already made eye contact with Dennehy, who gestured for Pazhman to roll down the window.

Pazhman glared at Mahmud.

Mahmud stopped the car. Pazhman lowered the window.

"Where are you trying to go?" asked Dennehy.

The men in the car seemed tense. He noticed that. They looked foreign, which probably explained it, and they were lost. He was immediately reminded of his first tour in Iraq, before Afghanistan, where he had spent countless hours at checkpoints, checking passing motorists for IEDs and weapons. There was something about the men that sparked this memory. They were like the thousands of Iraqis he had questioned: tense, polite, scared.

"We're looking for Lake Menahag," said Mahmud, though he already knew the way.

"You're in the right ballpark, you going to the hotel?"

"Yes, we're visiting a friend," said Pazhman.

"Follow the detour, it'll take you back to the Route 32, then just follow the signs."

Pazhman smiled. "Thank you!" he said, and the car drove away.

Lots of people drove nervously in the presence of law enforcement, but Dennehy had no reason to stop them for it. Still, there was no reason why he couldn't make a note of the license plate, for practice, if nothing else.

Then he returned to Mac, who was drinking his coffee. The men were talking about a recent trade made by the Red Sox, and Dennehy pretended he cared.

225

# CHAPTER 51

It had been Mahmud's job to find the house. The specifications, sent from Pakistan, were precise: a large barn with suitable open space, far from prying eyes. Mahmud had posed as a successful businessman, a foreigner who lived in the city and was looking for a weekend place where he could practice his hobby, sculpture. It wasn't much of a stretch. His business, which was, of course, a front, provided vague cover, International Equity Partners, Inc. He dressed the part: expensive Italian loafers, dress shirt, tailored trousers. He leased a Mercedes and spent a week scouting properties. The house he chose was slightly dilapidated, but the barn was enormous, and it had electricity. It was perfect, Mahmud told the realtor.

Then the cell waited. A year passed. Two. Mahmud furnished the house, and obtained the tools as instructed – he didn't know why. He even began creating sculpture according to the specifications that had been given to him. Angular structures made from wood and discarded metal. They didn't look half bad. Anyway, even if they did, they completed the narrative. He visited the house nearly every weekend and became known in the village. Occasionally he invited the others to visit, Hassan and Rodney, and they enjoyed barbecues and long walks in the woods.

Hassan hated his visits. Mahmud spoke of the struggle to come, and he drank heavily, even though it was forbidden. Once, there was a problem. Mahmud drank beer all afternoon, and after dinner, insisted they visit a strip bar in the neighboring town. Hassan did not think this was a good idea. Sometimes when Mahmud got drunk he said things he should not say. Besides, they didn't want to draw attention to themselves. Hassan took the car keys and threw them in the woods. The next morning, they spent two hours looking before they finally found them. Mahmud was furious. That was the last time Hassan had visited the country house.

Mahmud looked nervously at Pazhman when they pulled up the long drive that led to the house. He wanted Pazhman to be pleased.

226

"No one ever visits here, it is very quiet," said Mahmud.

Pazhman did not reply. Mahmud had been listing the property's virtues throughout the car ride, like a real estate agent, and Pazhman was tired of it. He would see with his own eyes, and know soon enough if the property was suitable. It had better be, he thought.

The dirt road was more than a quarter mile long, most of it through woods and heavy underbrush. It led to a long meadow with tall grass. Pazhman felt a rush of excitement when the farmhouse came into view. It was a moment he had anticipated for so long.

He saw Rodney rush from the house as they stopped in front of the barn. A few moments later, Hassan followed. They greeted Pazhman, and Mahmud eagerly gave Pazhman a full tour. He showed him the house, the barn and the meadows that surrounded it. When they were done Pazhman stood on the porch and once again surveyed the barn and the expansive fields bordered by dense woodland. He nodded. There were no visible neighbors, and the large clearing provided a defensive buffer against nosy intruders.

"You have done well," he said.

They unloaded the explosives and all the equipment they had accumulated, including the four cases smuggled in by the unfortunate Jemel. Under Pazhman's directions, they cut and installed a plywood floor in the van, then set to work building a counter top in the van to house the electronics. Hassan drilled a hole in the roof so an antenna could be installed on top of the vehicle. Two small office chairs were put in place. Pazhman climbed in and sat down at the counter. He examined the woodwork.

"It's good," he said. "Now run an antenna to the top of the barn."

It was late afternoon by the time Rodney set up a ladder and climbed to the top of the barn's roof, where there was a vent. He attached a metal bracket and then lowered a rope and pulled up a 6-foot antenna, which he bolted to the bracket. When he was done, he attached the wire to the antenna and climbed off the roof.

When he returned to the barn, he saw that Mahmud was already busy setting up the computer in the van. There were other components as well, quite a lot of electronics, and a TV monitor, which Rodney did not understand. He watched Mahmud and Pazhman work for the remainder of the afternoon, setting up the system and trouble-shooting. He realized Pazhman must be a brilliant man to understand such complicated electronics.

When they finished, as the sun was setting, Pazhman walked out of the barn and looked at the field. He walked into the meadow, paced all the way back to the woods, and returned.

"Have you a chainsaw?" he asked Mahmud.

Mahmud shook his head.

"Get one. These trees must come down."

# CHAPTER 52

Kim began her first loop of the reservoir at noon. She wanted to be finished with her run in time for visitors' hours at the hospital, so she could visit her father before she left town. She was going to take Gambler's advice. He was right, she needed to get out of town for a while. She would head to Wild Meadows, her family's retreat upstate. She didn't want to stay in town, the apartment building lobby was a shambles, and she felt guilty about bringing disruption to her neighbors. She decided to do her run, visit her Dad, and then throw a few bags in her car.

Jack waited by the granite pump house, leaning against the chain link fence that surrounded that reservoir. Kim saw him and stopped running. She interlocked her fingers and put her hands on top of her head, catching her breath. She didn't say anything.

"I'm sorry," said Jack. He was wearing a wrinkled polo shirt and khaki shorts and sneakers. "I didn't dare call. I didn't want to put you in a compromising position."

"You already have," said Kim.

"I didn't mean to. Look, I'm a journalist. I pick up on things. I see you're on to something, I connect the dots, discuss it with a few colleagues who have their own sources. That's how things work."

"It's not how they're supposed to work, Jack. We're supposed to be in this together. What you did endangered the investigation, not to mention my career, not to mention that there's a maniac out there who you've given aid and comfort to."

"Oh spare me that crap. The public deserves transparency."

She shook her head. "Even when it means helping terrorists? I hope you're proud of yourself. You got a scoop. Now go to hell."

She began running down the path, wiping tears from her cheeks. When she turned to look back he was gone.

Before leaving the city she paid a visit to the hospital. She decided she wouldn't tell her father about the bomb.

"I'll think you'll be surprised," a nurse in the hallway said before Kim entered her father's room. "We adjusted his medication, he's much more lucid now, but still very weak."

Benton Conrad looked like he had aged 10 years. He brightened when Kim entered the room. "Well, I guess I screwed up, I'm not as good a businessman as everybody said. I'm sorry."

"You don't have to apologize, Dad."

"Yes I do, and I'll make it up to you. I promise."

Kim smiled, "You just get better."

He took her hand.

"You know what, you don't need me. You never did, and for all the strings I pulled for other people, I never had to pull any for you."

He looked so frail, Kim felt tears welling up. You're telling me this now? she thought.

She cleared her throat. "I heard about the ambassadorship."

He made a dismissive gesture.

"I had to remove my name from consideration. Someone, I don't know who, leaked accusations out to derail my nomination. Probably for the best, you know how damp London can be. Still, I may have made some bad financial decisions, but I don't think I broke any laws. Proving it may be another matter."

"That's not fair," she said.

"It's the way the game is played, honey, and anyway, I'm no angel. There'll be other opportunities, don't worry." He smiled bravely. "They haven't seen the last of me."

Kim arrived at the family country home later that afternoon. Kim's great-grandfather, Cyrus, had purchased the nearly 300 acres during the 1920s. They called the house Wild Meadows.

She wandered the rooms, thinking that this would be one of the last visits to this house that held so many memories of her father and mother. It would have to be sold, she was sure, with all the other assets. She phoned the hospital to tell her Dad she had arrived. Her stepmother answered the phone. No, she said, her Dad was resting. Better that they didn't talk.

230

Kim sat on the sofa and turned on the TV. There was a summer corn festival going on. A corn festival? What in Christ am I going to do in Woodboro? she wondered. She turned off the TV and went to the house's secret room, accessed through a concealed door at the back of the cedar closet.

Her dad kept the shotguns there, and a few items that were too valuable to leave out in the open, like an antique clock and some family photos in heirloom silver frames. Her eyes settled on her dad's Beretta 9mm and ammo. She picked up the pistol and two boxes of ammo and left. She locked the door behind her.

She put her pistol and ammunition in a rucksack and went to her bedroom, where she changed into shorts, sneakers and a T-shirt. She found a bottle of her father's single malt whiskey and a shot glass in the bar and put those in the rucksack too, along with a bottle of water.

Kim put on the rucksack and a floppy canvas hat and hiked down the driveway and through the field surrounding the house. She knew where she was going, she had walked the fields, meadows, dirt roads and trails of the property countless times over the years. The place had once been a working farm, and some of the fields were still cultivated by neighboring farmers. The original farmhouse was long gone, but the old rubbish dump was still there. As a child Kim and her brother had explored it, finding discarded bottles and rusted hardware. Kim rummaged through the old rubbish tip looking for glass bottles to shoot at. She carried them to the edge of a nearby field and set them up on a fence and paced off 20 yards. She poured herself a shot of whiskey and loaded the pistol. The first bullet went wide. The second splintered a wooden fence rail. The third shattered a bottle.

She spent the rest of the afternoon shooting until she was drunk and out of bullets, and out of bottles to shoot at.

# CHAPTER 53

Neither Hassan nor Rodney had ever cut down a tree before. They argued over the best way to do it, and when they were finally in agreement, Rodney started the chain saw and began cutting. It was a locust tree, about 50 feet tall. Halfway through the trunk the saw got stuck.

Pazhman was in the barn's loft when he realized the saw had stopped. He heard shouting. He climbed down from the loft and walked outside where he saw they had failed to cut a notch and then back-cut the tree, as any fool would do. Now the full weight of the locust had clamped down on the saw.

"Go find a rope, quickly," he snapped.

After several minutes of frantic searching in the barn Rodney located a rope, and a ladder. Pazhman instructed Rodney to climb the tree as high as he could, which was done with great diffculty because there weren't enough branches to grab hold of. Rodney shimmied up, the rope tied to his belt. Hassan shouted advice as to which branches he should hold on to. When he was as high as he dared go, Rodney tied the rope to the tree and shimmied back down, scraping his stomach badly. Pazhman shook his head. Mahmud yelled at him for being careless.

The two men hauled on the rope. The tree swayed, and Pazhman was able to free the saw. Then he showed them the correct procedure for cutting down a tree. They watched as the tree crashed down in the field, away from the driveway.

"Now chop off the branches and then cut down the others," he said, handing the saw to Rodney.

They spent the rest of the morning cutting the remaining trees and carting away the branches. In the middle of the day when it was very hot they took a break from their work and drank water in the barn. They climbed to the loft to see what Pazhman was doing.

Hassan watched silently as Pazhman measured and cut strips of C-4 with confidence. He packed them in tin baking trays they had purchased at the supermarket. Hassan marveled at his skill as

Pazhman worked with speed and confidence making a trigger mechanism. He had never seen anything like it, it was ingenious, and Pazhman's fingers worked with such precision and confidence it was as if he had made hundreds of such devices.

After a while they returned to their work on the trees. Hassan was cutting a branch when he saw a car approaching. It was a BMW sedan driven by a middle-aged woman in a suit.

She stopped the car near where Hassan was working and got out of the car. She slammed the door shut.

"What the hell are you doing? Why are you cutting these trees?" She sounded angry.

"Who are you?" asked Hassan.

"I'm Gloria, I'm the real estate agent who looks after this place. Who are you?"

Hassan wasn't sure what to do. "Better you talk to my boss," he said.

"Where's Mahmud?" she demanded.

Hassan certainly didn't want the woman going into the barn, but she seemed brassy, judging from the way she had slammed the car door. He didn't want to have to kill her. He didn't want anyone to kill her. While he was struggling to find something to say, Mahmud appeared.

"Gloria, Gloria, what is the matter?" he asked.

"Mahmud, you can't cut down trees, what are you doing?"

He thought for a moment, than replied. "It's for my art, my sculpture, I need the wood."

The explanation seemed far-fetched to Hassan, but it was better than anything he could have come up with. Eccentric artist chopping down trees with a chainsaw. Chainsaw sculpture? Maybe. Hassan took a moment to absorb this. Gloria was also, momentarily, confused by the absurdity of his response. She quickly recovered.

"Mahmud, there's nothing in the lease that gives you the right to remove trees. That's damage to the property. You'll have to pay."

"Okay, so I'll pay, it's not a problem."

"It is a problem. These are grown trees. What good does paying for them do?" She walked around the downed trees, looking at them and shaking her head.

Mahmud shrugged. "Okay, I'm sorry. So what do you want me to do?"

Gloria looked flabbergasted. "In America we don't just cut down trees. I don't know how they do things where you come from. I'm going to have to tell the owner, I'm sorry."

"Okay, I'm sorry too, I didn't know. Now I know." It sounded pathetic, Hassan thought, but anything to get rid of her.

"I have to notify the owner," she repeated.

Pazhman watched the exchange from his perch in the loft. He was considering his options. The woman who had arrived seemed to be upset about something, perhaps there was trouble. But he couldn't hear what she was saying, so he wasn't sure what he should do. He suspected she was upset about the trees. He saw her get back in her car and drive away. He hoped she wouldn't return, not for another day, anyway. Mahmud and Hassan watched her leave, too. Then they went to the barn and explained the situation to Pazhman.

As soon as she was back on the main road, Gloria phoned Art Lewis, the owner. Lewis was a lawyer in town who had invested heavily in real estate with the idea of developing housing that would be needed as Yorke Aerospace expanded. Until the land was developed, he found tenants.

He was attending a conference on real estate investment in Las Vegas. There was a lot of noise in the background. It sounded like a party. Music. Splashing water.

"Art, it's Gloria."

"What's up?"

"I went to check at the Mill Pond property, you know the artist from New York, foreign guy?"

"What about it?" asked Lewis.

"Art, he had a chain saw. He took down a bunch of trees."

"What?"

"He's chopping down trees," she repeated.

"Did you tell him to stop?"

"Of course."

"Why the hell's he chopping down trees?" he asked.

"For sculpture, he said."

"Sculpture?"

"That's what he said."

"This is that foreign guy?"

"Yeah."

"Okay, you know what, I want him out," said Lewis.

"Art, he signed a lease."

"I don't give a shit. I want him out." Art Lewis was nothing if not decisive.

"On what grounds?"

"They're chopping down my trees."

Lewis was planning on breaking ground at the property in the coming year. He might want those trees. He hung up the phone and speed dialed Frank Burke, the Woodboro chief of police. He was nothing if not efficient, and was planning to meet friends in the bar momentarily.

"Ed, what can I do for you?" asked the Chief.

"I want to file a police report," said Lewis.

"What do you want to report?"

"I got a tenant, on the old farm on Mill Pond Road. The guy's chopping down my trees. I want a police report in the file, official."

"Can you stop by the station?"

"Frank, I'm in Vegas."

"Alright, I'll take care of it as soon as I can."

"Thanks."

Chief Burke put down the phone and scratched his head. He saw Dennehy talking to his secretary who was scheduling utility crew details. Maybe he could send Dennehy? He decided against it. Art Lewis was the richest man in Woodboro, and had considerable influence over the town government, which meant he had considerable influence over the police department budget and contracts with police officers, including the chief. If Art Lewis had a problem, he would take care of it personally.

235

# CHAPTER 54

Ed Robertson, a lanky pilot in khaki trousers, white shirt and aviator sunglasses entered the big hangar at Yorke Aerospace. He joined a knot of engineers who stood around the newest variant of Yorke remotely piloted aircraft, the XB-46. It looked sleek and lethal, like a shark. Robertson sometimes wondered if the design was all about aerodynamics and functionality or if the designers gave it features just to make it look more menacing. Maybe he was reading into it because he had worked on the XB-46 for the past nine months and knew what it could do. The XB-46 had more advanced navigation, communication, and targeting systems than any RPA Yorke had yet developed. It was stealthy too, and could fly longer, faster, and higher. It could also carry a heavier payload, which meant it would soon be the deadliest PRA in the arsenal.

"How's it look?" asked Robertson.

"We're good to go," replied Hank Goss, one of the engineers.

"Good day for it," said Robertson.

"Wind five to ten out of the northeast."

Robertson nodded and began his walk-around. He liked to do a thorough inspection before taking the controls. He had flown the XB-46 more than a dozen times since its initial roll-out. They'd already established, after the first couple of flights, that she would be a major success for Yorke Aerospace. Now Robertson was working his way through a long list of test procedures designed to measure the flight characteristics against the required military specs.

Robertson was a graduate of the Air Force Academy. Before joining the development team at Yorke, he had been one of the first generation to make the transition from manned aircraft (in his case, the F-16) to unmanned vehicles. He'd piloted RPAs on more than three hundred missions over Iraq, Afghanistan and a few other places. He was considered one of the leading experts on unmanned missions, so he figured he'd made a good career move coming to Yorke. The use of RPA's was skyrocketing, and Yorke was well poised to be a dominant force in the industry.

Just wait until the sky starts filling with civilian RPAs, thought Robertson, then his shares of company stock would increase further. Life was good.

After he had finished the pre-flight check, Robertson went down the hallway that led to the flight control room. He stopped at the men's room, as he always did (these aircraft could stay up a long time) and then, against his better judgment, poured himself a cup of coffee, stirring in a pack of powdered milk and sugar. When he was ready he settled into the comfortable leather chair at the console and powered up the flight controls and video monitors.

It won't be long before there are no more manned fighters or bombers, he thought. No more aircraft carriers. No more aerial combat as we know it. His own dad had flown 127 combat missions off the USS Forrestal over Vietnam, and his granddad had flown an F-4F Corsair in the Pacific. But Robertson had opted for the Air Force, not the Navy, and he flew an RPA. His father didn't understand, and still referred to them as drones. Robertson always corrected him. He didn't fly drones, he was a pilot, flying remotely piloted aircraft. Still, no matter how much he and the other pilots tried to convince themselves, it wasn't the same thing as a Corsair in a dogfight with a Zero, or an FA-18 operating off the pitching deck of a carrier. Sometimes he wished he had been born twenty years earlier.

Half an hour later the XB-46 circled at 10,000 feet. Robertson methodically worked his way through the test procedures while the computer recorded the flight dynamics. He checked the video feed, and adjusted the camera so it zoomed in on Yorke Aerospace with its sprawling facility, parking lots, hangars, manufacturing facilities and office buildings. He followed the main highways over the town of Woodboro. With his hands on both joysticks, he increased the speed and brought the RPA through a series of high-speed maneuvers. She performed flawlessly. He flew for 10 minutes over rolling farmland and forests, then it was time to bring her home.

Robertson set the controls to let the computer guidance system do all the navigation, calculate wind and weather, and land the XB-

46 without his help. All Robertson had to do was watch. He let go of the controls, sat back and took a deep breath. This was too easy.

He watched the monitor as the aircraft circled over the vast state forest, descending rapidly to line up its approach. He shook his head. *One day I'm going to be out of a job,* he thought, as he watched the trees fly by on the black and white video monitor.

Then the screen went black.

Perplexed, Robertson tapped on the keyboard, but quickly realized it wasn't the monitor. The camera had shut down.

*So much for a perfect mission,* he thought. He would have to check that out as soon as the vehicle returned to the hangar. He decided to switch to the back-up camera, but it was the same: a black screen.

Robertson checked another monitor which displayed a map of the area, flight data and location of the RPA. Video feed or no video feed, it was right where it was supposed to be, heading for home.

And then the screen went blank. Static. Then color bars. No signal. Robertson sat up in his seat, scrambling to reset the screen, but there was nothing. He picked up the phone and called the tower.

Hank Goss answered.

"You got a visual on 46?" asked Robertson.

"No, why?" replied Goss.

"It should be on the approach, 2,000 feet about half-a-mile out."

Goss picked up a pair of binoculars and scanned the horizon.

"I don't see it."

"It's gotta be out there."

Goss checked again. "Nothing."

Robertson punched up the control tower approach radar. It would show anything flying higher than 300 feet. The screen was clear.

"God damn it!" said Robertson, as the realization sank in. His heart was beating fast. He'd just lost a $4 million experimental aircraft.

\* \* \*

238

With a flick of his thumb, Pazhman activated the transmitter. The signal on the monitor flickered and a black and white image appeared. He adjusted the joystick and saw immediately that he had control. He felt relief and the men seated behind him in the van smiled at each other. It was just as it had been months earlier on the computer simulator in Peshawar. Pazhman had never doubted the genius of the engineers and computer hackers employed by Professor Al Fariz. He had risked his life because he had faith in it, but still, he was relieved.

Pazhman keyed in a command and watched as the image on the screen, an aerial view of the forest, became more defined. He turned his attention to the computer monitor, which indicated the guidance program was working.

He had practiced this more than a hundred times, but he had never actually done the real thing. Not like this. His palms felt sweaty as he gripped the pistol-handled controls. He pressed the joystick forward and watched on the monitor as the RPA dropped to 100 feet, as low as he dared. It reminded him, in a way, of flying his falcons as a boy.

Mahmud and Rodney rushed from the barn to the field outside to search the sky. They were like boys, excited. Hassan remained in the van, watching the monitor, and saw the forest canopy whipping by. Three minutes later Rodney shouted "I see it!"

Pazhman eased back the throttle and pushed the stick forward and watched on the monitor as the barn and the driveway came into view. The RPA slowed to almost a stall and then dropped down into the grassy field by the barn. Pazhman killed the power and released the controls.

They had done it!

The men stood around the aircraft, as if afraid to touch the beast. The XB-46 was cutting-edge, with carbon fiber wings angled back, and a sinister looking fuselage. The propellers were different too, fan-shaped like jungle machetes. Yet, despite its radical and obviously sophisticated design, Pazhman had been able to intercept it easily, just as the professor had predicted. The professor truly was someone worthy of following, not that he ever doubted that. He was right, too, when he had lectured him. America did not have a monopoly on advanced technology. Weren't most of the best science students from Asia, Pakistan, and India? But the Americans still thought they held the advantage, and that was a weakness to be exploited. The more reliant on technology they were, the more vulnerable they became.

"Quickly, bring it inside." Pazhman spoke harshly, and the men snapped into action.

They pushed the aircraft across the field to the front of the barn where, after several minutes, they figured out how to unlock the wings and fold them back. Then they wheeled the machine into the barn. Pazhman didn't want to waste any time. The interception program was designed to disable the guidance system and other functions, including its transponder. But he wanted to make sure. He used a square screwdriver to remove the cover to the main electronics panel and located the transponder. He cut the wires and removed it.

Hassan looked anxious.

"Will they be able to locate us?" he asked.

Pazhman shook his head. "No."

Pazhman hoped he was right. He was fairly certain he was. He looked at the others. "Now there is much work to do."

# CHAPTER 55

*New York Harbor*

Petty Officer Second Class Mark Rodriguez could think of worse ways to spend a summer weekend. The truth was he looked forward to his monthly duty, a few days away from his wife, Theresa, and the baby. But he didn't tell her that, of course. He pretended he hated having to leave them.

It was a break, and it sure beat the hell out of doing inventory at the Bed and Bath Emporium, where he was an assistant warehouse manager. His boss hadn't been thrilled when he reminded him that he had reserve duty, and that there was no way on God's green Earth, except maybe for death or an Act of Congress, that he could get out of it. Not with the G20 and the President in town. National security and all that.

"All right, all right, go and play with your little boats, we'll manage without you, somehow," his boss said.

And so he found himself not in a warehouse counting terry cloth towels and bath gel, but in New York Harbor on a sunny June day, on a Coast Guard Cutter cruising between Governor's Island and the Statue of Liberty.

"Showing the flag," his skipper, Lieutenant Emerson called it.

Rodriguez loved the Coast Guard. It wasn't like the Navy, where he'd spent three years out of high school. In the Coast Guard the culture was a little more relaxed, and Rodriguez liked that. The enlisted men were encouraged to think for themselves, to take responsibility. Not like in the Navy, where you were supervised by an officer at every turn. But there was one thing about the Coast Guard he didn't like. Their equipment was older, and budgets small, which meant they didn't get to practice on their weapons as often as Rodriguez would have liked. Hell, he hadn't fired the .50 caliber in more than a year, and he'd only fired the Bofors gun once. Still, they said it was the small budgets and crappy gear that made the Coast Guard famous for improvising, making do with less. It was why they were good in a pinch.

*Still, it's kinda screwed up. Here we are on picket duty, getting ready to guard the President of the United States and I ain't fired the machine gun in over a year.*

He looked at the foredeck and saw fellow crewman Dave Simmons studying the .50 cal.

"Hey Simmons, if you have to fire that, you know what to do?" he asked.

"Yeah, of course," replied Simmons.

"What do you do?"

"You pull this, then you squeeze that, and you look down at this doohickey."

"Doohickey?"

"Yeah."

"We call that the main sight."

"Whatever."

"Do me a favor," said Rodriguez, "the shit hits the fan, I'll do the shooting, you load."

242

# CHAPTER 56

*Woodboro, New York*

The farmland outside Woodboro always brought back memories for Chief Burke. As a boy, he must have traversed these fields and meadows a thousand times, sometimes with his .20 gauge, hunting doves. But those days were long gone, and he hadn't been dove hunting in ages. It still looked like the place he remembered, with the exception of a few new houses here and there.

But soon it would all be gone, the old fences and dirt roads. The bucolic atmosphere lost forever. The landscape would be graded, scraped of its natural character, new roads and sewer lines brought in for housing developments. He supposed it was for the best. It meant jobs and economic growth where jobs had been scarce and life tough, at least in his lifetime. If all this were developed, Chief Burke didn't think a few trees would be missed. He figured maybe Ed Lewis wanted an excuse to get rid of the tenants early, so they could break ground.

Mahmud and Rodney were putting up a large blue tarp near the end of the driveway, in front of the barn. It was the biggest tarp they could find, 40 by 20 feet. They had tied two corners to trees, and two corners to poles they had erected. The problem was the center of the tarp drooped down almost to the ground. Mahmud and Rodney were arguing over what to do. They didn't notice the police cruiser until it was halfway up the dirt road leading to the farm.

The chief pulled the cruiser to a stop and got out of the car. He took a moment to adjust his belt and put on his campaign hat before approaching the two men. As he walked toward them he noticed the tree stumps and sawdust by the side of the driveway. The two men were standing by the tarp, watching him.

"You the tenant here?" he asked. "Mr. Mahmud?"

Mahmud nodded.

"Don't think we've met. I'm Chief Burke, Woodboro Police."

He smiled and shook hands with the two men, who stood mute.

"How you getting' on out here?"

Mahmud nodded. "Very well."

"We love it," added Rodney.

"Yeah, good country." The Chief looked at the big meadow near the barn and took a deep breath. "This is quite a spread. What a day? Huh?"

The two men smiled and nodded in agreement.

The Chief continued: "Reason I'm out here is the owner complained about the trees, asked me to take a look. Doesn't want any more trees chopped down. You understand, I'll have to file a report, damage to property."

"I do understand, of course," said Mahmud.

"Whatch y'all do out here, anyway?" asked the Chief.

Mahmud had his answer rehearsed. "I am a sculptor."

"Sculpture, huh? You have a studio in the barn?"

A look of surprise, fear, flickered across Mahmud's face. Burke noticed it.

"Yes, a studio of sorts," he said.

"I'd love to see your work. There's something fascinating about the creative mind at work. Don't often get to see an artist's studio, except my Aunt Phyllis, she liked to paint landscapes. 'Course, she was just an amateur. May I take a look?"

Before they could answer, the Chief started toward the open door of the barn.

"Love these great old barns, and this one looks really old," he said.

"Yes, very old," said Mahmud, trying not to sound nervous.

Up in the loft, Pazhman lay on the floor and watched the policeman talk to Mahmud, then walk into the barn. The Chief noticed the scraps of lumber on the ground, and Pazhman realized he would soon see the wire that ran from the roof of the van to the window of the barn loft. Why didn't Hassan or Mahmud stop him before he entered the barn? The idiots stood there like statues. Now it was too late, Pazhman decided he must act. He stood up and began descending the steps from the loft.

The Chief looked at Pazhman, surprised to see someone in the barn. "Hello," he said.

"Hello there," Pazhman smiled.

"Love these old barns," said the Chief.

"Yes, it's quite a lovely old place, isn't it?" replied Pazhman.

At first the Chief didn't understand why there would be three foreigners staying here. Then he figured it out. They were artists. They were gay. Spending the weekend out of the city, perhaps they had friends who owned one of the antiques shops in town. He was starting to get the picture. But where was the sculpture, where was the studio? His eyes drifted toward the loft, saw the antenna wires running down from the loft to the van. Then he saw a stack of cardboard boxes against the back wall of the barn. In Magic Marker, on the side, the contents were spelled out: DANGER: C-4, Saltieri Brothers.

Saltieri Brothers, C-4? He had seen an advisory about that just the week before.

He looked at Pazhman as it dawned on him. The Chief reached for his pistol. Pazhman was one beat faster. The knife was out of his pocket. With a single unhesitating motion he plunged it directly into the Chief's neck. Burke's eyes bulged, he tried to speak and Pazhman gave the knife a determined, twisting push.


Hassan and Rodney lifted the Chief's body and placed it in the trunk of the cruiser. Pazhman would have preferred to wait until dark, but he had no choice. Almost all police cruisers had tracking devices, Pazhman told them, so it would have to be removed immediately.

Rodney drove and Hassan followed behind in the Toyota. There was a lake two miles away. The lake had a public landing with a boat ramp.

The roads were deserted on the drive, and Rodney was relieved to find that there was no one at the lake. He pulled to a stop at the top of the concrete ramp. He placed the car in drive, then opened the door and hopped out. He watched as the police car rolled into the water. Slowly, the car floated away from the shore. It continued to float, gently drifting away. But it wasn't sinking! Hassan held his breath, watching, waiting, until finally bubbles gushed from the trunk and the police cruiser disappeared below the dark surface of the lake.

# CHAPTER 57

Hank Goss had never lost an unmanned aircraft before, let alone one that cost $4 million. He and the other engineers were anxious to recover the aircraft and determine the cause of the crash. He had gone through the flight in his head a hundred times over the past 24 hours, worried that he had done something wrong. But as hard as he racked his brain, he couldn't come up with anything.

It was the strangest thing: the way they had lost all communication with the XB-46. Even the transponder, which should have been a beacon pinpointing the aircraft's exact location, had failed. The instrumentation had simply died. And so the tech team was in overdrive.

Crews searched for the wreckage in the vast state forests that surrounded the plant. They followed an elaborate search pattern that had been calculated and programmed into laptop computers. It was slow and tedious.

So far they had found nothing.

Then Robertson had an idea.

"Let's put up another bird," he said.

He remembered as a child, he had once lost an arrow from his bow and arrow set. His father had suggested he shoot another arrow in the same direction, and watch where it fell. The second arrow landed 10 feet from the lost arrow. They could therefore use the second 46-series prototype (there were only two, XB-46T1 and XA-46T2) to find the first. Somehow.

"Jeez, I don't know," said Goss. "We don't know what happened yesterday. You sure it's a good idea to launch another. We might lose 'em both."

Robertson smiled. "Hank, we've flown this bird a hundred times. What happened yesterday was a communications malfunction. There's nothing wrong with T1. Trust me."

\* \* \*

The aircraft, tail number XB46-T1, climbed to 7,500 feet and began flying figure-eights where the first aircraft had been lost. From his vantage point in the picnic grounds half a mile from the runway, Rodney had watched as the RPA took off. He alerted Pazhman with a rare, but necessary phone call.

In the control room, air-conditioned to 62 degrees to keep the banks of computers cooled, Robertson piloted the aircraft while three anxious engineers scanned the high-resolution imagery of the forest below.

He focused on the eight large color monitors mounted above the console. He noted two large ponds to the north, and made a mental calculation. There was a chance, though it was slim, that T2 had gone down in the water, in which case they might never find it. But it was more likely that it had crashed into the trees.

There wouldn't have been much of an explosion, so they would have to look carefully for signs of broken tree trunks and branches, maybe a portion of the airframe or wing resting on top. The XB-46 could stay airborne for up to 36 hours, depending on weather and wind, so Robertson sipped his cup of coffee and settled in for a long day.

The quality of the video feed was one of the major breakthroughs of the X-46. Highly classified, the XB-46 digital system processed ground imagery faster and with more clarity than any RPAs before it. If the T2 was down there, they would find it.

The pilot scanned the monitors as the aircraft continued its search pattern. The area had been charted on a map and divided into grids. As the RPA flew above each grid, the map on the computer was framed in orange, and when nothing was found, the grid became shaded, indicating that the search was complete.

That wasn't all. The visual imagery was being recorded, digitally, and fed into computers that analyzed it for any visual anomalies, using top-secret software. It could search the ground imagery better than any of the men who sat with their eyes glued to the screen, and it would do it in real time. If they missed anything, the computer wouldn't.

And then it happened. Again.

248

Robertson was watching the first monitor when it suddenly flickered, and went dark.

"What the hell?"

He turned to the computer operator sitting beside him. "Can you patch that up on monitor 2?"

The operator tapped a few keys on his keyboard. He looked confused when nothing happened.

"Huh? This is very strange," he said.

Then the second monitor flickered, and went dark, followed in rapid succession by the others. They were flying blind.

"What the fuck?" said Robertson, a sick feeling in his stomach.

He immediately looked at the flight data feed, which was really more important that the video imagery. It had stopped. The data was frozen.

Goss and the other engineers began to frantically pound keys on the keyboard, doing back-up checks, checking wire connections, rebooting computers. They checked everything they could possibly think of. But it was no use, and Goss knew it.

He took a deep breath and dialed the control tower.

Yorke Industries had lost another one.

# CHAPTER 58

Early the next morning, Mahmud and Rodney wheeled a portable gas-powered generator from the barn to under the large blue tarp. They returned to the barn and pushed out the XB-46. Pazhman unfolded the wings and attached the cables that would start the engine, then he returned to the van and turned on the computer. The back of the van was open so Pazhman could see the drone.

His drone.

Mahmud waited for Pazhman's signal. Pazhman felt a knot in his stomach as the computer monitor came to life. Intercepting the XB-46 had been a great achievement, to be sure. Landing it had been even more impressive. What he was now about to attempt was pushing the limits of what could reasonably be expected. But then what, after all, had they worked so hard to achieve? For years, the engineers at Pachaas Talwaray had studied the American drone technology. They had stolen data, or purchased it, and accumulated as much knowledge as they could. This, now, was the moment of truth. Perhaps the UAV would fail to start, or perhaps he would lack the skills needed to take off. Such an outcome would be a devastating setback, and humiliating in front of the others. He closed his eyes and said a prayer. Then he raised his arm to signal Rodney.

Rodney ran to the generator and turned the power on. The props on the aircraft began spinning. He disconnected the starter cable and went to the right wing tip, which he held. Mahmud did the same at the left wing tip.

Rodney felt the flying machine vibrate under his grip, gently pulling to get away. Mahmud knew all too well the power of RPAs, the important role they played in the American arsenal. He had been conditioned to fear them, but now he felt they had harnessed a new power, and he was excited. Soon the tables would be turned.

In the van, Pazhman pushed the throttle forward. The engine revved with a high-pitched whine and Rodney and Mahmud held it a moment longer and then, together, let it go. The aircraft rolled down the long driveway, its wings passing easily over the stumps of the trees they had cut. After a very short distance it was airborne.

\* \* \*

Despite the loss of two RPAs, and the ongoing search, operations at Yorke continued. There were 800 employees at work on dozens of defense and corporate contracts. Those contracts meant deadlines that could not be missed. The XB-48, the naval variant of the XB-46, was undergoing a lengthy series of launches and recoveries as part of its final testing, and a new prototype for a weather data-gathering RPA, designed to fly through hurricanes, was being readied for takeoff.

The staff manning the control tower (Yorke operations was busier than most small municipal airports) was also preparing for the arrival of a Gulfstream IV jet, due to arrive momentarily from corporate headquarters in Atlanta. It was carrying Bud Richardson, the company's CEO, and a posse of top brass who wanted a first-hand report on the previous days' mishaps. There was a meeting in Washington scheduled for later that week at which they would have to make a convincing case to Pentagon generals and procurement officers as to why the $730 million contract shouldn't be cancelled.

Mark Riley, the Yorke air traffic controller, monitored the arrival of the Gulfstream, still 45 miles out. He picked up his binoculars and scanned the horizon. He saw an approaching aircraft. At first he thought it was the Gulfstream, but it was much too low, practically skimming the treetops.

"Jesus Christ, we've got a 46 coming in, we can't have Goss running his tests on the approach. Tell him to lay off for a few minutes, will ya?" he said to his colleague, a former Air Force air traffic controller named Lou Meyers.

Meyers picked up the phone and dialed the test hangar. He exchanged a few words and hung up.

"Wha'd he say?" asked Riley.

"He said he cancelled all testing until you give him the okay."

251

Riley nodded. He put the binoculars back to his eyes and watched the RPA's approach. The Gulfstream was still more than 30 miles out, so he felt confident the airspace and runway would be clear by the time the big shots arrived.

He watched as the RPA approached the field, then dropped down, bounced a couple of times and rolled down the runway in not that straight a line. Riley shook his head and rolled his eyes as Meyers grinned. Not one of the smoothest landings he'd ever seen, but then again, there was the old saying, any landing that you could walk away from was a good one. And since these aircraft were remotely piloted, as long as the vehicle arrived safely, that was all that counted. In this case, he was happy as long as the runway was clear before that whopping big G-IV showed up.

He raised his binoculars again and quickly spotted the inbound jet. Before he could give final clearance, he had to make sure the runway was clear. He shifted his gaze to the end of the runway.

The RPA was just sitting there.

Riley turned to Meyers.

"Tell them to get that fucking bird off my runway," he said.

As the CEO of a Fortune 500 company, Bud Richardson was a busy man. Riley knew he wouldn't be pleased to be told he had to return to altitude and circle. Meyers picked up the phone just as the props on the RPA accelerated, and it turned and taxied off the runway. Meyers put the phone down. Riley keyed the microphone and informed the pilot of the incoming jet that the runway was clear for landing.

Mike Porterfield, the Yorke crew chief, squinted at the RPA on the apron and scratched his head. The air traffic controller may have been too busy with the arrival of the corporate jet, but Porterfield, standing in the huge test hangar, recognized the tail markings. "Well I'll be a son of a bitch," he said. "It came back."

Yorke RPAs could stay airborne for more than 36 hours, and if communications were lost they were programmed to return to home base. They could even land themselves, such was the advanced technology of the latest generation of Yorke aerial vehicles. But it still had the crew chief scratching his head. "Where the hell have you been?"

252

He and two colleagues walked up to the errant drone. It looked none the worse for wear.

"You sure this is XB-46?" asked the crewmember.

He shrugged. "Sure as hell looks like it, unless there's some mix-up, and this is one of the units they were testing this morning. Help me get it into the hangar."

The engineers arranged themselves behind the wings and began pushing it into the test hangar.

Back at the farm, Pazhman released his grip on the controls. He sat back in his chair, watching the monitor. He saw a man in coveralls walk in front of the lens, and then he could make out the hangar building, and the huge sliding doors. He smiled.

The Gulfstream was on its final approach. The engineers stopped pushing the RPA to watch as the super sleek jet touched down, the small puff of smoke coming from the landing gear on impact as the tires went from zero to about 100 mph instantaneously. The jet slowed and taxied to a stop near the main building. Almost immediately, the airplane's door opened and men in suits began getting out of the burlwood-paneled cabin. The small group of executives stood on the tarmac for a moment, unsure where to go. Then Richardson, the CEO, noticed Porterfield and the other engineers who had resumed moving the RPA into the hangar, and began leading his entourage in their direction. He liked to schmooze with employees.

"Whatcha got there?" he asked.

"Sir, to be honest, I'm not sure. It sure looks like T2, that's the bird we lost yesterday," said Porterfield.

By now more than a dozen of the corporation's top executives and an equal number of engineers and mechanics were clustered around the machine. For many of the men in suits, it was the closest they had ever gotten to an RPA. They were accountants and lawyers, not aviation experts. But Richardson was a former Air Force general, with an eye for detail. He was the first to notice the strange object that had been attached below the fuselage near the wings.

"What the hell is that?" he asked.

253

In the barn, Pazhman and the others were watching the video monitor. They could see more men studying the aircraft, standing very close. It was time. Pazhman put his finger on the toggle switch and pressed it. The video monitor flashed white, and then there was static.

The force of the blast blew out the west-facing glass in the control tower, knocking Riley and Meyers to the floor. Riley was dazed, he smelled acrid, choking smoke, and felt something warm and sticky on the back of his neck. He looked at Meyers, who was sitting on the floor, holding his face in his hands. There was blood smeared on his fingers. Riley couldn't hear anything. He said something to Meyers, who didn't reply. Then he got to his feet and looked through what had been a huge plate glass window. He saw the Gulfstream pilot running from the plane to the hangar. Only it wasn't a hangar anymore. The aluminum walls had been shredded and there were debris everywhere, and rags, and then he realized some of the rags were moving. The ground was littered with bodies, and body parts. He lifted the phone and dialed 911.


Kim was still in her robe, eating a cup of Greek yoghurt, when the local Albany news broke the story: major fire at Yorke Aerospace, outside Woodboro. Kim switched to CNN, which had picked up the same local story, the same looped helicopter video feed. Kim saw a complex of buildings, with smoke rising from one of them. Yorke Aerospace had a history of safety violations at the plant, the anchorwoman said. It had paid large fines to the government. Kim watched for a few minutes, then clicked it off and went for a walk.

# CHAPTER 59

*New York Harbor*

"That is one ugly ass boat, how much you say it cost?" asked Rodriguez. They were motoring off Governor's Island, looking at an enormous private yacht that had everybody talking.

"Newspaper said 250 million," replied Lieutenant Emerson.

"I believe it." Rodriguez shook his head. The yacht was too modern for his tastes – aluminum, angular, with a huge hangar in the transom for powerboats and not one but two helicopters on the stern deck.

"That's just showin' off," said Rodriguez. He himself had his eye on a used Bayliner for sale in Port Jefferson. The owner wanted $6,000 for it. Rodriguez thought it was a good price, but with the expense of the baby, his wife was against it. They'd had a few arguments over it already and he figured he better not bring it up again.

The enormous yacht was called Innovation, and belonged to Silicon Valley CEO Max Wilder. Wilder had loaned it to the US Government for a G20 luncheon. It was tied up at the pier on Governor's Island. Foreign heads of state could only be impressed so much by other politicians, but software titans, that was something else. It was an "in your face" opportunity to remind the rest of the industrialized world of American technical superiority and economic might.

"So that's what we're protecting?" asked Rodriguez.

"Yep," said the skipper. "Just pretend we're back in Bahrain, and that's a Navy frigate. It's the same drill. Nothing comes within a mile."

"That mean shutting down the harbor?" he asked.

"Pretty much," said the skipper.

"What happens if something gets through?"

The lieutenant shook his head. "Nothing gets within a mile."

"But if it does?"

"We order it away. If it comes within 500 yards, we blow it out of the water."

Rodriguez figured the operation would require multiple pickets to keep traffic away, and more vessels to watch out for a high-speed motorboat packed with explosives.

"Seems like a lot of trouble for one meeting," he said.

The lieutenant studied the yacht with his binoculars. "Yes it does."

# CHAPTER 60

*New York City*

Arthur and Hector Gutierez sat quietly in Team Omega's waiting room. Hector absorbed the details around them, the plush blue carpet, framed photo of the President, and carved emblem of the FBI. This was the big leagues, and he was excited.

Arthur felt nervous. He was ratting on his boss, which was wrong. Hector had convinced him otherwise, but he still felt nervous.

Mahan buttoned his suit coat as he walked from the Pit to the waiting room. He smiled. "Mr. Gutierez? I'm Special Agent Mahan, we spoke on the phone."

He led them to the conference room where the conversation could be recorded.

"So what's up?" Mahan asked.

"This is strictly confidential, right?" asked Hector.

"Of course," replied Mahan. "Anything you say will be kept private."

Hector nodded to his cousin.

"It's my boss, Hassan."

"Full name?"

"Hassan Khalifa, owns Midtown Shoe Repair."

"What about him?"

"He all of a sudden took off, closed the shop, acted very strange."

"He ever do that before?"

"Never. And he knows I make my money in tips, which I don't get if we're closed. Not just that, he closed the shop and we got shoes that customers want to pick up. It ain't right. Then I seen that picture in the paper, when I was riding on the subway yesterday."

"Which picture?" asked Mahan.

He produced a folded copy of the Daily News. There was the composite sketch of Pazhman.

257

"You know this man?" asked Mahan.

"That's the dude was in the shop. Few weeks ago. Freaked my boss out. Ever since then things ain't been right," said Arthur.

"In what way?" asked Mahan.

"He been in and out, taking days off, and I don't know, kinda seemed tired and depressed."

"Wait a minute," Mahan interrupted as a light bulb went off. "You said Mid Town Shoe Repair?"

"Yeah, why?"

"Address?"

"168 West 36th." Arthur looked confused, he shook his head. "Anyway, that ain't all."

He looked at Hector who gave him an encouraging nod.

"I looked in the back room and found a pistol and cash, a lot of cash, and a Pakistani passport with his photo but someone else's name. I don't want to get him in no trouble."

"Do you remember the name on the passport?"

Arthur told him, and Mahan made a note of it.

"How much cash?"

"I didn't count it, maybe five grand."

"Where does your boss live?"

"Woodside, I don't know the address."

"What does he do when he takes these days off?"

"I don't know. I do know he goes upstate sometimes. I went with him once. We delivered a computer, to a farm there. I remember the name of the town. Woodboro."

"Woodboro, New York?" asked Mahan.

"Yeah, upstate."

"You have an address of this farm?"

Anthony shook his head. "He drove, and I didn't pay much attention."

"Would he be there now?" asked Mahan.

"I don't know where he is."

# CHAPTER 61

*Woodboro, New York*

He was still a proby, so Dennehy wasn't allowed to go out on patrol alone yet. He rode shotgun with Bill Gastonberry, an old-timer. The guys with seniority tended to have more say over what shift they got, which meant the older guys got more day shifts, when the bad guys were asleep. Dennehy and Glastonberry had been on patrol since 7 a.m., and Gastonberry was hungry. He suggested they stop for coffee and doughnuts.

"You've got to be joking?" said Dennehy.

"What?"

"You actually eat doughnuts?"

"Yeah, why?"

"Just that it's such a cliché," said Dennehy.

"I know," said Gastonberry, "but they're really good."

"You eat a doughnut every day?"

"Pretty much."

"I don't want to get into that," said Dennehy. "You eat your doughnut, I'll just have coffee."

"What are you afraid of?" asked Gastonberry. "Getting fat?"

Dennehy didn't reply. He knew what he was afraid of. He was afraid of the utter predictability of the rest of his life. He could see the years unfolding before him. The night patrols, the speeding tickets, fender benders, utility crew details. Doughnuts.

"I'm just not hungry," he said.

The radio crackled. The dispatcher's voice came through. "All units, we have reports of a fire at Yorke Aerospace please respond."

Gastonberry looked at Dennehy. "Doesn't your girlfriend work at Yorke?"

"My girlfriend, my ex-girlfriend, I'm not sure."

Gastonberry picked up the mike. "Dispatch, unit two responding."

"Unit two, roger."

Dennehy switched on the lights and siren and they pulled out of the coffee shop parking lot.

A tall column of dark gray smoke rose from Yorke Industrial Park. As the two officers got closer Dennehy saw that the smoke was coming from an above-ground fuel tank, which had caught fire.

He pulled his cell phone from his pocket and dialed Jill's number.

"Hello, Lance?" she said.

"You're okay?" he asked.

"I'm fine, there was an explosion, they're telling us to stay in the building. What happened?" she replied.

"I don't know. As long as you're okay. I'll talk to you later," he said as the cruiser stopped near the burning building.

"Be careful," she said.

He heard the siren of a fire engine arriving as he opened the trunk of the cruiser and pulled out the medical kit. The building looked like it had been ripped apart from the inside. Then he saw a man in a suit holding a bloody towel to his forehead and moved toward him. Employees from the adjacent buildings were giving first aid. And then he saw the bodies. His mind flashed back to a suicide bomber attack at a police barracks in Iraq, on his first tour.

He'd seen this before.

* * *

Thirty seconds after the switchboard lit up at the police station, Sgt. Dennis Tratt, who had just arrived for work, realized he was the ranking officer in the station house.

"Where's the Chief?" he asked Rhonda, the dispatcher.

"Didn't say. He got a call, yesterday, said he had to check something out on his way home, left a little early. Never showed up this morning," replied Rhonda.

"A call from who?"

"Didn't say."

"Try his cell phone again, would ya?" asked Tratt.

She did, then shook here head. "Straight to his recording."

260

"Try his landline at the house."

"I did, twice," she replied.

Tratt considered the emergency calls coming in from Yorke, and made a mental count of the other officers on duty. The Chief lived alone in a small ranch house outside of town. Tratt figured he better send someone to check it out. Maybe the Chief had taken ill, or worse case, he'd had a heart attack. It wasn't like he was in the best shape. He decided to send Kendall.

Twenty minutes later Officer Kendall arrived at the well-kept ranch house. There was a Ford Expedition in the driveway. Kendall recognized it as the Chief's car, but his police cruiser wasn't there.

Kendall rang the front doorbell. No one answered. He walked to the nearest window and looked in. He could see the hallway and living room. No sign of life. He tried the back, checking a few more windows. The house was empty. He didn't want to have to break in, but luckily the kitchen door was unlocked. A lot of people in Woodboro didn't lock their houses.

He entered.

"Chief, you here?"

No answer.

"Chief?"

Kendall checked all the rooms, which didn't take long, since it was a small place, but the house was empty. He went back to his patrol car and radio'd Sergeant Tratt.

"Nada. Place is empty."

"Shit," said Tratt.

Tratt picked up the phone and called Chief Burke's girl friend, Virginia. She was a dental technician who lived in the neighboring town but she said she hadn't heard from him since the day before. Something was wrong, for sure, she said.

Tratt had no choice. He picked up the phone and called Buddy Lamott, the Woodboro fire chief.

"You gotta be kidding me!" said Lamott. "The shit's hitting the fan here. I got multiple fatalities."

"Don't know what to tell you. Chief is whereabouts unknown. Something must have happened to him."

261

"Okay, it is what it is. I'll notify Lieutenant Carlisle." He hung up the phone.

During an emergency, the police chief was supposed to man the emergency communications center at the station. Instead, Lamott had to put his deputy fire chief, Lieutenant Carlisle, in charge. But both departments were small, bare-boned, and he didn't have men to spare.

# CHAPTER 62

Kim returned from her walk after only a few minutes. She sat on the couch and thought for a moment, then reached for the remote control and punched in CNN. They were running video of the fire at Yorke. "Investigators on the scene reported a loud explosion, followed by a fire. Yorke, as you know, is a major defense contractor in the aeronautics field."

What had Colonel Aronson said? The terrorist Pachaas Talwaray was interested in unmanned aircraft. The group had been attacked, maybe almost annihilated by them. And now they had explosives. There had been maps and tourist guides to Ulster County in Jusef's apartment. Was it possible? She pulled her cell phone out of her pocket and dialed Mahan.

"Mahan, it's me, Kim."

"I know who it is. I was about to call you."

Kim continued. "I was thinking, remember what Col. Aronson said about Pachaas Talwaray? I'm wondering if this fire at Yorke Aerospace might be connected. I don't know, just a thought."

"Fire?"

"There's a fire at Yorke Aerospace, not far from here, I saw it on the local news. They're a big defense contractor, they make drones."

"Well, we just had a walk-in. He said the man he works for met with a man who looks a lot like our guy, Pazhman. He said a few months ago he and his boss delivered a computer to a farm in Woodboro."

"So Pazhman is here."

"He might be."

"Did he say where this farm was?"

"He didn't remember the address, I referred it to Gambler. He said he'd send a team. But that team doesn't include me. Gambler said he wants fresh brains on Pazhman. I've been reassigned."

"Reassigned to what?"

"G-20 security. The city's practically on lock-down."

"Mahan, this is G-20 security. You better get on this."

She hung up on Mahan and dialed the Woodboro Police Department.

"This is Special Agent Conrad, FBI, may I speak to the Chief?"

There was a pause.

"Chief Burke?" Rhonda, the dispatcher asked.

"Is he in?" Kim asked.

"Well, no, we're not sure where the Chief is at moment, he hasn't checked in."

"Maybe he's at the fire," said Kim.

"That would make sense. He may have his hands full, and he may be having communications problems," said the dispatcher.

"Communications problems? Well, please tell him I called." Kim left her number and jumped in her Range Rover.

By the time Kim arrived at Yorke Aerospace's sprawling complex there were dozens of rescue vehicles and fire trucks on the scene. Departments from half a dozen neighboring towns had responded. She showed the guard at the gate her FBI I.D. and was directed to the emergency response center that had been set up. Kim approached the nearest uniformed officer.

"Excuse me, Officer, I'm Kim Conrad, FBI, is the chief around?"

Dennehy shook his head. "He's not here yet."

"Can you tell me what happened?" asked Kim.

"There's a report of an explosion. From the debris field, and the way this building got totaled, I'd say it was a pretty big one. Must have been some kind of weapons test that went wrong. Just a whole lot of confusion right now," said Dennehy.

Dennehy saw Jill in a group of employees organizing first aid.

"Jill!" He shouted across the parking lot.

She turned, a look of confusion on her face, saw Dennehy and hurried over to him.

"They let you out of lock-down?" said Dennehy.

"I insisted. The entire marketing department is away and we need a spokesman, and no one can seem to locate our top management. They must have been in the hangar."

"So who's in charge?" asked Kim.

"One of the engineers, an assistant VP named O'Brien, as far as I can tell." She lowered her voice, "He's in a little over his head. I'm

264

trying to coordinate with him to get a statement for our headquarters in Atlanta."

"Where is he?" asked Kim.

Jill led Kim and Dennehy to an area near an ambulance where people were being treated for minor injuries caused by flying glass. The seriously injured had already been evacuated. O'Brien was talking to a man with a bandage on his head and blood on his shirt.

"Mr. O'Brien?"

"Yeah?"

"Kim Conrad, FBI. I need an initial assessment of what happened," she said.

O'Brien stood up. "We have no idea. The tower tells me the test division was landing one of the new RPAs, remotely piloted aircraft... drone."

"I know what they are," said Kim.

"Apparently our CEO's corporate jet had just landed, and they went into the hangar, next thing you know there was an explosion."

"Were there weapons involved in this test? Did the RPA carry a missile or something?"

He shook his head. We never test live munitions here. That's done at the Air Force proving grounds out west."

"So could this have been a bomb?"

He shook his head. "I don't know, I don't know. All I know is they were running tests. They'd just landed their test bird, then the jet came in and then kaboom."

"Could it have been the fuel tank or something?" asked Kim.

The engineer shook his head. "It doesn't make sense. Pilot said everyone who was on the plane was killed, except him."

"Who were they?" asked Kim.

"The whole top management team. Everybody. Gone."

"What were they doing here?" asked Kim.

"I guess they were looking into the problems we've been having. We lost two vehicles in the last two days. Went down, probably in the forest. We haven't located them so we don't know what the problem is, looked like something with the guidance system. Not a good development considering we're about to go into production for the Defense Department."

"What do you mean, you lost two drones?" Kim asked.

"They just disappeared. Poof."

# CHAPTER 63

"Agent Conrad?" said Dennehy, when they entered the hangar.
"Yeah?"

"I don't know what you're thinking, but I've seen this before, in Iraq and Afghanistan. This is high explosive."

Dennehy's cell phone rang. Kim listened as he spoke.

"Where? Are you sure? Dammit," he said and flipped the phone closed.

"What is it?" asked Kim.

"Some kids just found the chief's cruiser. In Lake Nashauna. Shit, I gotta go," said Dennehy. He looked for his partner, and saw him helping injured people.

"I'll go with you," said Kim.

She left her car in the Yorke parking lot and rode with Dennehy in the police SUV, siren and flashing lights on.

"When was the last time anyone saw him?" asked Kim. Dennehy drove fast over speed bumps on the approach road to the plant. Kim gripped the handrail as she bounced up and down.

"He was in his office yesterday, about 5 o'clock, then he got a call and headed out. He didn't report for duty this morning, then the fire at Yorke, and we all figured he went straight here."

"Did they log the call?" asked Kim.

Dennehy picked up the radio. "Dispatch, Unit 2, come in."

"Dispatch go ahead two."

"Rhonda?"

"Yeah?"

"Can you tell me who the Chief spoke to last night, before he went out?"

"Sure, it was Ed Lewis, I put the call through myself."

"What was it about?"

"I don't know, a problem with one of his tenants, I think. You want me to call him?"

"Yeah, and call me back." Said Dennehy.

It took them less than 10 minutes to get to the lake. A tow truck had already arrived. Two bass fishermen in waders were standing with the tow truck driver, looking at the car.

"No one's in the car," said one of the fishermen, an older man with a white moustache. "One of the kids swam down and looked."

The tow truck driver waded into the water and fastened his cable to the rear axle. While Kim and Dennehy waited for the car to be hauled out, Rhonda called back.

"What did you find out?" asked Dennehy.

"Well, I spoke to Ed Lewis, he said he asked him to check out his farm on Old Mill Road, because the tenant there chopped down some trees, and I guess Ed didn't like it."

"Who's the tenant?"

"I heard it was some fancy guy from the city, an artist."

"I'll check it out," he said.

"Be careful," said Rhonda.

The tow truck pulled the police cruiser up the ramp. Dennehy waited for the water to drain, then opened the driver's door and popped the trunk where they found the Chief's body bathed in bloody water. His throat had been cut.

\* \* \*

What is this farm?" asked Kim as Dennehy drove, this time with the siren off, but just as fast.

"Rental property, no one farms out there anymore. It's about ten minutes away. Rhonda said it was leased to some artist types from New York."

"She know anything about them?"

He shook his head. Kim removed her pistol, her Dad's Beretta, checked the safety and chambered a round.

While they drove Dennehy radio'd Rhonda again. He told her the chief was dead, and where they were going. He said he'd call for back-up if they needed it. When they arrived near the farm Dennehy turned off the main road and followed the long driveway through the woods. They came to the open field and a meadow and in the distance, saw the barn and farmhouse.

268

"Stop," said Kim.

Dennehy hit the brakes.

She found a pair of small binoculars in the glove compartment and scanned the property.

"Anything?" asked Dennehy.

"Place looks deserted. I see where they chopped down some trees. I can see the stumps."

"So let's take a look," said Dennehy.

"Hang on, let's see what we have here first."

She was still looking at the tree trunks. And then she realized why they had been cut.

"Oh my God," said Kim under her breath.

"What?"

She handed him the glasses. "They used the dirt road as a runway."

From inside the barn, Mahmud watched the police SUV.

"We have company," he said.

Rodney was at work on the second drone, checking the electrical cable.

"They get any closer you know what to do," Rodney said.

Mahmud smiled. He moved to a switch connected to a wire that led out the front of the barn.

"Not yet," said Rodney, "wait for it."

Dennehy started cautiously down the long driveway. This time he saw it before it was too late: disturbed earth by the side of the road.

Instinctively, he turned off the road. The heavy truck suspension of the police SUV bounced on the rough ground and dipped down an embankment into the field.

"What are you doing?" asked Kim, holding on as the vehicle rocked sideways. Before Dennehy could reply, Mahmud pressed the switch.

The earth erupted around them. The blast hurled the SUV into the air. It rolled twice before coming to rest upside down. The window by Kim was broken, and she was covered in dirt. Her ears were ringing and her shoulder hurt. She unclipped her seat belt and dropped onto the ceiling. She felt a sharp pain in her ribs and winced in pain.

"You okay?" she asked, coughing dirt and smoke.

"I think so, you?"

"Think I broke a rib," she said as she crawled between the seats and the roof and pushed open the rear window. She still held her Beretta, and crouched low as Dennehy emerged beside her.

He scanned the barn in the distance.

She started to stand up and Dennehy grabbed the back of her belt and pulled her down.

"Whoever detonated that is probably still watching us," he said.

"So what do we do?" she asked.

"Call for back up and wait. Probably get the bomb squad in here," he replied.

"There's no time for that."

Kim remembered she still had the binoculars around her neck. She crawled to the edge of the road, raised her head to see through the tall grass.

"Anything?" asked Dennehy.

"There's a loft in the barn, with a big door. They could have been watching us from there, but, wait a minute."

She saw two figures on the far side of the barn. They were pushing something.

"Holy shit, it's the other drone," she said.

Dennehy crawled up beside Kim as she stood up and began working her way toward the barn.

"Dammit," Dennehy muttered. He followed Kim as she moved closer. He couldn't keep up.

Mahmud and Rodney rushed through the launch procedure. As soon as they had the aircraft in position in front of the barn, they let it go. With the local police closing in, Mahmud knew they had little time. He prayed that Pazhman, who was already miles away, would realize the problem and not delay. To his relief, the props began spinning faster and the drone sped down the drive.

Kim stood up and leveled her Beretta. Dennehy saw what she was doing and did the same. They each managed to squeeze off three shots as the drone, moving very fast, lifted off and flew over them.

"Shit!" said Kim.

She crouched on the ground and took out her cellphone and speed-dialed Mahan. She waited a few second until he answered.

"Kim, where are you?" asked Mahan.

"I'm at a farm on Old Mill Road. They've got another drone in the air, repeat drone in the air. Somehow they must have intercepted them. It just took off. It could be headed anywhere," she said. "Warn everybody. We're moving in."

She ended the call.

"What the hell's going on?" asked Dennehy.

"It's a terrorist sleeper cell, they intercepted the drones," said Kim. Hunched over, she moved toward the barn. A car engine started and Kim suddenly saw a Toyota. The car skidded in the dirt courtyard outside the barn as it turned and headed straight for Kim.

Dennehy rushed toward Kim, his legs somehow finding strength, and speed. He pushed her out of the way as the car hurtled by. Then he was up again, firing his police issue Glock at the fleeing vehicle. The rear window shattered and the car lurched into the field and careened into a massive oak tree.

The driver, Rodney, sat slumped over the steering wheel. He was dead. Mahmud started to stagger out of the passenger side. He had a knife.

"Out of the car and on the ground, now!" Dennehy shouted, the familiar adrenaline coursing through his body. Mahmud looked at him and smiled. His mission was fulfilled. He stood up out of the car and limped toward the officer. Dennehy fired.

Kim's heart was beating fast, too fast, as she and Dennehy entered the barn. They saw the wires, explosives and tools. It was like what Dennehy had seen in the cave in Afghanistan. A bomb factory.

They returned to the Toyota.

"You think this thing still drives?" asked Kim.

Dennehy pulled Rodney's body out of the front seat and got behind the wheel. He put it into reverse and backed away from the oak tree. The front of the car was smashed in, and steam was

271

venting from the radiator, but it was moving.

"It should get us to where we need, which is where?" he asked.

"Back to Yorke."

"Keep your fingers crossed," he said.

Her phone rang. It was Mahan. Kim gave him a quick update.

"Pazhman wasn't at the farm?" he asked.

"No. Just two guys, they're both dead."

"Where are you now?" he asked.

"On my way to Yorke, we need to figure out how we stop one of these."

"I'll call you back," he said.

She turned to Dennehy. "We need to talk to someone who knows about drones."

"I know someone," replied Dennehy. He dialed Jill and quickly explained. "Hang on, I'm putting you on with Special Agent Conrad," he said.

Dennehy passed Kim the phone.


Back at the Yorke Aerospace, Kim frantically scanned the chaos all around her.

"You need to talk to one of our engineers," she said.

She saw someone she knew named McHaskell, who was a supervisor in the engineering department. She hurried up to him and gave him her phone.

"I don't have time to explain, but your drones have been intercepted by terrorists, and they're relaunching them," said Kim.

"Relaunching ours?"

"I need to know about the one that's missing, the one that supposedly crashed," said Kim.

"What do you want to know?" he asked.

"If it's still up there, how do we find it?"

He shook his head. "The new ones use stealth technology. Can't really explain it, it's highly technical, but you can't find them, not unless you see one with your own eyes."

"So who controls them?"

"We do, from a control center in the hangar. Well, there used to be a control center, anyway."

"So we have no way of knowing where it's going?" asked Kim.

"No."

"How do we stop it?" she pressed him.

"You can't, they have their own internal navigation systems, and they can be controlled by encrypted terrestrial signals."

"What does that mean?"

"I mean, you want to stop one you gotta shoot it down."

"How fast can one of these things fly?" asked Kim.

He hesitated. "Cruising speed is 200 miles per hour, but it depends on the altitude. If it's flying low, like it's designed, it's about half that."

Kim made a quick calculation. It could be in New York City in less than half an hour.

She hung up and dialed Mahan.

"Warn the Secret Service. This thing is headed for the G20 meeting. You've got to get them somewhere safe."

There was silence on the other end.

"I just spoke to Gambler, he said they shoved off in a yacht 15 minutes ago. They're already eating lunch."

"Tell 'em lunch is over, he's gotta get 'em out of there."

# CHAPTER 64

*New York Harbor*

Hassan found a parking space near a playground in Fort Lee overlooking the harbor. From here they could see everything: Governor's Island, Lower Manhattan, Staten Island, the Statue of Liberty, and up the Hudson, the George Washington Bridge.

Pazhman could have directed the RPA from miles away, but he wanted to see the destruction with his own eyes. He wanted to savor and enjoy it.

He scanned the harbor through the van's windshield with his high-powered binoculars. Such an abundance of targets, he thought, but he mustn't be distracted.

Hassan did not share Pazhman's excitement. He sulked behind the wheel. *How can you be so happy,* he wondered. *Do you not see that we will die today?*

"What's the matter?" asked Pazhman sharply, irritated that Hassan's mood was dampening the moment.

"What will we do? Mahmud and Rodney are almost certainly dead. They will find us soon."

"Not now," commanded Pazhman.

"We cannot return to my apartment," said Hassan.

"No," replied Pazhman, trying his best to ignore him.

Hassan could see it was hopeless. *Perhaps I should accept my fate, and be at peace. Unless...* then a thought occurred to him. *Perhaps if I prevent this, they will not put me in prison, I will go to work for the Americans.*

*But what of my family in Oman? They are old, they would not be harmed, and perhaps no one would find out.*

He turned this new idea over in his head, then turned to Pazhman, energized by his newfound clarity.

"I cannot let you do this," he said.

274

Pazhman glanced at Hassan. "What?"

"We must not do this!"

"Are you mad?"

"We cannot," said Hassan.

Pazhman looked at Hassan. He saw that Hassan had his pistol out, and aimed at him.

"Hassan, what are you doing?"

On the flat screen monitor behind Pazhman, Hassan could see the skyline of lower Manhattan as the drone approached fast.

"Let go of the controls," said Hassan.

Pazhman laughed. "I always knew you were a fool. You have lost control of your senses." He had always suspected there was weakness in him, but he had not come this far only to be betrayed.

"Yes, a fool to associate with you. Move away!"

Pazhman swiveled in his seat. Hassan's glance was diverted momentarily by the image on the screen. Pazhman took his hand off the joystick and held it up. "There, I have done as you asked."

But with his other hand he reached for his belt.

He struck with the speed of a cobra. Hassan saw the flash of steel, felt the searing stinging pain in his neck. He tried to scream but heard only the gurgling of blood as Pazhman twisted the knife.

Petty Officer Rodriguez was in the ship's mess of USCG Cutter Reliance when General Quarters sounded sharply, the horn reverberating off the steel bulkheads. He dropped his lunch tray and ran to his gun station. He was there in seconds. He quickly put on his helmet and life jacket and began scanning the skies and waters around him for threats.

He saw Navy ships, Coast Guard vessels and police boats, maneuvering at full speed. Some pulled alongside the yacht Innovation, and guests were being hurriedly transferred to the other vessels.

The speaker at Rodriguez' action station crackled. It was the skipper, Lieutenant Emerson.

"Keep your eyes peeled for a possible air attack imminent, maybe a missile or something, that's all I know."

Twenty seconds later, Rodriguez saw it: just a speck on the horizon. But it was a spec that wasn't supposed to be there. He saw the RPA approaching from the direction of the Hudson River, saw it dip and turn and then resume course. It was headed straight for the President.

"Incoming 4 o'clock!" he shouted.

Emerson didn't hesitate. Rodriguez gripped the rail around the gun mount as the cutter increased speed and turned hard to port. The skipper was placing them directly between the yacht and the approaching drone. Rodriguez sighted his .50 caliber gun.

In the van, eyes fixed on the monitor, Pazhman saw the river give way to New York Harbor, filled with ships and boats. He saw the massive yacht and smiled. He was seconds away. He would pilot his weapon into her side, amidships, and the charge would detonate, obliterating the vessel. He was almost giddy with joy, too bad it was happening so fast.

Then, to his horror, he saw a Coast Guard cutter slide into the frame in front of the yacht, blocking his angle of attack! There was a man on the foredeck manning a machine gun, white tracers arced toward the camera mounted in nose of the drone. Rodriguez fired a long burst as he tracked the incoming aircraft.

The RPA exploded less than 200 feet off the cutter's bow, the force of the blast enough to shatter the glass on the bridge and knock Rodriguez off his feet, pushing the cutter over on her side. As he fell, the Coast Guardsman saw a section of the drone's fuselage pass above him like a spear, slicing into the aluminum hull of the yacht at the waterline.

Rodriguez staggered to his feet as the cutter righted itself, aware that his uniform was covered in blood. He lurched to the rail where he saw that the yacht, Innovation, was badly damaged, settling low in the water and heeling sharply to starboard. She was sinking fast. Rodriguez saw civilians in the water, and realized they had been on the yacht's stern deck, waiting to transfer to a high-speed launch, and had been thrown overboard by the blast. He saw a man in a suit, struggling, then disappearing below the surface.

Rodriguez threw off his life jacket and dove in. He surfaced, took a breath, and dove again. Twelve feet down he saw him, a man in a

276

silver grey suit, arms and legs spread eagled, motionless, sinking. Rodriguez felt his lungs burning, desperate for air, but swam deeper. He looped an arm around the man's chest and started kicking toward the surface.

When the two men were hauled out by a Coast Guard launch, Rodriguez saw that the man in the suit looked as pale as a ghost, and wasn't breathing. He did mouth to mouth resuscitation, as he had been taught in basic training. The man spat up seawater and slowly regained his senses. He said something the Coast Guardsman couldn't understand.

"Holy moly, you know who that is?" ask the boatswain's mate on the launch.

Rodriguez shook his head, he was exhausted, unable to speak.

"I've seen him on TV, you know who this guy is?"

"Who?"

"You just rescued the freaking President of France."

# CHAPTER 65

Through his binoculars, Pazhman watched the scene in the harbor. He was confused, the explosion hadn't been as he expected. He saw rescue vessels plucking people out of the water. The yacht was low in the water, and tipping to one side, but it was intact. It hadn't been destroyed. He saw men on the deck, and others in the water, swimming.

He realized he must get away. He got out of the van and walked around to the driver's door. He opened it. Hassan's dead body slumped out onto the parking lot. Pazhman took his place and drove away.

Avoiding the major highways, he snaked slowly along on surface roads. On the outskirts of Newark it occurred to him to turn on the radio.

"This is what we know now," said the newscaster, "a yacht carrying the President and world leaders for a G-20 meeting has been attacked in New York Harbor by what witnesses describe as a military drone. No word on injuries yet."

Cut to audio of an eyewitness: "I seen it comin' across the harbor. It was like a cruise missile or somethin', and then it exploded. I heard machine gun fire and that's all I seen."

Pazhman tuned the radio....

"...reporting from Lower Manhattan, where world leaders from 20 leading nations embarked earlier today for meetings on Governors Island. All are believed to have boarded the yacht, 'Innovation,' owned by Silicon Valley billionaire Max Wilder, for lunch. At approximately 1:15 p.m. witnesses described a flurry of activity in the harbor, then gunfire, and some described a low flying aircraft or perhaps a drone crashing into or near the yacht, which appears to have been damaged. Rescue vessels are on the scene."

The newscaster began repeating what he had just said. They don't know anything yet, thought Pazhman. He turned off the radio so he could think. He had not made plans for anything beyond the attack, all his thoughts had been focused on events leading up to

278

this moment. Now it appeared the plan had failed to achieve complete success. The authorities would double their efforts to find him.

Pazhman knew he must reach the safe house as soon as possible, while there was still confusion. The safe house was in Trenton. He arrived late in the afternoon at a small, detached brick house on the wrong side of the tracks, with an overgrown lawn and a cracked cement walkway. Pazhman knocked on the door. No answer. He looked up and down the block, there was no one in sight. He knocked again. Presently he heard movement in the house. The door opened. A barefoot old man with thick black-framed glasses stood before him. He was short, and bent over, in a cap and robe. The house smelled strongly of tobacco. He looked at Pazhman and nodded.

"I thought you might come."

The old man, whose name was Haj Mir Kasi, prepared tea which he served to his guest. Pazhman and the old man had first met more that 20 years earlier, when Pazhman was a student, and Kasi ran a cultural exchange program, long since closed down.

The old man knew better than to ask questions. Together, they watched CNN. The cable news channels were covering the breaking news with video footage taken from a tall building in Lower Manhattan. Someone in an office building had taken a cell phone video of the strike, but the quality was grainy and very poor. Still, this was endlessly repeated.

The anchorman reported that there were no reports of any fatalities. So far, he said, it appeared all heads of state had been accounted for, though some had been taken to area hospitals.

Pazhman's face turned red with anger.

The anchorman continued. "This was the second of two attacks today, and for that we now go to the town of Woodboro, New York, where law enforcement officials are preparing to brief the press on a deadly bombing that took place just hours ago."

A reporter was on the scene at Yorke Aerospace, and inset in the

279

screen was the aerial footage of the hangar on fire. Behind the reporter was a row of emergency vehicles.

"We're waiting for a briefing by the FBI any moment now, but meanwhile I can tell you that by latest count more that twenty-four people have been taken to area hospitals, and firefighters say the blaze has been extinguished. That means this is now a crime scene, and investigators have cordoned off a large area in order to safeguard evidence. As it stands now, at least a dozen people have been killed, among those, we can confirm now, the CEO of Yorke Aerospace, and other top management and engineers who were working in the hangar when the explosion occurred."

The reporter stopped talking when the press conference began. Someone from the State Police introduced special agent in charge Neil Gambler, who stepped to the microphone. Pazhman and Hassan watched closely.

"Good afternoon ladies and gentlemen, I'm Neil Gambler, special agent in charge of the New York Special Joint Anti-Terrorist Task Force; I have a brief statement. At approximately 10:15 this morning there was an explosion outside one the hangars here at Yorke Industries. We believe the explosion was the result of a bomb that was placed on an intercepted unmanned aerial vehicle that had been reported lost several days earlier. There have been a number of fatalities and injuries, and local law enforcement will give out information on that as soon as families are notified. We believe this attack was facilitated by the same individuals responsible for the attack this afternoon at the G20 conference in New York Harbor. We believe that two members of what we are describing as a sleeper cell were confronted by law enforcement late this morning and that confrontation resulted in the two subjects being killed. A third suspect was located in a parking lot in Fort Lee, he was deceased. I'm now going to turn the microphone over to State Police Major Andrew Feeney."

Pazhman showed no emotion over his dead cohorts. Better dead than taken alive, he thought.

"Could you repeat your name, please?" a reporter asked.

"Andrew Feeney, New York State Police." He spelled his name. "I have a short statement. At approximately 11 a.m., responding to a call from local fisherman, local law enforcement officers recovered the body of Frank Burke, Chief of Police of the town of Woodboro. The location of the body was in Lake Menahag. This is an apparent homicide. We are working on the assumption that the murder was connected to the terrorist events that took place today."

"Do you have any suspects?" A reporter asked.

"Other than the three deceased individuals, not at this time," he replied.

"What are their names?"

"We're not releasing that information at this time."

"What can you tell us about them?"

"We believe they were foreign nationals who were living in this country on work visas, we have no information on the other yet."

"Are there other suspects?"

"Yes."

"How do you know?"

"I can't get into that."

The state trooper turned to Gambler, who stepped back to the podium.

"We have a suspect who we think is the leader of what the public would refer to as a sleeper cell that we are actively investigating," he said.

"But you don't have them in custody?"

"Not at this time."

"Can you explain how the three suspects were killed?"

"Yes, and I'd like to single out the efforts of local law enforcement and special agent Kim Conrad, who were instrumental in connecting the dots early on and interrupting activities at what we believe to be the launch site for these attacks."

Pazhman was stunned. That woman, special agent Kim Conrad, was standing among a line of law enforcement agents behind Gambler and Feeney. He couldn't believe it.

Gambler continued. "Special Agent Conrad was very quick to ascertain the threat and warn law enforcement in the harbor. Her actions, together with that of Deputy Sheriff Lance Dennehy played a critical role in preventing more wide-spread destruction," he said.

The news ran non-stop. Pazhman watched all of it. Every angle examined, repeated. It was reported that they were believed to be part of a hitherto little known but insidious terror network known as Pachaas Talwaray. A narrative emerged: the plot had been foiled by the quick thinking of an astute special agent, a woman, Kim Conrad, who was hailed as a hero. The media seized on her story. The public ate it up. It was good luck, a break in the case, she had discovered the farmhouse and issued the warning. Remarkably, she had been part of the investigation, but was off-duty, at her family's country house, and put two and two together after the first explosion. Kim's photo was splashed on the TV. The bureau was happy to promote the story, it made the FBI look good, the bureau had saved the day, spoiled the plot in the nick of time.

For the next weeks, a massive manhunt was launched. But it turned up nothing.
Pazhman Khan had vanished.
Like a ghost.

# CHAPTER 66

*Woodboro, New York*

Mahan sat on the porch and pulled off his hiking boots. He looked over the rolling farmland.

"You gonna check your messages?" Kim asked.

"No."

"Seriously?"

"I will later, I don't want to spoil the day."

"Maybe there have been developments," said Kim.

"I want to just enjoy the scenery, and the moment."

"Well I'll check," said Kim.

After two weeks non-stop searching for the fugitive, the work had shifted to another unit, and Gambler had given Omega Team a week off. Kim had invited Mahan up to Wild Meadows. Her dad was out of the hospital, and she needed a break.

"I'm told there are mountains nearby. You can hike," Kim had told him.

"I think there are, they're called the Adirondacks," said Mahan.

"I've heard of those," Kim smiled. "Maybe I'll even go with you."

Kim went into the kitchen to pour iced tea. When she got back she had her iPhone.

"I checked my messages," she said.

"And?"

"Nothing from the office. We're good. I had a call from the policeman who helped me, Lance Dennehy. He's coming by with his girlfriend to say hello."

"Do I have time to go swimming in your lake?"

Kim smiled. "That sounds great. I'll come with you."

It was a very hot afternoon. Mahan stripped down to his drip-dry hiking shorts and emptied his pockets on a rock ledge overlooking the pond. There was a rope tied to a tree branch hanging over the water.

"That rope good?" he asked.

"A neighbor puts it up every year for his kids. I used to swing on it was I was little," she said.

Mahan put his weight on the rope to test it and Kim laughed. She had dirt on her face and still wore her hiking clothes and boots.

"You going to kill yourself," she said.

"It's just like the obstacle course at Quantico," he said.

He looked at the lake to make sure it was deep enough, then pulled himself up on the rope and swung out over the lake and let go.

The water was clean and cold, he flung his head back and looked up at Kim.

"Woohoo! It's gorgeous, come on."

"You've got to be kidding me," she shouted.

"Just do it."

Kim rolled her eyes and sat down on a boulder to take off her boots and socks. She hesitated, then stripped down to her underwear as Mahan watched.

"This is not a good idea," she shouted down from the rock.

"Yes it is."

She took the rope in her hands and held on.

She screamed as she swung just a few feet out, then back over the rock.

"Push off!" shouted Mahan.

Kim gripped the rope again and ran off the edge of the cliff, then screamed again as she swung over the water and let got, dropping ten feet in the lake.

"It's freezing!" she screamed.

"I may have forgotten to mention that," said Mahan.

Kim swam toward him and put her arms around his neck. "I guess we'll be seeing a lot of each other, now that I'm reassigned to Team Omega."

"And received a commendation to boot. But you're still a terrible shot. We'll have to work on that together. And by the way, Special Agent Conrad, you're out of uniform," he said.

"So are you," she said as she kissed him. Then kissed him again. "I wanted to do that all day."

"Race you to the middle of the lake?"

"Nope," she kissed him again.

Concealed in the underbrush on the hillside overlooking the lake, Pazhman Khan watched.

*"I have found you, you slut, and soon you and your lover with feel the edge of my blade,"* he said to himself. He looked at the sky. It would be dark soon enough.

Kim and Mahan lingered in the cold water, and on the grassy shore. Too long.

"My God," said Kim, strapping her watch on her goosebumped wrist. "It's almost 6 o'clock, Lance and his fiancée will be here."

They dressed quickly and rushed home.

Kim hopped in the shower first, then pulled back the curtain. "Put out the cheese and crackers, if you want something to do."

She got no answer, and quickly showered and stepped out into her room.

"Shower's all yours," she called out.

She toweled off and pulled on a skirt and T-shirt.

"Tom?"

Kim opened her bedroom door and walked into the kitchen. She saw Mahan sitting on the floor. There was blood on his face. His hands and feet were bound behind him and there was a dishtowel stuffed in his mouth. When he saw her he made an urgent muffled noise. She saw something out of the corner of her eye and turned.

Pazhman was on her, smashing her sideways into the kitchen cabinets. She felt the wind knocked out her as she fell to the tile floor. Pazhman grabbed her hair and dragged her back up like a maniac gone berserk. But he didn't want to kill her. Not yet. She saw Mahan frantically trying to get loose, then drifted quickly out of consciousness.

Jill's Austin Mini Cooper sped down the old lane that led through the farms outside Woodboro. Lance looked uncomfortable in the passenger seat.

"I feel like we invited ourselves," said Lance.

"We did not. She called to ask about you. You guys worked great together, for God's sake."

"I don't know about that."

"Well she seems to think so. You want to talk about a job at the FBI. You said so, right?"

"Yeah."

"Well then doesn't it stand to reason that maybe you should network with them? You are getting a special award, right?"

"Well yeah, but FBI agents all go to college," said Dennehy.

"And your point is?"

Lance smiled. Jill had been pressing him to return to the state university. Funny how she had maneuvered him into this. She already had him enrolled at an online college course on criminal science. He took a deep breath, he felt self-conscious.

"Just relax, and be yourself," she looked over at him as she drove. "You look nice."

When Kim regained consciousness her head was leaning forward, her chin resting on her chest. She opened her eyes, saw blood, and looked up. She was tied to a kitchen chair and couldn't move. Her arms were behind her back, and something had been stuffed in her mouth and packing tape from the utility drawer in the kitchen was wrapped around her mouth.

Pazhman saw that she had come to and approached her.

"Oh good, just in time to see your friend die." He smiled.

He raised his knife to within inches in front of her face, then rested the blade on the bridge of her nose. He laughed.

"Not so good, huh?"

Behind him, she saw Mahan frantically trying to loosen himself. She saw the knife rack on the counter. Maybe if she could somehow loosen her hands enough to get to that....

Pazhman moved over to Mahan and put the knife blade on his naked chest, the same place where Kim had cut Pazhman when they first met. With a quick motion he slashed the knife. Mahan grunted as blood oozed onto his chest. Pazhman looked at Kim and smiled.

"It only gets worse," he said.

There was the sound of tires on the gravel driveway, a car coming to a stop. Pazhman listened. "Company?" he asked, a smile on his face.

He went into the living room and looked through the window. He saw a young man and woman getting out of a car. Were these the first of many guests? He remembered the man in the kitchen had been preparing food. He considered his options. Perhaps I should kill them quickly and leave.

Pazhman hurried back to the kitchen where Mahan was still bound and gagged on the floor. His eyes rested on the kitchen chair. It was empty. But it wasn't possible! The bitch was gone! Pazhman looked at the back door. It was open. A look of fury in his eyes, he turned to Mahan.

The doorbell rang.

On the front steps, Jill and Lance waited.

"Do I look alright?" she asked.

"What would you do about it now?" asked Lance.

She smiled and fixed her boyfriend's collar. Lance looked at his watch.

"6:30 right?"

"Don't worry, we're on time," said Jill.

The sun was softening over the tops of the pine trees surrounding the lake.

"Should we ring again?" asked Jill.

"Maybe they're on the patio out back, let's walk around," said Lance.

"Ring once more," said Jill.

Lance rang the doorbell.

He looked at Jill. "Maybe they're in the bedroom, you know."

She slapped his arm. "Stop that."

"What?"

Pazhman thought of cutting Mahan's throat, letting him bleed out, but that would mean blood, and time, when every moment counted. Mahan watched as Pazhman stepped quickly out the back door. Mahan quickly struggled to his knees and then to his feet and reached his bound hands around his back, fumbling to get a knife from the knife rack on the counter as the swinging door to the pantry pushed open and Kim entered, shuffling on her tip toes, still bound. Mahan leaned against the counter and reached for the bread knife.

Outside the house, Pazhman followed a brick path that led from the kitchen door to the driveway. Frantic, he scanned the shrubs near the house. Where was she? He was breathing heavily. Suddenly in a panic, he realized his mistake. He turned back toward the kitchen but stopped when he heard a woman's voice.

"Are we in the right place?"

Pazhman turned. A young woman in a white skirt and orange T-shirt stood with a man, tall, short hair, in khakis and a golf shirt.

He smiled. "Of course, everyone is waiting in the back," he said, realizing this was going to become messy, very messy indeed.

Dennehy smiled. "I'm Lance, this is Jill, are you friends with Kim?"

"Yes, yes, old friends. My name's Rafael."

Dennehy was about to ask if they had met before, there was something familiar about him. Then he realized the connection: the composite sketch. Dennehy held his smile.

"Oh heck, I forgot the bottle of wine in the car. Jill, hang on a minute, I'll be right back."

Jill looked confused. "What wine?" she asked.

"There's plenty of wine," said Pazhman, but Dennehy was already hurrying back to the car. He hated the idea of leaving Jill alone, but he knew how dangerous Pazhman was, and had to have his weapon.

Kim ripped the packing tape off her mouth and pulled out the gag. She took the knife from Mahan and began work on her feet.

Pazhman hurried back to the kitchen. He was starting to panic, sweat dripping down his head. People were becoming too spread out, he was losing control. He must act now. It was time to start slitting throats. In five minutes, it would all be over.

Back at his car, Dennehy threw open the door. He opened the glove compartment and let out a sigh of relief as he felt the reassuring textured weighty grip of his Sig Sauer.

At the kitchen door, a sixth sense told Jill that something was wrong. Where was everyone, for starters, and what was all that about the wine? Pazhman turned to her.

"Come in," he said.

She shook her head, "I'll wait here."

Pazhman had no time to waste. He grabbed her by the arm. Dennehy was halfway back to the house when he heard the scream.

Kim sliced through the last strand of rope binding Mahan's hands. She looked up to see Pazhman entering the kitchen. He was dragging Jill on her knees. Jill pulled back and tried to get up. He gave her arm a jerk like he was trying to control a dog on a leash.

Then he produced the knife.

"Let her go, she's not who you want," said Kim.

It was too late. Pazhman grabbed Jill's hair and yanked her head up, exposing her throat. Kim lifted the kitchen chair she had been tied to and hurled it at Pazhman, then grabbed his wrist with both hands.

Once again, this bitch is getting in my way, but this time she will die, he thought. He swung his arm back, slamming Kim into the refrigerator, but he couldn't shake her loose. Jill was now free, looking on in horror, and Mahan was on his feet, hopping toward the melee. He lunged at Pazhman but fell to the floor.

The shiny blade flashed inches away from Kim's face. Then they were on the floor, frantic, smearing blood on the vinyl tiles. Kim saw Dennehy in the doorway, trying to get a bead on Pazhman as they rolled and turned. Before she could stop him, Pazhman had his arm around her throat.

She could hear Pazhman breathing heavily as he looked at the others in the room. He held the knife to her throat as he began backing out of the room.

"Kill him!" Kim shouted.

Dennehy aimed the pistol at Pazhman. "Let her go," he shouted.

"Take the shot!" yelled Kim.

"Let her go," said Dennehy.

"Take the shot!"

Dennehy's eyes locked on Pazhman's and in a split second, he was aware of nothing else in the room. No noises, no people, just the space between his target's eyes. He squeezed the trigger.

# CHAPTER 67

Six weeks later, a discreet ceremony took place at the French Embassy in Washington. The ambassador presented Petty Officer Second Class Mark Rodriguez with the Ordre du Merite Maritime. The event was attended by Rodriguez' wife and baby daughter, along with his commanding officer, Coast Guard brass, and the Secretary of State.

Seven thousand miles away, in the skies above Miramshah, North Waziristan, an MQ-9 Reaper circled. Its pilot, in a control room at Clovis Air Force Base, watched a monitor. He could see a large house with several vehicles parked outside. The pilot turned to the intelligence officer standing behind him.

"Cyber terrorists, huh?"

"So they say."

An SUV stopped in front of the house. They watched as three men got out of the vehicle and entered.

"Looks like it's go-time," said the pilot.

The intelligence officer picked up the telephone.

Inside the house, Professor Al Fariz was dismayed by the limited progress his programmer and engineers had made. The latest last-minute move had set them back weeks. Men were busy setting up his computer network, and there were wires and cables everywhere. He was weary, and he was old, and yet still be was forced to live like a criminal, always in the shadows, always on the run. Still, he thought, I must continue the struggle for as along as I can.

In the control room at Bagram, the Intelligence Officer hung up the phone.

"All clear. You're good to go."

The pilot raised an eyebrow. "Roger that."

The pilot's index finder pressed down on his mouse, and a 500-pound JDAM dropped silently from the Reaper.

"I guess that's one way to deal with computer hackers," he said.

Eight seconds later the house was obliterated, and with it, the last of Pachaas Talwaray.

The early fall weather was cool and sunny when Kim arrived at the New York State Supreme Court on Center Street. Her father was waiting for her. He stood next to his attorney, Marvin, who wore his usual rumpled pinstripe suit and carried a sheaf of legal documents under his arm. Her father put on a brave face and smiled, but his heart attack, and the legal mess, had aged him considerably.

"You sure you don't have someplace else you ought to be, chasing bank robbers maybe?" he asked.

"No Dad, not today."

This isn't likely to be pretty, you know."

"I know."

They turned and walked up the steps together.

## THE END

If you enjoyed SLEEPER CELL, please consider ordering a copy of DEVIL'S REEF. Go to www.DEKarlson.com.

What readers said about DEVIL'S REEF:

"A stellar literary debut."

"Pulse-quickening…"

"… [a] swirling vortex of memorable characters, delicious settings and shocking twists…"

"Compulsively readable!"

"Strap your air tank on extra tight for this one and remember to come up for air."

"…a wild ride."

"Harry McCoy promises to entertain and enthrall."

"… a great read, hard to put down."

"Solid entertainment."

"In Harry McCoy, we have a new kind of hero – circumstances have put this laconic, well-educated former DA beyond the emotional reach of lesser men."

25695887R10167

Made in the USA
Middletown, DE
08 November 2015